"O" FACE

HEATHER
HILDENBRAND

Cover by Mayhem Cover Creations
Editing by SF Benson

ISBN: 1978217102
ISBN-13: 978-198217102

CHAPTER ONE

LIAM

THE exhaust from my borrowed pickup was the only familiar scent as I slid into the narrow parking space and cut the engine. The last chug of the motor echoed off the garage walls—thick, gray cement that was too perfectly constructed to exist anywhere except good ole' America. The empty tobacco case lying in the space next to mine suggested it couldn't be anywhere but downtown Charleston. Home sweet home. Sort of. But even though it was familiar enough, the lack of crumbling edges and rotting rats in the corners left me unsettled. I'd spent four months diving off the coast of Africa and the Middle East before that. South Carolina was terrifyingly luxurious by comparison.

Was it insane to miss the pickup truck beds full of government gangbangers rolling through town with guns raised? Probably. But then it was even more insane that I was here of all places. Even before the military, I'd never spent any time in the world of corporate America, and I knew I wasn't going to fit in now. But a promise was a promise.

I paused inside the cab long enough to roll up the windows. Manual windows took more elbow grease than pushing a button. A familiar for both of the worlds I'd lived in. At least some things were universal.

Just fucking breathe, man. I inhaled. Exhaled. Got out.

Shoving the keys into my pocket, I started walking.

The closer I got to the street—and the view of the skyscraper across it with the words Franklin Industries mounted over the front—the faster my heart pounded. The more my irritation bubbled up, threatening to boil over.

I didn't want to do this shit. I wanted to go home. To Summerville. To the house my parents had raised me in. They were gone, retired and living on the coast of Florida. Purchasing my childhood home was the first step I'd made toward building a life for myself after almost losing it. Well, surviving that IED had probably been the first step if you asked anyone else. But "surviving" and "making a life" were two different things. And it was the former that had brought me here—all the way to the doorstep of the last place I ever expected to visit.

Just one meeting, I reminded myself now. One dog and pony show. Kiss a few babies. Shake a few hands. And then home to the peace and quiet of Summerville.

In a blur of forced will and silently repeated responsibilities, I made it into the building and through the security checkpoint.

"You're Liam Porter," the security guard said, his smile friendly. Open. Not murderous. Not radicalized. But I hated his enthusiasm. I did not want to be recognized. Not here. Not anywhere, really, but especially not here on my own turf.

"Yeah."

"I graduated from North Summerville too. Three years ahead of you. Wow. It's an honor, man." He put out his hand, and I shook it, gritting my teeth to bite back all the asshole things I wanted to say.

"Thanks."

"Your meeting's on the fourteenth floor. You can just go right up," he said, releasing my hand and nodding at a bank of elevators behind him.

"Thanks," I said again. Better a repetitive monkey than a cursing ass.

I spun on my heel and headed for the elevators. Maybe I should have brought Sophie after all, like she'd begged me to. "Just for backup," she'd said in that voice that always sounded like a warning of some kind. "Just in case."

"I survived an IED at forty feet," I'd told her with more than a little sarcasm. "I think I can handle this."

The words were true enough. One visit to Franklin Industries should have been cake. But Sophie and I both knew, for me, this sort of thing was worse than death. Even as I thought it, I tugged on my collar. I'd vetoed the tie Sophie had tried forcing on me. A dress shirt and slacks were bad enough.

I stepped into the elevator, reminding myself it was more than a fair trade. Not exactly an eye for an eye. More like a mouth for an ear. This company had done more for me than technology should have allowed. Definitely more than the military would have. The least I could do was stand up beside them and tell the world who'd given me a second chance at life.

They'd get one speech. That was the deal. After that, I could fade into obscurity. I was already well on my way with the stubble on my face and longer hair hanging over my forehead. After a few more months, with any luck, no one in town would recognize me ever again. I wouldn't be "Liam Porter, war hero." I'd be "that guy who never shaves and spends all his time carving out rocking chairs."

Sophie probably had a warning for that too, but I didn't

3

give a shit. The idea of taking over my dad's old workshop, of losing myself in the sound of the saw, the smell of the sawdust... It was exactly what I needed after the stress of the last few months. Between the explosion, the subsequent surgeries, and now the spotlight, I just needed to lose the spotlight for a while. Get some peace and quiet. Move on.

But first, I had to pay my dues.

The elevator doors dinged, the yellow light indicating I'd arrived on the fourteenth floor. When the doors slid open, the first thing I saw was the view. Floor-to-ceiling windows ran the length of the foyer, offering a look at a cityscape that was too far away to look anything less than pristine. Even the silence ringing in my ears had a tone to it that screamed *money*.

I stepped out into the hall, caught up in the cityscape of Charleston as it stretched as far north as I could see. I knew Franklin's office wasn't at city center, that behind me, the city limits gave way to forest and from there, only winding back roads leading straight home to Summerville. But from here, all I could see was the bustle of a city too bloated with people and pollution to comfort me just now.

I thought of my dad's shop again, still full of half-finished passion projects from the last time I'd come home for a visit. It smelled of sawdust that burned my eyes and reminded me of the life I'd had before I'd almost lost it all. I'd left town as a player looking for glory, but four years later, I had returned as something else. I just didn't know what yet.

I took a deep breath and turned away from the window, walking slowly to the other end of the hall and the office that awaited me. Plush carpeting lined in gold trim led me straight to a reception desk made of glass and marble.

"Can I help you?" A bright-eyed twenty-something with gold earrings that glinted off the harsh lights greeted me.

"I'm Liam," I began and her eyes went even brighter.

"Liam Porter, oh my God!" She jumped up and raced around to shake my hand, gushing in a way that made her look even younger.

I nodded a lot, and when it was clear I wasn't going to encourage her any further, she led me to a conference room and plied me with coffee without waiting for my agreement. The low buzz of muted voices and dollars wrung from desperate hands hovered everywhere. If my mother could see me now…

I was glad in this moment that she couldn't.

One press conference, I reminded myself.

Finally, the chirpy receptionist left me alone.

I sipped the coffee. The fact that it was good pissed me off somehow. I set it aside, pretending to study the artwork on the walls mixed with various awards given for Franklin's research and contributions to global causes. A pat on the back made out of paper and ink. I snorted, ready to turn back and find a seat again, but a photo on the side table caught my eye.

Shit. I'd almost forgotten.

Okay, not really. But I hadn't expected to see a photo of her here. It had seemed too simple, somehow. Just because her father owned this place, and just because she was heir to it all, didn't mean I'd actually see her—photo or otherwise. But there it was.

I got up and wandered closer, reaching for the glass frame and holding it closer to get a better look. And sure as shit, there *she* was.

Cassie fucking Franklin.

If that wasn't her middle name, it should have been. Thick blonde hair that made your fingers itch to grab a handful of it. Full lips that were made for kissing. A body with curves in all the right places and legs for days. But it was the eyes that stopped traffic. Blue as glaciers and just as cold. She was the ice princess that had ruled men's daydreams and fantasies probably the world over. I'd known her in high school. Okay, *known* was a strong word. Everyone knew Cassie Franklin. But no one really *knew* Cassie Franklin.

In the photo, she stood next to an older man in a gray suit. He was smiling, his shiny, bald head glinting in the sun almost as sharply as the private plane parked behind them. Mr. Franklin himself: CEO of Franklin Industries.

I'd met him once at a school fundraiser. He'd been friendlier than I'd expected from the stories I'd heard, but then I hadn't been old enough or rich enough to have something he wanted. If I had, rumors suggested he would have been less inclined to talk and laugh and shoot the shit with the kid hauling his donations from the trunk to the gym.

On Cassie's other side stood two other men, both expensively dressed. Both smiling the smile of men with money and a never-ending drive to accrue more of the same. The one closest to Cassie had his arm slung a little low on her waist. Possessive. But something glinted in his eye as his lips curved upward. Something twisted I'd come to recognize in my years facing off with pieces of shit that I was forced to be diplomatic with. Something dark I didn't like, not with him standing so close to Cassie. But I shrugged it off, and when I blinked again, I wondered if I'd just imagined the cruel twist to his smile.

Maybe blowing out my eardrums had lost me more than my balance. The guys back at the dive locker had given me shit about also losing my good sense and maybe they weren't wrong after all.

When I looked again, it seemed less menacing all around. In fact, the whole picture was predictable, and yet nothing about the photo told me a thing about the woman in the center of the group. Cassie Franklin had clearly grown up since high school, but from the shuttered, distant expression on her gorgeous face, she hadn't changed a bit. Still as untouchable as ever.

Had I thought of her when I'd learned it was Franklin's medical technology and surgeons that had saved my life three weeks ago? Hell yeah I had. Was I thinking of her today when I'd purposely left my little sister at home this morning and come here alone secretly hoping to catch a glimpse of the only girl I'd ever wanted yet never managed to have? Damn right.

But one look at the photo, and I knew all the answers to all the questions that had made me wonder about her more times than I wanted to admit over the years. Cassie Franklin was still a frozen wasteland. Unreachable. Untouchable.

And despite all that, I still wanted to get my hands on her.

A soft noise made me turn. The door to the conference room opened, and I glanced at the newcomer, my mouth open and ready to offer a stiff greeting. The email hadn't said which snot-nosed executive I was meeting with today to prep for the speech they wanted from me, but it really didn't matter. They were all the same stuffy, condescending assholes. I was going to make this as short and sweet as I could. In fact, even as I turned, I pasted on a sour expression just so the asshole knew I wasn't going to be impressed by the large numbers that made up his bank account or his waistline.

But I stopped short at the sight of the face that stared back at me, my voice drying up in shock. Definitely not the corporate idiot I was told to expect. In my right hand, I still clutched the photo, my knuckles tightening as I realized what was happening here. Maybe it was fate or karma or whatever—not that I believed in any of those, though now I had to wonder. Whatever it was, I knew this was my lucky day. Staring at her phone, hovering just inside the conference room where I stood was the blonde bombshell from the picture I still held. Close enough for me to smell her perfume. And damn if it wasn't sexy as hell—just like the rest of her. If I'd ever wanted a chance to get my hands on Cassie Franklin, now was my chance.

CHAPTER TWO

CASSIE

I scratched absently at my elbow and shoved open the conference room door, my phone clutched tightly in my hand. Bev, my assistant, was trying to catch my eye from down the hall, but I ignored her. My ten o'clock appointment wasn't on the books so the fact that she'd beat me to it by escorting him to the conference room could only mean questions I wasn't ready to answer. Without acknowledging her, I stepped inside and let the door click shut behind me, pausing to send Bev a quick text message with clear instructions: *In a meeting. Do not disturb.*

I had no doubt she'd take that as an order.

With that done, I dropped my phone onto the table and shoved aside every single misgiving I had about this crazy idea. Besides, the level of crazy didn't matter. He was already here; there was no going back now.

It was a good thing retreat wasn't in my nature, I realized, as I got my first look at the man waiting for me now. Because the reality was nothing like I'd imagined. In fact, in a lot of ways, it was a whole lot better. Now that I was meeting him, I wasn't even sure what I'd expected, but it hadn't been this. The man standing before me was straight up eye candy.

He wore heavy boots with utility pants and a fitted long-sleeve shirt that seemed to accentuate every line and ripple of his muscular arms and broad chest. Displaying his assets as it were. I tried not to roll my eyes—or drool. But the stubble and longish dark hair sweeping down over his forehead was better than every alpha male love interest on any magazine cover or action movie I'd ever seen. Jess would have called him an ovary melter or something similar. My own sex drive wasn't nearly so creative. But even I could agree this guy was hot.

Business arrangement, I reminded myself. This was just business.

I cleared my throat, scratching again at my arm. It was beginning to redden and swell into what I already knew would become hives if I didn't chill the fuck out. But between Dad's lecture earlier and this … relaxing wasn't an option.

"Glad you found your way," I said, striding across the room and offering my hand to the man standing near the window. The sunlight streaming in behind him was partly shaded by clouds, casting his silhouette in a gray glow that made him feel even more dangerous up close.

I suppressed a shudder, hiding everything I felt and thought behind the mask I'd perfected a long time ago. Neutral. Give nothing away. That's what Dad had taught me. And I was a pro.

"Sure," he said uncertainly.

He took my offered hand, shaking it slowly. Our gazes met, and I found myself caught by a pair of dark brown eyes that seemed at once both familiar and strange. I shifted my weight, the itching on my arm intensifying as I arranged my features carefully and drew my hand away. There was something about him… Something I thought I recognized. And that was not okay considering what I was about to ask him to do.

"I see Bev got you a coffee," I said, my voice strained as I realized she'd spent a few minutes with him. Damn. I should have met him after work at some darkened dive bar after all. But if this worked out he needed to be seen here. Besides, I couldn't get a contract notarized at a bar.

He didn't answer, so I gestured to the chair closest to where he stood. "Let's get right to it then."

He started for the chair and then doubled back. I didn't notice the photo he'd been holding until he reached over and set it back on the table, returning it to its place.

I blinked, remembering the day captured in the picture. It had been a high note for Dad. He'd made a deal with a foreign investor that had saved us from nearly losing everything when he'd put all of our money into bad tech; a project that had failed even before it began when the FDA banned it from public sale. My smile was tight in the picture thanks to all of that—and thanks to Evan trying to grope me while everyone's attention had been on the camera lens.

God, I hated doing business with him. Not that my own father was much better. His pressure to see me "tied down" was what had led me here in the first place.

The guy across from me cleared his throat, and I realized I'd been silent too long. "So," he began. "I'm not really sure what made you decide to meet with me—"

I leaned in, splaying my hands on the table. "Look, this is obviously a bit strange for us both. But desperate times call for desperate measures. I need someone who understands nuance and has strong boundaries. Based on my information, you seem like you know how to handle yourself in hard situations." I tried for a smile, mostly to put him at ease, and knew I'd failed miserably. Smiling wasn't exactly my strong suit. I went with serious but friendly instead. "I trust you understand my need to meet you in person before we…well, it's imperative that we have at least some sort of chemistry for this to work out, don't you think?"

My attempt at cheerful seemed to confuse him more. "I'm not sure chemistry matters."

I sighed, leaning back in my chair. "Fair enough. What questions do you have?"

His dark eyes followed the movement of my hand like a hawk as I ran my fingers through my hair impatiently. The urge to check my phone was strong, but I managed to keep my attention on him while I waited for him to answer. This wasn't going nearly as well as I'd hoped. But then, it wasn't like I had much experience with this particular sort of negotiation.

It's just like any other, I told myself.

Yeah. Right.

"No questions. Just want to get this over with and get back to my life."

I blinked. Not what I'd expected him to say. Was this really such a bad offer for him?

"Right. Okay. Let's talk about frequency and duration. I'm not sure of your availability, but I was thinking three times this week and three or four next week depending on how it goes over—"

"Wait. What? Are you serious?" He sat up straighter, his expression morphing into hard irritation. I wondered at the glint in his eye—at how many people had flinched from being the cause of it.

"Completely serious," I said, my voice hardening underneath the weight of his glare. Who the hell did this guy think he was? God's gift to women? "We'll need people to really take notice so the message is received. This was all laid out in the original paperwork I sent over."

He frowned. "I must have misread it. I thought this would be limited to one appearance."

"One? No, I'm hoping to keep it short, definitely, but I think it'll be at least a month or so total with a few appearances each week until I can—"

"Whoa." He held up a hand and shook his head, adamant. "I can't do a month of appearances. I need to get on with my life."

I bit back a sigh. "I was assured your schedule would allow—"

His brow shot up, wrinkling that perfectly tanned forehead. "Oh you were assured, were you? Did your people get with my people?"

I ignored the flip in my belly at the sight of his mouth twisting. A fantasy flashed in my mind of his mouth moving and twisting as it explored my own. The image was enough to send a shot of heat into my belly.

I blinked, shocked to realize I'd just felt a tug of lust over this stranger before me. Lust in itself wasn't alien, but the urge to act on it was. I looked up and found him studying me, clearly waiting for an answer. Clearly, not imagining what it would be like to kiss me right now. Because that would be insane. And I was pretty sure insanity wasn't far off for me either. Forcing myself to refocus, I licked my lips, trying to remember what he'd just said.

Schedules. Right.

I flicked my shoulder back, tossed my hair, and feigned a confidence that I absolutely didn't have. "I didn't have my people get with anyone. I handled this personally. Discretion is paramount to this arrangement." My chest tightened at the truth in my words, and my voice lost some of its chill. "Look, I'm going to be blunt with you. My situation is tenuous. Frankly, I don't have the time to shop around or else I would. You're already here and if you can find room in your schedule, I can absolutely make it worth your while."

"You're asking a lot," he said, his voice rough with irritation.

"I know." I twisted my fingers together then flattened them again, willing myself to hold still. This was a negotiation. A standoff. I would not show my nerves and give this guy the upper hand. God, what had my life come to? Instead of securing funding for cutting edge med-tech permits, here I was facing off with a damned gigolo of all people.

"Look, I'll add another hundred thousand if that helps," I said, hating to concede even that much. But I needed this. And now the asshole knew it.

"A hundred grand?" His eyes widened.

I grimaced. "Fine. Two. Look, I'm not asking you to marry me or anything. And if you're worried about public perception, I think you could do a hell of a lot worse than me for a fake girlfriend for a month. Now, do we have a deal or not?"

"Wait. You want me to be your... boyfriend?"

My left eye twitched, and I blinked against the tic. Holy shit, why was he making this so hard? I assumed this wasn't his usual proposition but still. It wasn't fucking rocket science either. "Yes. Hired boyfriend. But absolutely no sex. I want to be clear on that."

He stared at me for another beat and then finally, he tossed his head back and laughed. Loudly.

Asshole.

I shoved to my feet, my face flushing with what I knew was a hot blush. "You could have just said no if this arrangement isn't something that interests you. Clearly, I need to look for someone else with more class, anyway. In the meantime, I'm sure you can find your own way out."

I was halfway to the door when a hand closed around my wrist, spinning me around.

"Don't touch me," I hissed.

I yanked my arm out of his grip, and he took a step back as if the contact had surprised him just as much as me.

"Sorry," he said, still staring intently at me.

He was close enough for me to catch the scent of him now. It was woodsy but raw like sawdust or fresh cut firewood and underneath that, skin and soap and something else I couldn't name.

I sniffed again, wondering vaguely if it was some new cologne I'd never heard of because the scent was nothing like I'd encountered with any of the men I'd dated before. Not that there'd been many. And not that I'd gotten close enough to smell them often. But this guy…everything about him was different. His smell, his clothes, his attitude. His lack of manners and consideration made me want to punch him or cuss him out. But the way he swallowed me up with his eyes and that scent rolling off him now weren't making it easy to do either one. Even as I tried to resist, the same spear of heat hit me again between my legs. Lust.

Goddammit. Why, after literally years of being immune to it, did I have to be attracted now? And to such an asshole?

"Look, Cassie. Can I call you Cassie? I'm sorry for laughing at you," he began. "But you have to admit, the whole idea *is* kind of crazy."

I shook my head. "I'm not discussing this with you any longer. You've made your position clear. I have important things to do."

His brow rose—a perfect arch that caused the same twisty feeling in my stomach as it did when he stared at me. "Things like hiring a boyfriend?"

I glared at him.

He held up his hands. "Right then. None of my business. But before I go, can we just confirm once and for all what I actually came here for. Am I still giving that speech tomorrow night? Or was that all a ruse to get me to go out with you?"

His lips twitched, and I almost went off on him again for being so damned smug. But then his words sank in. Speech. Tomorrow.

Holy shit. This was not my ten o'clock from the escort agency. This was—

"Your speech…?" I trailed off, my face heating and my blood going cold as I gave him another once-over, this time seeing him with new eyes. The utility pants that suggested they'd actually been worn for function rather than some hipster kind of look. The boots that had a real layer of dirt on them. The military haircut albeit quickly growing out to something shaggier in the weeks since he'd been discharged. And those haunted eyes…

Fuck me. I was an idiot. And he was just going to stand there and make me say it. "Liam Porter," I said quietly.

He smiled, but it was too amused at my blunder to be considered friendly. "The one and only."

"I didn't recognize you." And now that I had, my heart was racing along double time. Propositioning someone I knew—someone who knew me—was the worst possible scenario for what I'd attempted. No. Scratch that. Propositioning Liam Porter was definitely the absolute worst.

"You know who I am?" he asked, and the surprise registering was nearly as much as when I'd offered to pay him to be my boyfriend.

I frowned. "Of course. We went to high school together. My best friend and your best friend are siblings."

"And yet, despite all those things, we've never actually held a conversation."

"Well, you're clearly barely capable of one now." The words were out of my mouth before I could stop them, and if I was being honest, after watching him laugh at me earlier, I couldn't bring myself to take them back. Petty? Yes. Regrettable? Not really.

But instead of looking pissed off or storming out, he snorted, clearly amused by my insult. For some reason that irritated me. "What?" I demanded.

"I'm just surprised you knew who I was back then. Never thought you could see so far down your nose."

I glared. "That's rude. You don't know anything about me."

"True." He hesitated and then added, "Does anyone?" And the smile he was failing to hide made it clear his question was meant to be rhetorical.

What argument could I possibly make when clearly Liam knew more about me now than anyone else in the world? What were the odds he'd keep this particular secret to himself? Probably not as high as our entire hometown hearing about this by dinnertime.

I groaned. "Look, this was just a giant misunderstanding."

"Right. I misunderstand women offering me thousands for dates all the time." He shook his head. "I mean, you wouldn't believe the offers I've had. In Africa, they offered me grains of rice and in—"

"Okay. Fine. Not a misunderstanding. An unfortunate case of mistaken identity."

"Funny. I knew who you were the entire time."

I gritted my teeth and tried to think of something to say that could possibly smooth this over. The truth was one possibility, but I couldn't shake the sound of Liam laughing at me. And I couldn't risk it happening again. Finally, I sighed and when I spoke again, I made sure my voice was as no-nonsense as I could make it. "Your speech is on schedule for tomorrow night. The party starts at seven. The press wants you there thirty minutes before that for a few photos."

"Just the one appearance then?"

My cheeks heated as I thought about what I'd tried to talk him into just now. "One and done."

"Mmm." His lips curved, his gaze lingering on my lips. "My favorite."

He stepped around me, and I spun, watching him go and wondering what the hell I'd just done.

CHAPTER THREE

LIAM

THE twang: another thing that hadn't changed in this town. I hated country music, but tonight I didn't mind the familiarity it provided. Drinking slowly, I watched the crowd with a lazy stare. Millie, a girl I recognized from my senior class, was here along with her husband, some rancher transplanted in from Texas according to Jess who hadn't stopped chattering since she'd popped up an hour ago. Chatter: another thing I didn't love but had also decided to let slide tonight.

Sophie caught my eye across the table and grinned. I wiggled my brows back at her just to get a reaction—and to let her know I wasn't brooding over her choice of entertainment for the night. I knew she was just glad to have me home. Hell, I was glad to be home. And alive. Since the moment I'd awakened from the IED blast to find my hearing gone, I'd known two things. One, I wasn't going to be in the military much longer. Busted eardrums tended to end in medical discharge regardless of whether the surgery had worked. And two, life wasn't something I would take for granted ever again.

If that included letting Sophie choose the venue, I'd do it, especially if it resulted in seeing her smile.

"Your welcoming committee has arrived." Jamie, my best friend, returned from the bar, hands full of precariously balanced shots. He grinned at me and set the drinks down, one for each of us—all except me.

"Why do I get four?" I asked, narrowing my eyes.

"Because you were gone for four years," he explained as if I were the slow one for not automatically putting the two together. Leave it to Jamie to come up with a good reason for getting me wasted the moment I returned. Looks like something else that hadn't changed since high school: Jamie was still the partier. I'd always been the tamer of the two of us though not by much. And I'd also been the one most likely to be found in the backseat of a car instead of the center of the party. But Jamie had happily taken over my role the moment I'd left. And he hadn't let up if his stories were true.

Fine by me. I had no intention of ascending that particular throne again. Almost dying had given me a new perspective— one that didn't include seeing the world from the back of a car or the inside of a random hotel room. In fact, I hadn't been tempted by a single woman since I woke up in the military hospital four weeks ago. Not until today anyway.

"Uh-huh. Well, I would argue your logic," I said, shoving aside my thoughts about Cassie Franklin—again, "But since your version of a welcoming committee involves liquor and not more people, I'll concede." I picked up the first shot and held it high. Sophie picked hers up and joined me followed by Jamie and Jess.

"To homecoming," Sophie said, smiling at me with eyes that sparkled.

I offered a lopsided smile back. Yes, this was why I'd come

home. And it was a good damn reason.

"To partying with your sister," Jamie added eyeing Jess.

She gave him the finger. "To friends who are not your twin," she said pointedly. Clearly, their sibling rivalry hadn't changed.

I shrugged because where Jamie and Jess fought like cats and dogs, Sophie and I got along great. Jamie swore it was a twin thing. Jess swore it was a Jamie thing. "I'll drink to that," I said, but no one moved to drink.

"You're supposed to add something," Sophie said.

"Oh." I tried to think of something fun and light and not about friends getting killed right in front of me or handling explosives at forty feet underwater. "To... beards," I said finally.

Jess and Sophie shook their heads. Jamie grinned. "I'll drink to that. Cheers, brothers and sisters."

In unison, we all drank our shots and slammed the empties against the table. The rest of them went back to their beers, and I followed suit.

"So. When can we plan the party?" Jamie asked.

I was shaking my head even before I'd put my beer down. "Never."

"Come on, man. We can have it at our place so you don't have to worry about a mess or anything," he said. But Jess balked.

"Uh, no we can't said your roommate. Yeah. Remember me? I'm the sister that moved back in with you last year to help with the mortgage? You're welcome for that. And I get a say," she reminded him.

Jamie rolled his eyes. "Okay, fine. We'll keep them in the backyard. Limit the damage," he said but Jess shook her head.

"Not happening. Your friends are all gross. They pee

everywhere but in the toilet. I'm not cleaning that shit up."

Jamie opened his mouth, eyes narrowed now, and I knew an argument was coming.

I cut him off. "We are not having a party anywhere."

Jamie drew back, still frowning, and Jess turned away, muttering about being "on the same page with the idiot for once."

"We have to do something to celebrate," Jamie argued. "You've been gone for four years."

"We're celebrating now," I pointed out.

Jamie was unconvinced. "What happened to the Liam Porter I knew?"

"He's old," Sophie said, and I grinned at her.

"Exactly," I agreed. "So if you want to take me to bingo and then use my military discount at the early bird buffet, I'm your guy."

Sophie giggled. Jamie looked scandalized. "I don't even recognize you," he said.

Jess rolled her eyes. "It's called adulting, Jam. Try it sometime."

"Don't call me Jam," he muttered. And then louder, to me, he said, "Fine. What exciting thing are you going to do for your first weekend back in Summerville?"

"Uh, video chat with my mom? Work in the shop?" I said, listing everything like a question or the answer to a quiz. "Take Sophie to buy her books for next semester?" If it had been a quiz, based on Jamie's expression, I'd just failed.

Jamie looked from me to Sophie, eyes wide. "Holy shit, I think there's an alien living in Liam's body."

Sophie laughed and shook her head. "I'm with Jess on this one. It's called being an adult," she said.

Jamie shot her a look. "Traitor." Then he gestured to my

second shot, still waiting. "You're behind, old man. Let's see it." I grabbed the shot, raising it to my mouth, but Jamie stopped me. "Hang on. What's the toast for this one?"

"I have to toast for all of them?" I asked.

He nodded, clearly about to tell me yes, but Jess cut him off. "You could dedicate the next one to the girl who saved your life." Her eyes shone with what could only be mischief and nefarious intent.

I had a bad feeling about where this was going. I'd hoped it was just coincidence and friendly nostalgia that had made her come along tonight. Jess and I hadn't run in the same circles four years ago. Mainly because her circle was more like a two-point line: Jess and Cassie Franklin. Despite Jamie and Jess being twins, or maybe because of it, he and I had pointedly steered clear of the duo back then. But I did know that since their parents had passed, Jamie had been spending more time with Jess. Maybe adulthood had mellowed her.

I looked back at Jess, noting the calculations going on behind her sharp gaze. Huh. And maybe not.

"I don't know who you're talking about," I said. Before she could answer, I raised shot number two high in the air and added, "To not ironing a uniform ever again," before tossing back shot number two.

Jess smirked and sipped her beer.

But Jamie wasn't letting it go. "The girl who saved your life? Who is she talking about?"

I didn't answer.

Jess, however, was more than happy to jog his memory. "Cassie. Franklin Industries. The company that supplied Liam's doctors with the tech that saved his hearing…"

Jamie's eyes widened as her meaning finally struck him. I'd already explained to him how the military had only been willing to buy me a top-notch hearing aid and a bottle of Motrin on my way out. It had been Franklin who'd donated the implant as part of a trial they were doing. "Shit balls. I totally forgot. You have to give that speech and kiss babies and whatever as thanks."

"As my plus-one, I urge you to find a more diplomatic way of describing our presence there."

He pinned me with a devilish grin. "Did you see her when you went over there today?"

I sighed, suddenly glad for all these shots. A buzz was going to be the only way to survive this conversation. "Yeah."

Jamie's eyes widened. Clearly, he hadn't expected me to say yes. Even Sophie looked interested now. Probably because I hadn't mentioned that fact to her when she'd asked me about it earlier. Now, she put her phone down, listening intently.

"Hot damn," Jamie said. "And? Is she still hot as hell?"

"You tell me," I said. "I've been gone for four years. You've lived in the same town as her—"

But Jamie shook his head, cutting me off. "She doesn't go anywhere except for the office. No one sees her anymore. Not even Jess."

My gaze flicked to Jess who looked away now, troubled.

Jamie was oblivious. "Does she still have ice in her veins?" he asked, leaning toward me.

"She didn't smile at me if that's what you're asking."

Jamie snorted. "Maybe with all that medtech her daddy owns, they could do some sort of smile transplant. Make her at least appear happy."

I thought about the offer she'd tried to make me earlier. It was definitely all about appearances with her, though considering her terms, I wasn't sure happiness was her end goal. I still couldn't believe she'd tried to pay me to pretend to be her boyfriend. Or, not me, exactly. But someone. She was going to pay someone. Pretend with someone.

Just not me.

And I remembered her making it clear sex wasn't included, but I wondered how far the fake relationship was really going to go. It was hard to picture Cassie intimate with anyone. Since the moment I'd left her office this morning, every time I tried to, it ended up being my face on the guy's body. And it was really starting to piss me off.

"I'll drink to that," I told Jamie, though I wasn't even sure which part I was agreeing with. Cassie smiling, maybe? That would be a new one. In all the time I'd watched her growing up, I'd never seen her smile. No one had. Except maybe Jess.

At my words, Jess scowled. I raised the third shot to my lips and offered her an evil grin in return before I tossed the drink down my throat.

"She's not as much of a bitch as you guys like to think," Jess said.

"She's not as much of a saint as you like to think either," Jamie shot back.

They glared at each other, and I shook my head. I still couldn't believe those two were twins. Different as night and day. And not just in their choice of friends. Sophie looked up from her phone, her expression apologetic and I knew she hadn't heard a word of this, not really. "Guys, I'm sorry. I have to go."

"Work again?" I asked.

She nodded, wincing. "I know tonight was supposed to be our big celebration," she began.

I waved her off. "Sis, anytime you need to bail on me to save someone's life, do not apologize. Besides, we'll always have Florida," I added, citing our recent family gathering at our

25

parents' new place.

When I'd flown home to recuperate from surgery, I'd done it there and Sophie had flown down for the last week or so. It had kept my parents happy and given me time to pay for renovating the house I'd just bought from them up here. The money the military paid out as a parting gift was getting put to good use.

"Thanks. I'll see you at home." She planted a kiss on the top of my head, grabbed her purse, and headed off, waving at Jamie and Jess as she went.

When she was gone, Jamie's brows knitted. "I thought your sister worked for a divorce attorney."

"She does," I told him. "Can you imagine how many lives have been spared by divorce?"

He snorted, but he wasn't looking at me anymore. Instead, his gaze was locked on something across the bar. I followed it and shook my head. "Nancy Miller, huh?"

Jamie whipped around to look at me. "What? No. We're, ah, just friends."

Nancy waved and Jamie's answering smile was more than friendly.

Jess rolled her eyes. "You have the worst taste in women ever."

He smirked at her. "We have that in common then, because your best friend is a glacier."

"Ugh." She groaned. "Why did I even come here tonight?"

"No idea." He shot me a look that seemed to ask for permission.

I sat back and gestured toward Nancy, whom I remembered for her love of flavored lip glosses back in the day. I decided not to mention that part just now. "Go with God," I told him.

"His name will be called upon later." Jamie grinned, grabbed his beer, and disappeared.

Jess stared back at me, her expression sulky. "And then there were two."

"You don't have to stay," I told her.

"Thanks, Dad."

I debated flipping her off and then decided against it. Irritating or not, she was Jamie's little sister. And they had just lost their parents last year in a car accident. Besides, I knew I was just grumpy from all the hands I'd shaken today trying to navigate the hardware store. That and my mysterious meeting with Cassie earlier. What the hell was happening in her life that made her want to hire someone for something like that, anyway? Was she in some kind of trouble?

Not your problem.

"You know, I can see why you and Cassie are such good friends," I said dryly. "Your knack for deadpan sarcasm is unmatched except for each other."

I waited, expecting some pissy retort for the dig, but she only studied me intently, her expression growing thoughtful as she cupped her beer. "Tell me, Liam Porter, what else do you see?"

"What do you mean?"

"When you spoke to Cassie today, what else did you see?"

"It's Cassie Franklin. I saw what she wanted me to see." I shrugged. "You of all people should know that."

She wasn't put off. "I do. But not everyone else realizes how much of a front it is."

My brows shot up. "Then they're idiots."

"Exactly." She leaned forward, and I knew I'd just fallen into some sort of trap. "Which is why I was hoping you would agree to a favor."

Fucking A. "What favor?"

Jess hesitated, her gaze flicking down to stare at her beer, and I knew whatever this was had been carefully planned. No wonder she'd agreed to join us tonight. I should have known it wasn't to finally become friends with me. But I'd forgotten how devious Jess could be. "Look, Cassie and I have been friends for a long time, but even I don't get to see everything," she said.

I grunted. No surprise there. One conversation with Cassie and I knew instinctively she was a private person.

"There have always been limits to what Cassie shares," Jess went on. "I've known that. Always been fine with it. She's a private person, I get it. It's not exactly easy for me to share about some of my stuff, either. But a couple of months back, something changed. Cassie shut down. Like completely. She stopped telling me stuff and then she even stopped hanging out with me. Won't return my calls. Won't get together. No explanations. She's been distant—even for her."

"I'm sorry for your...issues," I said, making it sound like a question. When the hell had this become a sharing circle? I cleared my throat. "But what does this have to do with me exactly?"

"You're smart, Liam. And you're good at reading people. Jamie told me about some of the stuff you did while you were in the military. The interrogations and investigations."

"What the hell? That's top secret—"

"Yeah, yeah." She waved a hand. "Your secrets are safe. Who the hell am I going to tell in Summerville, anyway?" She snorted, and before I could answer, she'd leaned in, turning serious again. "My point is that you're qualified. You know how to watch people. To read them. But besides all that, you don't have any preconceived ideas about Cassie. And you don't want anything from her so you won't hurt her."

I couldn't help but choke on that last part—the part she'd said with particular force. Who did she think I was—some sort of saint? Oh. Right. Liam Porter, war hero. Apparently that title knew no limits in Summerville. Goddammit it all. Although, apparently it also canceled out my previous reputation with the ladies. A point in its favor.

I reached for shot number four still sitting in front of me on the table.

"What exactly do you want from me?" I asked, holding the small glass between my fingers.

Jess eyed me, gaze imploring. "I just want you to talk to her. To make sure she's okay."

"And what makes you think she'll tell me?"

Jess softened, the first hint of a smile since she'd brought it up. "Because there's another thing I know about you, Liam Porter."

"What's that?"

"If anyone can get Cassie Franklin to talk—or do anything else—it's you."

"What the—?" I stopped, the last shot halfway to my mouth.

Jess looked smug. "So. Will you do it?"

"Are you going to explain what the hell you meant by that last comment if I say no?"

She rolled her eyes as if I'd just asked the world's dumbest question. "Of course not."

I could feel Jess watching me, but all I could think about now was a certain job offer. Clearly, Jess knew nothing about it, but I wasn't naïve enough to think Cassie had been kidding around or acting on a whim. That offer, combined with Jess's suspicions, suggested Cassie probably *was* in some kind of trouble. And Jess wanted me to help get her out of it. When all

29

I wanted to do was go hide in my damned woodshed.

But how could I say no to Cassie Franklin?

I stared at Jess, willing her to blink or back down. But I should have known Jamie's sister would have a killer poker face. This was going to be a damned disaster. I could feel it. And yet, I couldn't seem to think of a reason to say no.

"Fine. I'll see what I can do," I said finally.

Jess lit up, turning her usual scowl into something actually pretty attractive. I decided not to tell her that and risk the wrath I was sure would follow. "Thank you," she said, her voice genuine for the first time since I could remember. At least when she spoke to me.

"Don't thank me yet," I said, bringing the fourth shot to my lips and tossing it back. Not that I needed it. I was already buzzed, and the tingling brought on by the alcohol had less to do with the drinks and more to do with the idea that I could possibly affect Cassie in any way—especially the way Jess had just implied.

"Why not?" Jess asked, wary now.

I smiled, knowing full well it was a predatory sort of smile and not caring in the least. Jess had asked for a favor—and she was going to get it. "I've been away for a long time. And I think you'll find I've become a different person than the one you remember. If Cassie needs help, I'll help her. But I'm not going to lie and say there isn't something in it for me."

"Liam, I'm serious. If you hurt her—" Jess warned.

"You have nothing to worry about there," I said, and I meant every word. "I have no doubt if anyone's at risk of injury when dealing with Cassie Franklin, it is not her."

Jess couldn't argue that. "What's in it for you then?"

"The opposite of pain, actually," I said, already enjoying the look on Cassie's face when I accepted her offer. Aside from the time it would require in the spotlight, which I hated, this might actually be fun. Cassie had always been an enigma. A puzzle that was too untouchable to put together. But earlier, she had made me an offer that, as it turned out, I couldn't refuse. And maybe after all these years of her face stuck in my mind, I'd unravel her enough to let go of the curiosity. Answer all the questions. Satisfy all the wanting.

"Pleasure," I said finally. "Lots and lots of pleasure."

Jess snorted, her expression going from concerned and wary to amused and almost inviting. Her eyes glinted in challenge. "If you think you're up for it, good luck," she said.

"What is that supposed to mean?" I asked, more thrown off by her blessing than if she'd tried to argue with me.

"If there's one thing I know for absolute certain it's that Cassie Franklin doesn't do pleasure. But you go ahead and give it your best shot." A small smile played at the corners of her mouth, covered finally by her beer as she brought it to her lips. She paused, her next words nearly lost to the music as she added, "This is going to be fun to watch."

CHAPTER FOUR

CASSIE

I gritted my teeth, pressing my lips together to keep from spewing profanities. My hands clutched my thighs, squeezing hard until my fingernails dug into my skin and sent a sharp pain all the way to my ankles. This was torture. All I'd wanted was to be taken seriously. No, scratch that. All I'd wanted was freedom. But my father wasn't capable of giving it just like he wasn't capable of running our company into the black again, apparently. No, that was up to me.

And thanks to the debacle earlier with Liam Porter, I also had no other options left. When he'd left, I found out the guy from the escort service had tweeted a photo of the building as he was trying to get through security. A big no-no according to all the signage posted in the lobby. When they'd detained him to question him on it, he'd blurted out the entire thing. Cassie Franklin had called for a hired date. I'd denied it, of course, and he'd been thrown out and labeled "crazy," but I couldn't afford to try that again. And now, here I was with Evan—the absolute last person I wanted to admit my problems to or ask for anything from. But I had nowhere else to go.

My life was a shit show.

I was the star.

"Cassie, if you just hold still—"

"I am still. I'm a fucking statue here," I snapped.

The pressure on my shoulders lifted. Evan drew back and leaned around to look at me, frowning in a way that made his disapproval clear. I hated that frown almost as much as I hated my current predicament. "I'm getting a lot of hostility here."

I rolled my eyes. "That's because I'm giving a lot of hostility."

Evan sighed and went back to rubbing and poking at the knots in my shoulders—a horrible attempt at a massage I'd let go on for way too long already. And not just because he was awful at it but because of the invitation he would take it for. The way his fingertips prowled over the skin along my neck made me want to deck him. But I couldn't. We both knew it. I also couldn't bring myself to let him touch me for another second, not even if it meant saving my future.

I yanked free of his touch and stood abruptly.

"Where are you going?" Evan asked, wearing that frown again.

"Home," I said tersely.

I was moving fast for the door—but he was faster.

"Alone? Cass, do you think that's a good idea with your stress level so high?"

I stalled as he moved to block me, his entire expression drooping to appear concerned. All it did was put me on edge. Evan was literally the only person in the world who knew my stress had reached levels requiring prescription drugs. And he used every opportunity he got to remind me he knew.

"You're crowding my space again," I said, using a phrase

I'd gotten from a self-help book as a trigger for anxiety.

But he didn't move. If anything, he only sagged more, intent on appearing to care. "Cass, you can't just walk out of here when you have a flare-up like this. Let me take you to dinner first. Get some food in you."

"I'm not hungry."

He pressed his lips together, the entire thing reminding me too much of my father to be of any help. "Evan, I mean it. Get the hell out of my way. I'm leaving."

"At least let me drive you home." His voice was full of patience, but it was also full of false charm. I knew that better than anyone.

"I pay a driver for that." I pressed my fingertips to my temples, massaging in vain.

I shouldn't have come here. I should have known Evan wouldn't help matters. He never did. "We can't just leave it like this," he said quietly. There was an edge to his voice now that I recognized all too well.

My head snapped up. My eyes met his.

His entire expression had shifted. He looked deceivingly calm.

Alarm bells sounded in the back of my head. "Evan," I began, measuring my words like one would measure poison. Or the few remaining bullets in a gun fight. "Did you take your meds today?"

His eyes narrowed fractionally, almost quick enough to be a tic. "Did I...? Are you fucking serious right now?"

Shit.

He definitely hadn't taken his meds.

I should not have come here.

"Look, I just want us to help each other," I said, backing away, my thoughts racing as I tried to remember if I had a backup bottle still buried in my purse from the last time we'd gone through this. Evan hadn't ever hurt me physically but there were times his temper made me wonder what he truly might be capable of. Especially considering the reason I knew he'd lost his last job.

"I thought that's what I was doing with your massage."

"You were," I said quickly. "Are."

He folded his arms, feet planted. His hazel eyes glinted with a stony look I knew well. Fuck my life. Today was not my day. "I spoke to your father today."

Now it was my turn to look pissed. "Why would you do that exactly?"

"Cass, let's not beat around the bush any longer. We both know what you came here looking for tonight." His eyes sparked with twisted satisfaction. "It's nothing to be shy about."

He took a step forward.

I took one more back.

"I don't know what you think I'm asking or what my father told you but—"

"He told me about the merger deal with Nichimoto. And about their refusal to work with you as the future CEO."

"It's not a refusal. It's a stipulation," I said, clinging stubbornly to some modicum of dignity.

He folded his arms over his chest. "A husband isn't what I'd call a stipulation."

"Boyfriend," I corrected.

"Excuse me?"

"Nichimoto's people are the ones making waves. And they just want me to appear attached. To make me appear stable, I guess. I don't know. But I'm not marrying anyone. And I have it handled so I don't need your help."

"Of course you do." His lips twitched—a direct

contradiction to the false sincerity in his tone. "And this doesn't have anything to do with the male escort that was tossed out of the lobby this morning, right?"

One look at the wolfish grin he was trying to hide, and I knew I'd made a mistake. Evan was not an option—not even a last hope. He was the enemy. What the hell was I thinking? "That doesn't concern you, Evan."

"No?" He frowned, but it was all acting now. I could see it in the way he'd shoved his hands into his pockets and rolled back on the balls of his feet.

Posturing. It's what Evan Swindell was good at. Probably the only thing he was good at. "Funny because I think your father's exact words to me were 'you're her only hope, son'." He tilted his head at me. "Your father already clearly thinks of me as family. Is it really so far-fetched that we might get together?"

"Since I've already made it clear to you a thousand times that I'm not interested, yes, Evan. It's far-fetched."

Evan's father had been friends with my own back in college. They'd made their fortunes shoulder to shoulder through a series of investments that intersected then forked then intersected again before Evan's father had died of prostate cancer two years ago. When Evan found out he only stood to receive a monthly check until his mother stepped down, he was furious.

Six months ago, he'd taken me to dinner—our one and only date—where I'd learned he'd only used me to get information on a deal we were brokering. Then he ran to his mother with the info and made the same deal behind our backs.

Instead of being furious, my father let him come to work for us. Something about keeping enemies close. I preferred slaying my enemies, but apparently I had no say. And now,

Evan's office was four doors down from mine. The only thing I'd gotten out of our shared workspace was to learn that Evan also had an anger management issue. One that required medication to prevent lawsuits, apparently.

"Cass, you're being so dramatic," he said in a tone that suggested he'd convinced plenty of other women, and maybe even men, of the same thing before. Not me. I'd had enough patronizing for one night.

"I am not doing this with you," I muttered, shoving past him. "Good night, Evan."

A hand closed around my wrist, squeezing tight. I whirled, the temper on my tongue momentarily cooled when I saw the rage in his eyes. "Do not walk away from me, Cassandra. We're not done here."

"You're right." I yanked my wrist free, pulling hard enough to send a pain up my arm, but I hid it and glared at him, pretending I wasn't about to have a panic attack from the whole thing. "We won't be done until the rest of the world knows what you really are. And if you don't leave me alone that will happen sooner rather than later. Now, if you'll excuse me, I have a life to get back to. People I care about in the present, not a guy still living in the past."

I whirled and marched for the door.

"Your father's lost his money again, hasn't he?"

I paused, not bothering to turn around. We both knew Evan wasn't wrong. But I wasn't going to give him the satisfaction of seeing the fear I knew I wouldn't be able to hide as I admitted the truth. "That's not your problem," I said quietly.

"It's not fair for him to ask you to do this just to fix his fuck up."

Now, I did whirl, my temper sending heat into my cheeks

and dialing back the fear. "And it is fair for you to use my predicament to wedge your way back into my life?"

"That isn't what—"

"You can fool a lot of people out there," I said, nodding at the rest of the office. "But you can't fool me. Stay away from me, Evan."

"Cass, get back here," he called behind me.

But I was already on the move, tucking my arm behind me to hide the stress rash that had reared up in all its crimson glory. A consequence of my crawling back to a crazy ex just to solve money problems. Evan had been insane and controlling from the moment I'd agreed to that date. Our relationship, not that you could call it that after one date, had ended abruptly the moment I'd realized he was only using me.

Since then, I'd stayed away. But now, I had only dear old dad—and my own idiocy—to blame for coming back. I'd been deluded to think he'd be different now. Or willing to really help me without helping himself.

What a train wreck that had just been.

Then again, it didn't top trying to hire the high school playboy as your pretend boyfriend—for lack of having a real one.

I grimaced as I stomped toward the elevator, hating the fool I'd become—and in front of Liam Porter, no less. I still couldn't believe I'd failed to recognize him this morning. He'd been the hottest guy in my senior class four years ago. Time had been kind, and now, he was even more delicious if that were possible. The fact that I hadn't recognized him had less to do with his maturing hotness and more to do with the haunted look in his eyes and the sharpness in his movements. Even the way he'd stood had suggested he knew how to hurt—and I didn't mean the heartbreak kind. Liam Porter was danger wrapped in sex. I wanted none of either.

So why couldn't I stop thinking about him?

CHAPTER FIVE

LIAM

I stared, open mouthed, as Cassie walked into the hotel's ballroom, complete with an entourage and a few local reporters acting as her very own paparazzi. She didn't have a date, but she also didn't need one. No one could have shared that spotlight anyway and the shadow that girl cast wasn't one I wanted to be caught standing in.

Beside me, Jamie whistled. "Damn. The ice princess still knows how to fill out a dress."

He spoke loud enough to be heard over the band. Even so, I pretended not to notice. Or at least not to care. But the truth was I did on both counts. "Meh. She's okay." I felt Jamie's incredulous gaze swing to me, but I kept my eyes on the drink I was swirling. Rum and coke. To take the edge off my nerves. I'd rather go up against the ice queen herself than deliver a speech I was about to give. Although, the alcohol wasn't helping my shaky sense of balance and if I tripped while walking onstage, that wouldn't be a great impression either.

"What do you mean? She's a ten across the damned board. Or did too many months in Africa's heat boil your brain?" Jamie elbowed me in the ribs. "Unless I've got it all wrong and you've gone to play for the other team. Was there not enough booty in Djibouti?" He nudged my shoulder, hooting like he'd just told the most hilarious joke ever conceived, and I decided to go classy by not punching him in the testicles.

"Man, do not talk to me about booty right now. I had more than my share. And where were you? Oh yeah, here. In the same damn town we grew up in. Playing on your computer."

"Talk shit about my IT skills one more time, bro." Jamie glowered at me, but I wasn't looking at him. I was looking at her. Again.

Weren't the hottest girls in high school supposed to peak and fizzle out by the end of college? Apparently, Cassie hadn't gotten that memo.

"You going to talk to her?" Jamie asked, catching the direction of my stare.

"I was thinking I'd let her come to me. You know, celebrity status and all."

Jamie's brows shot up. "Yeah, blown out eardrums really impress the ladies."

"Who said anything about impressing?"

"Dude, do not act like you don't want her. I see that look in your eye, and you're not fooling anyone."

"Why did I bring you here again?" I asked as the song changed from faster to slower—a strange sort of soundtrack to the way Cassie moved through the crowd.

Jamie grinned. "Because you've already dated everyone else in Summerville. I'm the only one left."

He made kissing noises, leaning in, and I shoved him away. "Not everyone," I shot back. "I haven't dated your sister."

"Funny. I've dated yours and she—"

"Do not even joke about that shit. Sophie is way too good for your ass, and I would hate to have to cut off your dick." I chugged what was left of my drink and shoved the empty glass against his chest. "I'm going to find more liquid courage for this speech I was blackmailed into giving."

Jamie snickered. "If by blackmail you mean a procedure that saved your hearing."

"That's exactly what I mean." I took off for the bar.

"Godspeed," he yelled after me, drawing a few stares.

I ignored them, plowing my way through the throng of Summerville's socially elite—and morally ignorant. Otherwise known as: charity donors. Every one of them was here to soak up all the positive press about a medtech company that had manufactured the hardware that saved the hearing of a war hero. My story would touch hearts and open checkbooks, I was sure. And Franklin Industries would be that much richer.

I was like the damned pig on a spit at the company barbeque—and I wasn't nearly drunk enough for any of it.

Three people stopped me as I attempted to navigate my way along. Two were Franklin donors who wanted to tell me how proud they were to have me home. As if my absence had somehow disturbed their quality of life for the past four years. The third, a reporter from the local paper, promised dinner in exchange for my life story. When I refused, she'd upped the stakes to box seats for the Gamecocks. I'd almost choked, thinking she'd referenced a different cock, and promptly walked away.

Was this how hookers felt?

Finally, I managed to secure another drink at the bar and tossed a bill into the tip jar. When I spun, my arm collided with a collage of glitter. The collision tossed the contents of my drink onto the shimmering fabric that probably cost more than my severance package from the military and the net worth of Switzerland combined.

"Shit, sorry," I muttered, trying to decide whether to reach out and swipe away the liquid. Considering it was currently running down the front of a dress worn by a well-endowed female, I decided to at least make eye contact first. When I saw her face, my arm dropped to my side in instant defeat. "Oh."

"Oh?" Glacier eyes flashed with irritation. "Oh?" she repeated. Full lips twisted in distaste. "You just threw cheap rum on Dior and all you have to say is 'oh?'" Cassie fumed.

The girl beside her rolled her eyes, and I recognized her as the receptionist from yesterday's meeting. The one who assumed everyone in the free world drank coffee. I looked from her to Cassie, trying to think of what else to say, but it was hard to concentrate under the full weight of that stare.

"Sorry?" I couldn't help but make it a question. Everything about her commanded attention and seemed to beg for apology. Like her very existence anticipated others' failures.

"Ugh. Bev, find me some sparkling water to get this stain out, would you?"

I watched as the receptionist ran off in search of said liquid treasure. Then my gaze swung back to the ice princess herself. "I think we got off on the wrong foot," I said.

"Or drink," she muttered.

"I meant yesterday."

Her cheeks flushed with the barest hint of pink, and she looked away for a split second before raising her chin and meeting my gaze head-on. Oh yeah, ice princess was embarrassed.

"I would prefer not to mention it," she said stiffly.

"Really? That's too bad. I was going to tell you I've had a

change of heart." She blinked, and I enjoyed the dumbfounded look my words caused.

"A change of heart?" she repeated, clearly unsure what to think.

"Yes. I've thought it over and I'd be happy to be your boyfriend."

She stared back at me, unyielding. I searched her blue eyes for some clue, but it was impossible to read her. "Fake boyfriend," she amended in a hard voice. "It wasn't an actual offer for—"

"Tomato, potato. My point is that I'd like to take you up on it after all."

"You…" Her forehead creased into delicate lines that seemed to clash with the smoothness that made up the rest of her. "Look, I think we can both agree that yesterday's meeting was awkward, but I don't think an arrangement between you and me would work out."

"An arrangement between you and me," I repeated slowly. "Wow. You know, I wonder, were you born with your nose that high in the air or is it a learned skill?"

"You're insulting, and I don't like your tone," she said in a low voice, her lips pulled back in a snarl. Something about the heat of her made my hands itch to touch her. Was her skin just as hot as her temper? Or was it cold like the dead gaze she had trained on me now? And why the hell did I need to find out so damned badly?

I heard a clicking sound, and Cassie's eyes flicked to something over my shoulder. Her jaw flexed, but otherwise, her expression didn't change. Still, something about her was stiffer. Tenser. More careful.

I turned and found a woman approaching with a dog-hungry sort of look. She wore a reporter's credentials around her neck. Behind her, a younger photographer was snapping photos of us as she followed the older woman. "Cassie Franklin," the reporter said with sugar-sweet manipulation dripping from her words.

Whoever she was, I didn't like her.

"Janice," Cassie said flatly. "What can I do for you?"

"Oh, I just wanted to tell you how beautiful you look tonight. You're positively sparkling," Janice said with a wink and an air-kiss aimed at Cassie's cheek.

"Thank you." Cassie's tight smile proved she agreed with my assessment.

"She does look beautiful, doesn't she?" I cut in, drawing Janice's sharp eye as she gave me a once-over.

"And you are…?"

"Liam Porter," I said, offering my hand. She took it, her eyes lighting up at the name I gave.

"Liam Porter, war hero? I didn't recognize you with the longer hair."

"You could have shaved," Cassie said, too low for Janice to hear but loud enough to drown out the rest of Janice's introduction as she kept talking.

"Your job offer didn't stipulate anything about facial hair," I whispered back.

Meanwhile, Janice had let go of my hand and gestured to the photographer who promptly got to work clicking away. "Darling," Janice said, and I realized she was still talking to me, "I've been looking everywhere for you. Care to give me a quick interview before your speech?"

I bit back a groan. The last thing I wanted to do was give a speech before a speech, but I was cornered now. And with only a few minutes to go before I had to be on stage, there was nowhere to run. Besides, Janice had a look in her eye that suggested she'd just chase me down, anyway. "Sure. What would you like to know?"

"Well, I was going to ask you about your ear implant courtesy of the Franklins' medtech program." She leaned in and winked conspiratorially at Cassie and me. "Although, now that I've caught a glimpse of the two of you, I can see I should be asking about another organ entirely."

"Uh, excuse me?" Had this brazen woman just asked me about my dick?

"Your heart, silly," she said, smiling brightly. "I saw the way the two of you were looking at each other when I walked up."

"Actually…" Cassie began.

I swallowed my laugh. Cassie was still stiff as a damned board beside me and for some reason that decided it. I slipped my arm around Cassie's waist, pulling her against me. A tiny gasp escaped her parted lips as I did, and Janice's smile widened. "We're just not ready to go on the record about it just yet," I told her, letting my tone match hers. "I'm sure you understand."

Janice nodded. "Of course, of course." She looked away, too smug about it though, and I knew it would take all of five minutes for her to blast this out to the Internet. "You two just call me when you are ready to talk. How about that?"

"Sure thing." I squeezed Cassie's waist, surprised she hadn't already screeched at me and threatened to have me arrested for assault or slander or some such. But she was utterly still against my arm and way too quiet to predict. "We'll catch up later," I told Janice, using my arm to steer us away.

"Yes. Let's do that," Janice called, giggling knowingly.

I didn't look back as I steered Cassie and myself around the corner to the backstage area. There were less people here which meant less chance for someone to overhear whatever happened next. Because even I couldn't be sure after that.

"Holy fuck that woman is scary."

Cassie grimaced. "She's the only one of them I never quite know how to handle."

I exhaled heavily. "I can see why. She's like a damned piranha."

I looked over in time to see Cassie's lips twitched.

Holy shit. Was that the hint of a smile I'd just seen? On Cassie Franklin?

"Whoa, was that a smile on the lips of the ice princess herself?"

She flashed me a quick glare but there was a twist to her mouth that felt like some version of silent laughter. "Curious. Exactly what organ did you think she was referring to back there?"

I licked my lips, purposely drawing her gaze to my mouth for a beat before leaning in and saying, "Make me your boyfriend and you'll find out."

"What?" Her cheeks flushed deliciously. Score. I waited for the rest of the reaction that always followed. And sure as shit, her expression shuttered into something cold and unreachable. "I meant what I said before. We can't—"

"Uh, I think we already did." I pointed, and we both watched as Janice's photographer continued to snap photos of us from the other end of the hall.

"Dammit."

"I think this means the cat's out of the bag," I said.

Cassie folded her arms and glared up at me. I tried to remember if irritation had ever looked so hot on anyone else. "You did that on purpose."

"It's possible."

"Are you getting off on humiliating me or something? Did I offend you in high school? Is this some weird grudge or revenge thing?"

I was thinking about getting off all right. But it had nothing to do with offending. Or high school. I shrugged. "Maybe I'm just bored."

"Right. Because war couldn't hold your attention so you thought you'd come back here and stick your nose in my business."

I stepped in, closing the distance so that we were nearly nose to nose. "You don't know shit about me or war, and I'd be careful about making any assumptions about either if I were you."

She blinked and her shoulders sagged a little. "Shit. I'm sorry. That was rude."

I forced myself to calm my breathing, a little taken aback at my own sudden reaction. A moment of silence passed between us. I concentrated on deep breaths and when I looked over, Cassie seemed to be doing the same. When she caught me watching, she stopped scratching at her elbow.

I cocked my head as her words finally sunk in. "Did you just apologize?"

She shrugged, still managing to keep her nose high. "When the situation calls for it, I'm capable."

"You're full of surprises."

She sighed. "Not really. I know what they say about me. And I'm not going to argue it." She spread her hands out as if offering herself up on display. "What you see is what you get."

"Somehow, I doubt that."

Someone with a headset microphone walked up and nodded at me. "Hey, Liam. They're almost ready for you." The guy gestured for me to join him near the curtain's edge.

"I'll be right there."

He walked off, eyeing me impatiently as I turned back to

Cassie. "Look, I have to give a speech. Can we figure out the terms of this later?"

"Liam, this is crazy. I can find someone else."

"Just tell me one thing. Did you have a thing for me in high school?"

"A thing?" she repeated, clearly trying to play it off. But the heat that crept into her cheeks gave her away. Interesting. Jess hadn't lied. Not about this anyway. And I knew—I wasn't taking no for an answer. "Even if I did, this isn't—"

I hesitated only a split second before interrupting her with a kiss.

Her lips were warm but stiff against mine. Even with the rigidity that never left her, in that split second, I found myself enjoying her. There was heat here. And something bubbling underneath that surface—something wild.

Cassie, I was pretty sure, did not feel the same.

I pulled back, the kiss over before it began, really, but it had lasted long enough for three things. First, I caught sight of the photographer lowering his camera and scurrying back to the party when we were done. Second, Cassie had finally been rendered speechless. And third, I'd had just enough of a taste of that girl to know I wouldn't be walking away anytime soon.

Jess was right. Cassie was trouble. And I was in it now.

I kept my voice low and my mouth close enough to breathe her in as I talked. She didn't pull away as I said, "Pretty sure Janice's photographer is tweeting that little treasure as we speak. Which means you're stuck with me now. Maybe after my speech, you can explain to me what this hired boyfriend stuff is all about."

I didn't give her a chance to answer before I walked away, joining the stage guy as my introduction was given for the crowd gathered on the other side of the curtain.

Just before I took the stage, I glanced back one last time.

Cassie was still standing in the same spot I'd left her, arms wrapped around her middle like a hug. In that split second, her carefully constructed mask slipped, and I saw what she was hiding: pain, fear, desperation—and attraction.

I went still, shocked at the raw emotion she'd let leak out. So she was capable of deep feelings after all. The public would have been thrilled to know it. Too bad I wasn't doing this for them. And suddenly, I wasn't doing it for Jess either. Maybe doing Jess a favor was how this had started, but it wasn't how it would end.

In the back of my mind, some voice warned me against giving in to that look. The girl capable of that kind of raw feeling was probably just as dangerous as the ice princess had been with the lack of it. But I ignored the voice and waited for Cassie to notice me there. When our eyes met, her mask shuttered instantly back into place.

But it was too late. I'd seen it. I'd seen her. And she knew it.

Desire shot through me, fast and hard, and I sucked in a breath as I rode the wave of it. It'd been a long time since I'd wanted a woman this bad just from looking at her. It was enough to knock me off balance in a way that had nothing to do with my recovering eardrums.

Oblivious, Cassie glared back at me. Just like earlier, her cheeks flushed, but this time, instead of amusement or uncertainty, her pale skin burned with rage. It was mildly terrifying, that look. But it was also sexy as hell. I still hadn't seen her smile, but the longer I looked at all that passion stored tightly inside that amazing body of hers, the less I cared about a smile. In fact, when it came to Cassie Franklin, there was only one expression I wanted her to wear for me. Cheeks warmed with rage or irritation was fine—as long as she was coming hard in my arms while she glared. An O face like Cassie Franklin's was hotter than anything else I could possibly imagine.

Turning slowly for the waiting crowd, I went to give my speech—as Cassie Franklin's boyfriend. Jess had been right. This was going to be fun to watch.

CHAPTER SIX

CASSIE

I glared at the phone display as if it were the villain, debating whether to even take the call from my father. After months of hearing him tell me how dire things were for the company, this conversation was stale—and yet, it hadn't lost its sting yet. Everything was still on me. And I was still stalling. But I couldn't hide forever.

"Hi, Dad," I answered.

"Cassandra. I need to see you. Come to my office."

"I'll be there in five," I said on a long sigh.

He disconnected.

"Nice to hear from you too," I muttered into the silence.

I got up from my desk and stopped on my way out to tell Bev where she could find me. Then, I made my way to the fifteenth floor. It was made up of only a conference room and a lounge on one end. To other end was my dad's suite of offices. I'd suggested a thousand times that we consolidate. Maybe even rent out some of this unused space to another company, but he wouldn't even consider it. He was too concerned with appearances.

"If you don't have money, at least make people think you do," he'd told me when I was a little girl. That was the perfect summation for my father's character. And the explanation for why he'd almost lost our company going on six times now since I'd come to work for him four years ago.

When I arrived, his secretary waved me in.

"Thank you for not dawdling," he said, waving me into a chair as I entered. "Time is money."

I rolled my eyes. If my father was ever a broken record about anything, it was that phrase.

"What's so pressing?" I asked.

"The status of this deal has me a little nervous," he admitted. "Particularly your part in it."

"Well, I wouldn't have any part in it if you'd lift this insane stipulation about my dating status."

"You know I would if I could," he said, but we both knew that was a lie. He could. And he wouldn't.

"I'm not going to use Evan," I said.

I hated the words my father was about to say even before they left his mouth. When he launched into another diatribe against the pharmaceutical company who had called in his bad debt, I tuned out. I still couldn't believe my father was blaming everyone but himself, but then he always had. How we hadn't lost everything before now was a mystery. My mother had done more to hold it together than I'd realized. When she'd died, my father's timeline for me had sped into light speed. I'd been officially hired on just out of high school, fitting in college classes at night, and between the two, I'd certainly gotten an education. The men in this family had put their name on the sign out front. The women kept it there.

"Evan's got himself under control," Dad was saying in

another attempt to talk me into his favorite solution to Nichimoto's reticence.

"Dad, you didn't see how he was with me yesterday." So far, I had kept my voice controlled and the longer this went on without me losing it, the more my arm itched. The rash from yesterday had morphed into full-blown hives. I knew if I wasn't careful, it would spread up to my chest and throat—and then a long-sleeved suit wouldn't hide the stress from prying eyes any longer. I'd even worn a gown with sleeves to last night's party to cover the evidence.

"I'm sure Evan was just excited about the idea of the two of you getting back together," Dad said.

I rolled my eyes. There was no point reminding him we couldn't be *back* if we were never together in the first place. "Or he's off his anger meds and his temper is a ticking time bomb. Again."

Dad had never acknowledged that Evan had narrowly avoided a lawsuit at his last job, and I knew he wasn't going to start now. I braced myself for whatever he tried to come up with instead.

"Cassandra, this situation is bigger than Evan's temper. It's bigger than you or even me. Think of all the good this company does. You want us to lose that? To default and let it all go to Big Pharma? Because that's what will happen and we all know what kind of monsters they are, flubbing the safety protocols and making drugs that kill people... Only private research firms like ours give any hope to a public too beholden to their prescriptions to do anything about it. Think of all the people we help. Think of Liam what's-his-name. He's alive because of us."

I sucked in a breath. Dad had always been willing to use anything in his arsenal to get the result he wanted, even when it came to me. And lately, guilt was the prime weapon. Probably because it worked better than anything else. But using Liam right now was not cool.

"Trust me, I am thinking of those people," I said. Especially Liam Porter.

Dad sighed. "I know you think Nichimoto's terms are old-fashioned."

"Stipulating a woman can't step into the role of CEO without being romantically attached goes beyond old-fashioned. It's practically illegal."

"I didn't make the rules."

"But you can change them. You're the CEO for God's sake. This is Neanderthal."

"It's not about your relationship status, Cassandra. Or your stability."

I blinked. This was the first time I'd heard him offer any sort of explanation. "Then what—?"

"You know what they call you?"

My jaw hung open for a moment as I floundered. "They call me the ice princess," I said, sitting up straighter and offering a cool expression. Not because I gave two shits about the nickname. But this was the first time I'd ever heard my father refer to it. Even when manipulating me for his own ends, he'd never brought it up. "I don't see what that has to do with the deal."

"The board doesn't want someone so cold running a public company who depends on investors." He grimaced as if he really didn't like the taste of his own words as he added, "I can't say I disagree with them."

"You …" I blinked as it all sank in. "This is why you won't fight for…? This is why I have to prove I'm romantically attached? To show that I'm *nice*?" I spat the words, making it clear how fucking ridiculous all of this was. But it didn't matter what I thought.

He didn't answer.

After a long silence, I knew he wasn't going to either. Another stalemate. Only now, I knew why. God, this was embarrassing.

My cell rang, buzzing quietly where I clutched it tightly in my hand. Without looking at the screen, I rose. "I have to go." I started for the door.

"What about the board—?"

"Tell them I have it handled," I snapped.

"You do?" The surprise—and relief—in his tone was palpable. Which only made me more pissed.

"I'll call you later with the details." I slammed his office door hard enough to make his assistant jump and picked up the incoming one on my cell. "Hey, Jess."

"Whoa. You answered."

More guilt. "I know I haven't been around much. I'm sorry." Jess was the one person in the entire world I could apologize to—and mean it—without feeling like I'd lost something.

"It's fine. I just miss you. Is everything okay with you?"

There was enough hurt hidden in her casual words that my chest ached. Fuck, I was failing at this. At everything. "Yeah, it's just… There's a lot going on right now with work. We're in the middle of an investment deal that I didn't realize had so many twists to the terms and it's been a huge time suck."

"That sounds shitty. I understand, though. Listen, I wanted to see if you had a chance to see Liam Porter yet."

"Liam?" My breath caught. "Why do you ask?"

Her voice turned light and teasing. "Because Summerville's most gorgeous playboy is now highly skilled at explosions if you know what I mean. I thought it might be fun for you to get to

"O" FACE

know him finally. Maybe put an end to your losing streak."

"It's not a losing streak."

"Trust me, honey. It really is. But if anyone can ruin that record, it's probably Liam Porter. Just sayin'."

"Jess, I didn't have time for that sort of thing before, and I still don't."

"Do not give me that shit. You had a major crush on him in high school."

"Major might be stretching it."

She snorted, and I knew I couldn't bullshit Jess. Not on this. But I also couldn't tell her about my meeting with Liam— either of them.

"I saw the video from his speech last night on the news this morning. I swear, that stubble combined with all that muscle made my ovaries hurt."

My lips curved at that and some of the stress melted away for the moment. "Dramatic much?"

"Are you kidding? He's a war hero with a hot body and a bionic eardrum. You don't get any sexier than that. Well, until he opens his mouth, anyway."

I laughed. "I take it you two still get along just as well as before?"

"Jamie still loves the guy. I guess he sees something I don't. Anyway, if you do decide to live out your high school fantasy, just don't let him speak."

"Jess, you're crazy."

"Right. But I'm your kind of crazy, bitch. Call me when your deal is done. We'll get drunk and skinny dip in my neighbor's pool again."

"That was one time, and you swore you wouldn't tell anyone—"

"I haven't," she promised. "Yet." Then she hung up.

57

Back in my office, I set the phone aside and dropped my face into my hands. Jess was a great friend. Actually, she was my only friend. I'd steered clear of kids in school after they'd either demanded too much time—time I didn't have after all my lessons, training, and grooming thanks to Dad—or they'd used me for popularity or to paint an image that only my father's money could provide. But Jess had never pretended to be anything other than herself. She was also the only other person I'd met who wasn't looking to over share about her feelings every chance she got. We were both allergic to vulnerability thanks to a few bad experiences.

But after so many years of her putting up with my shit, I owed her more than this. I owed her the truth. I just couldn't bring myself to admit to her what I'd been reduced to. Maybe when it was all over and I had it figured out. But not yet.

A noise at my office doorway made me look up. I froze, my jaw half-open and ready to offer up some quick order to my assistant. But it wasn't Bev. Not even close.

"What are you doing here?" I demanded.

"I thought I'd catch you before you drove home. See if you wanted to stay in the city tonight for our date." Liam strode in without waiting to be invited and sank into the chair across from my desk. He looked smug and sexy as hell in his boots and a button-up, but the combination—and his words—put me on edge.

"Date?" I repeated warily.

"You made it sound like you needed a boyfriend immediately. Am I wrong?"

"No, you're not, but—"

"Don't bother telling me you'll find someone else. I've already seen the article in the paper and that picture of our kiss was retweeted more than enough times to make us officially a thing."

Dammit. I'd seen the article this morning but when no one else mentioned it today, I thought maybe it had gone unnoticed. I made a mental note to grill Bev about it later.

Suddenly, the call from Jess didn't seem so innocent. Had she seen the picture? Had the board? Had Dad? Why hadn't he said anything?

I looked up to find Liam studying me. The shape of his mouth mesmerized me. What would it feel like to have his mouth on my skin? To let him kiss me again and really kiss him back? Even from that split second of contact, I knew he kissed with the same intensity he used to stare at me. Just the thought of it made my skin tingle.

"Fine," I said, nearly surprising myself at my own agreement. "I'll let you play the role of my boyfriend. But we can't take this out in public until we work out the terms."

"I agree. The terms are this: I pretend to be your boyfriend, and in exchange, you pretend to be my friend."

"Excuse me?"

"Look, the ice princess schtick has to be old by now, right? I mean, you've clearly been at it long enough to master it, and I'm sure you've got everyone around you fooled. But I saw behind your mask the other night. We both know there's more to you than that. So, I'll let everyone think I'm your boyfriend if you let me see the real Cassie Franklin. Just until our deal is done."

I stared at him, at a loss for words.

Liam waited, clearly not bothered by my silence.

I wanted to go off on him for the way he'd just spoken to me. He'd called me an ice princess which was probably the nicest way he could think of telling me I was a bitch. But he also wasn't wrong. And truthfully, deep down, I really was sick of freezing people out just so I didn't have to try to decipher their true intentions. At least this time, I already knew what he wanted from me.

Besides, after the deal was done, he'd go back to his own life, and I could go back to mine. We lived in two different worlds, so it wasn't like I'd run into him at parties or something. Not like with Evan.

"Okay," I said.

"Damn." Liam straightened, grabbing the armrests as he sat up. "That was easier than I expected."

I reached into the drawer on my right and pulled out the contract I'd prepared when I'd first come up with the idea. "You just have to sign here."

"No." I opened my mouth to argue, but he cut me off. "That's my other term. No contracts."

"We have to make this official. To protect—"

"I can protect myself. And I swear not to use you or take this any farther than you want me to. But I'm not signing a contract. Or taking any money."

"Liam, I have to give you something for your time."

"Give me you."

"What?" I asked, startled. Was he asking what I thought he was asking? Because I'd already made it clear sex was not on the table.

"Friendship," he amended but the glint in his eye told me he'd said it that way on purpose. "The real you. That's payment enough, trust me, I've wondered about the real Cassie Franklin long enough."

My mouth went dry. I wasn't even sure what to say to that. Did that mean he'd thought about me? His words sent a warning bell off in my mind, and I knew I should refuse this. It was crazy. But then so was hiring a boyfriend. And I didn't have any other choice. Apparently, my problems weren't going to go away until I proved I was capable of making someone like me. Basically, I had to prove I was nice.

And here was a perfect opportunity to practice just that.

Slowly, I pushed to my feet and came around the desk so that we stood eye to eye. I extended my hand, offering it in a hand shake to seal our agreement as officially as we could. Something told me this was enough of a promise for Liam. I just hoped I could trust it. And him.

"It's a deal," I said, watching as his lips curved upward into a smile that lit his eyes and sparked a warm tingle from my hand straight into my lower belly. My knees threatened to buckle.

"I'm glad to hear it," he said in a low voice that was predatory enough to make me shudder in anticipation. Of what, I didn't know.

"Now what?" I asked, shocked to hear how breathless my voice sounded.

"Now, let's eat."

CHAPTER SEVEN

LIAM

THE restaurant was crowded, but then I'd expected nothing less. Besides the fact that it was the dinner rush, this place had the best reviews online for fine dining in Charleston. And I knew without asking that Cassie would want to be seen. It was also the thing I wanted least in the entire world, but I'd already made my peace with it. At least for the next few weeks while I played my role. I'd even worn the blazer she'd dug out of some intern's closet, because even I knew better than to argue with her about proper attire for a restaurant like this one.

I still wasn't entirely sure why I'd agreed to this. But it wasn't like I had anything better to do. That was the thing with my medical discharge. It wasn't just about the fact that I'd nearly died or that I had a second chance. I was literally starting over from the ashes of a life I'd had to leave behind. Sure, I was grateful I wasn't a statistic. Or an obituary. I was lucky. I knew that. Appreciated it. But I had absolutely no idea what to do next. Besides, Cassie Franklin was a puzzle too intriguing not to solve.

Who in the hell hired a boyfriend so the gossip rags in our tiny town would talk *more* about your personal life? Didn't most public figures want less press? More privacy. Then again, Cassie Franklin wasn't most people. And I was dying to know what was driving her.

"We have your usual table, Miss Franklin. Right this way," the hostess said the moment we entered.

Of course she had a usual table.

I followed Cassie back to an intimate table for two in the corner. It was dimly lit and offered the illusion of privacy even though the entire restaurant had a clear view of us as we sat and ordered wine. I felt like a toy on display, especially as I noticed the stares and whispers we drew just from sitting down together.

Cassie didn't seem to notice or mind.

"This is your usual, huh?" I asked, my tone teasing—or at least challenging. I couldn't help but wonder how many men she'd brought here before me. But she pretended not to hear me and picked up her menu instead.

I tried another angle. "So, what have you been up to since high school?" I asked, purposely focusing on her rather than the busy dining room. It wasn't a hardship either. She'd kept her jacket on for some reason, but the way it covered her up only made me want to see more of her.

I'd lain awake for a long time last night picturing her in that sparkly dress she'd worn to the party. All those sparkles and all that smooth skin flushed with irritation at me—it wasn't an image I'd soon forget.

"Working mostly," she said and her clipped tone made it clear she didn't want to talk about it.

But I wasn't giving up that easily. "Right. Developing cochlear implants and other life-saving technology."

Her smile was tight—and fake. "Precisely."

The waiter arrived and took our order. Cassie gave hers in a brisk tone that bordered on rude. The waiter either didn't care or was used to it. Probably the latter. I offered him an apologetic smile and handed him our menus. After he was gone, I poured a generous amount of wine for us both. We were going to need it at this rate.

"What about you?" she asked, and it wasn't hard to see she was trying to take the spotlight off herself. But I ran with it.

"You already know most of my story. Four years in the service. EOD—"

"EOD?" she repeated. "That's bomb tech, right?"

"Explosive Ordnance Disposal. Bomb tech is close enough I guess. Although we purposely set off just as many as we shut down." I grinned just thinking about it, but Cassie looked horrified.

"Isn't that the opposite of keeping the world safe?"

"Not if they're too sensitive to deactivate safely. Sometimes it's safer to blow it up under controlled conditions than risk it detonating accidentally in a high-risk zone."

"Is that what happened when you…" She trailed off, her gaze dropping from my eyes to my ears and then my chest.

"When I nearly died," I finished, noting her discomfort. Interesting that she could be rude so easily to the waiter and show compassion for me now. "Sort of. The blast happened underwater, and it was spontaneous which means no one set it off on purpose."

"And you were too close?" she asked, her blue eyes wide as she undoubtedly tried to picture something that was, frankly, unimaginable.

"Yes and no. I was about sixty feet above it."

Her brows furrowed. "Then how did it affect you—?"

"Pressure," I explained. "Underwater, the pressure from an explosion is magnified. The momentum tossed me toward the surface, and I ascended too fast. My lungs expanded and I surfaced with a tension pneumothorax and blown eardrums. I was so dazed, I didn't even realize it had affected my ears until after the needle decompression procedure."

"That was for your lung, right?" she asked.

I blinked at her in surprise. "You read my file?"

She picked up her wine, sipping slowly, and I wondered if it was just a diversion while she collected her thoughts. Damn, this girl was good at hiding her thoughts. No wonder people thought she was cold. "I was interested to see if our tech actually worked."

"Obviously," I repeated quietly.

Her gaze snapped up and met mine. My brows rose in a silent challenge I had no doubt she understood, but she didn't offer any more explanation.

I decided to let it go. For now. Instead, I sipped my wine—liberally.

"I don't know how you do it."

I looked up to find Cassie studying me intently. "Do what?" I asked.

"You tell your story like it's no big deal."

"Did you want me to dissolve into a fit of tears as I relive every moment until my team was able to pull me from the brink of death as I nearly drowned in my own fluids?"

"God, Liam. No. I... I was just wondering how you ended up out there. Your bio said you were stationed at a base in Djibouti. That's not where the medical report lists your initial hospital stay."

"My bio was partly correct." And how in the hell did she get hold of a document that actually listed my hospital's location?

Her eyes narrowed fractionally as she attempted to read between the lines. "Is this the part where you tell me 'if I told you, I'd have to kill you'?"

I offered a telling grin. "Precisely."

I watched as she fidgeted with the stem of her wine glass, momentarily losing myself in the image of her dainty fingers wrapped instead around my—

"What about girlfriends?"

I blinked, my gaze snapping up to hers. "What about them?"

She hesitated, her cheeks flushing deliciously as she asked, "Did you have any while you were away?"

"Well, considering there was an average of one woman for every twenty men at my various posts, no."

She didn't look convinced which amused me. "No one serious all this time?" she pressed.

"No one special enough, I guess." Would she have cared if there had been?

"From what I remember during high school, they were all special to you."

"You kept tabs on me?" I raised a brow, trying not to show how much I liked the idea that Cassie had noticed me just as much as I'd noticed her all those years ago. Interesting. Maybe Jess had been more serious than I'd realized about me being the one to get Cassie talking.

She rolled her eyes. "You were hard to miss."

"Direct hit." I clutched dramatically at my heart. "I don't know if I've just been complimented or insulted."

"If you pretend it's a compliment, they usually won't have the balls to correct you." The way the words just fell out of her mouth, I knew the phrase was something she'd been told often.

I smirked. "Spoken like a true ice princess."

She looked abruptly away, and I instantly wished I hadn't said anything. We'd actually been inching toward flirting for a moment before I'd ruined it. To make matters worse, the food arrived, interrupting whatever backtracking I might have done.

I sat back, watching her as our plates were set in front of us. When we were alone, she picked up her fork, and I did the same, still watching her. The sound of her voice caught me off guard.

"It doesn't bother me, you know."

I looked up at her, guilty again of staring at her hands for some reason. They hadn't stopped moving since we'd sat down. Twirling her glass, scratching her arm, wielding her fork. And it was riveting. Pathetically so. "What doesn't?" I asked, trying to refocus on what she was saying.

"The title. Ice princess. I've always known that's what they call me, and honestly, if it keeps the users away, I don't mind."

"The users?" I repeated.

"The people who pretend to be your friend so they can get a free lunch."

"Ah." I nodded. "You had a lot of that?"

She shrugged, but it was a sharp movement. Too forced. "I had enough."

"Is that why you don't have friends?" The question slipped out before I could stop it; genuine curiosity getting the better of wisdom.

"I have friends," she insisted.

But I pinned her with a look. "Jess doesn't count."

Her lip curled in an expression I remembered as classic Cassie. "She'll be thrilled to know you said so." She speared a piece of potato.

"Let's not talk about her. Let's talk about you. While I have you willing to share, tell me something about yourself."

Around a bite of food, she said, "I like drinking wine in nice restaurants."

I pointed my fork at her. "Very funny. You agreed to be my friend," I reminded her.

"I agreed to pretend to be your friend," she corrected.

I huffed. Maybe I should have had her sign something after all. Clearly, she was better at this than me. "Pretending and lying are not the same. If I ask a question, you have to tell the truth."

Her mouth tightened, making it hard to look away from her lips. "Fine. You have five minutes."

"Deal," I agreed. "Favorite movie."

"Um." She looked like a deer in headlights. It was sad, actually.

"Never mind. I haven't seen a movie in like three years, anyway. Favorite song."

"I…"

This was really pathetic. Coming from a guy that had been out of touch with pop culture for years that said a lot. "Favorite food?"

"Macadamia nut cookies," she said with no hesitation.

I grinned. "At least you know what you like to eat."

She shook her head. "I don't eat them often. Too many calories. When I was a kid, I used to sneak out of my room at night and creep down to the pantry for one. I would take tiny bites, and then, I would just hold it in my mouth until it dissolved."

I looked up from my plate. "You wouldn't chew it?"

"I wanted it to last as long as possible."

"You could have just eaten two."

"No way." She shook her head vehemently. "Mom would have lost her shit. She was constant about me staying in shape.

And Dad was the same way. Keeping fit meant staying healthy longer. God, I think he was grooming me for an eighteen-hour work day from the time I could talk."

I shook my head in commiseration, but secretly, I felt like I'd just won. Cassie Franklin had shared something personal. With me. I decided not to push about her mom, too afraid it would shut her down. "See? Was that so hard?"

Her brows dipped in confusion.

"You just told me something about yourself that no one else knows. And you were nice about it. And no one died."

Her lips curved into the hint of a smile. Another point for me. "Whoa. Calm down. If you smile now, it'll give me too much too fast," I warned.

"Very funny."

"I'm serious. Your smile is like the holy grail of Summerville. If I get it tonight, I'll have nothing left to live for."

"What are you talking about?"

I stared at her, brows raised. But she seemed genuinely clueless. "Uh, just the fact that no one has ever seen you smile."

"Yes, they have. You're being ridiculous."

"I'm being dead serious. It's like one of the constants in life. Death, taxes, and Cassie Franklin not smiling."

Her amusement faded. "I have a lot going on," she muttered.

"Is that why you had to hire a boyfriend? Too busy to go out and find a real one?"

Her expression hardened. "I've had a real one."

"And?" I looked around, knowing full well I was baiting her temper. But if I couldn't get her to smile at me, getting her pissed was the next best thing. "Where is he now? Because all I see is your hired help."

"He's at home. Hopefully taking his medication."

I waited, but she didn't say more. In fact, she'd gone so quiet I wondered if she'd even meant to tell me that much. "You know, I really want to make a joke about how impossible you must have been, but I'm taking the high road here."

"Ha ha. For your information, he was diagnosed as bipolar last year."

"Damn. Wow. Sorry." Her shoulders sagged, but she didn't answer. "I didn't mean to be an asshole," I added. "Mental illness sucks."

She cocked her head at me.

"What?" I demanded. "Do I have food on my chin or something?"

"No, it's just… You're the first person to be so easy about it."

"The media wasn't so easy," I guessed. She huffed in clear agreement. "Is that why you hired me? To take the pressure off?"

"No. Although, it's refreshing to talk to someone who doesn't think they know all the details just based on what they read in the papers."

"Yeah, my being out of touch with reality is a real perk."

Her lips twitched again. "Actually, I hired you because my father is out of touch with reality."

"What do you mean?"

She sighed, and we both fell silent as the waiter appeared to refill our drinks. I didn't press the issue. Even after the waiter left us, we ate in silence and I waited. Whatever she'd been about to tell me was serious. It was also decidedly in the realm of private. And one thing Cassie Franklin had never been was open.

I hadn't even technically included it in our terms. I'd used the word *friend* instead of *open* on purpose. Partly because I didn't think she'd have agreed to spilling her secrets. And partly because I'd been too focused on the physical perks that would hopefully come from this arrangement—another reason I hadn't let her pay me. The last thing I wanted to become after leaving the military was Summerville's resident gigolo.

"We're broke."

I stopped, my fork halfway to my mouth with the last bite of the best chicken I'd had in three years—I'd already made a mental note not to tell my mother that. "What?"

She picked up her wine, holding it close without actually drinking it. "Franklin Industries. We had to pay out a settlement for a drug trial that went really wrong last year. And then we invested everything into the new implant program. But then the FDA still hasn't approved that even after your successful surgery. And my dad...he has a habit of pissing off the investors which makes it hard to get funding renewed. So, now we're broke. If we don't find new funding, we're going to lose the company."

"Shit, Cassie, I'm really sorry," I said, unable to picture her without her living in the shadow of her father's company. The heir to Franklin Industries had been her identity for as long as I could remember. Her whole life had been a preparation for running the place when her father retired. He made no secret of it. I could only imagine how Cassie felt knowing it might not make it that long. "Is there anything else you can do?"

"Not without an investor. They found one actually. A Japanese company that has all the resources we need to go back into R and D *and* contract to produce more of the drugs that we know would put us in the black again."

"That's good news," I said, but the look on her face told me it was anything but.

"It would be. Private funding is the only way we stay out of the government's pocket. Otherwise, we end up like any other Big Pharma research firm, ripping off the customers it's supposed to heal. But…"

"But?"

Her shoulders sagged and she let go of her wine long enough to scratch at her shoulder. I noticed her chest had reddened and now she scratched at that too. "Mr. Nichimoto is from a very conservative Japanese family. He's very old-fashioned and doesn't think a woman should have control of an entire company. He's pressured the board by stipulating the only way he'll invest is if I'm married by the time the deal goes through. And a week ago, the board agreed."

"Holy shit. Is this guy for real?"

"Apparently."

"And your dad is going along with it?"

"He offered a compromise," she said wryly. "If I can show that I have a boyfriend and we appear serious enough, he'll sell that to Nichimoto and we can make the deal to save the company."

"That's insane."

"I know."

"So, you need the media to see us and run with it so that it gets back to Nichimoto."

"Exactly." She took a deep drink of wine, the rest of her dinner clearly forgotten.

I studied her. "Can I ask you something?"

"Sure." She set the wine down but didn't let go.

"Why bother?"

Her eyes widened. "Are you asking me why I care about losing everything that matters to me?"

"No. I'm asking if it really matters as much as you think. Look, this company is your dad's. And I know he's your father, and I know losing his company would be hard, but he's retiring in a year, anyway. I'm sure he has savings. I'm sure you're both going to be fine if things don't go your way here." She didn't answer, but the pain in her expression spurred me on. "If it were up to you, is running this company what you really want?"

Her eyes glinted like I'd just challenged her entire existence. "I've been training for this my whole life."

"That's not what I asked."

"I know what you're asking, and I don't appreciate it. I promised to be friendly, but I don't owe you any explanations. Besides, I just shared something very personal with you, and you're throwing it in my face." For a split second, I expected her to get up and walk out. But she surprised me. Instead, she leaned in so that I caught a whiff of expensive perfume, her eyes blazing with the kind of fury meant to send a message: I am not backing down first. "Of course I want it. I wouldn't be here—with you, doing this—if I didn't."

I threw up my hands, surrendering underneath the heat of her glare. Wisely, I decided not to mention the rash that was spreading across her chest and up her throat. A rash that was looking more and more like hives. If I hadn't seen it the other day in her office, I might have assumed she had an allergy to something she ate. But I already knew, this was stress. Anxiety in its purest form. Cassie Franklin was a ticking time bomb herself. I had to tread carefully here.

"Sure," I said lightly. "Of course you want it. I'm sorry, I didn't mean anything by it." I raised my wineglass in a peacekeeping toast. "You convinced me."

It wasn't a lie, I realized as we finished our drinks, and I paid the bill. Cassie had definitely convinced me of something, but it had nothing to do with her father or his company. I'd come here thinking a dinner would be enough to satisfy my curiosity. That I could get to know the real Cassie Franklin and once my questions were answered, I could walk away for good. Go live in my parents' house on the outskirts of a tiny town and ignore the world.

But after everything she'd told me tonight, I was nowhere close to being done. More than ever, I wanted Cassie Franklin; in my bed, sure. But more than that, I really did want to earn her friendship. There were secrets buried in her. Surprises and sides to her that I was convinced no one else in the entire world had experienced including Cassie herself. Cassie Franklin was uncharted waters, and that was something I couldn't walk away from. I'd pretend to be her boyfriend for as long as she needed me, but before it was over, I planned to experience Cassie Franklin as a lover—and maybe even as a friend.

CHAPTER EIGHT

CASSIE

TWO nights after our fancy dinner, I let Liam take me out again. I wasn't sure what I'd expected when I'd agreed to another date, but it definitely wasn't this. Liam's truck was a throwback to our high school days, and I had a feeling his flannel shirt was too. I had no problem with casual, but this was a little too laid back. I tried not to show my disapproval but Liam was more perceptive than I gave him credit for.

"Do you want to change?" he asked when I greeted him at my front door.

"Me?" I blinked, looking down at the black dress I'd chosen and then at his flannel and jeans.

"Well, it's a little late for me," he said with a playful grin. "Unless you want me to wear something an old ex of yours might have left behind."

"I don't have any ex's clothes," I mumbled. What I'd meant was that I didn't have any exes. Not really. I'd been a little generous at dinner the other night, calling Evan an old boyfriend. But Liam didn't know that, and I wasn't about to admit my lack of sexual experience to a guy who'd probably slept with half our town four years ago.

"Well, we could both go nude and give them a real story."

"Let's just go," I snapped, cranky from being grilled by Dad about Liam and our fake date the other night. Dad wanted me to use the publicity to bring in more investor cash. He wasn't convinced we had enough to keep us afloat until I could find a way to satisfy Nichimoto. I couldn't bring myself to tell him that I wasn't even sure I wanted to anymore.

My words came out even sharper than I'd intended, though. Liam complied without another word about our clashing wardrobe.

Twenty minutes later, the truck idled annoyingly loud as I sat and stared out the window at the club across the street. The bass coming from within was loud enough and strong enough that I could practically feel it shaking the pickup truck. Rock music. Not my favorite. Around the side, I spotted an outdoor area that had some sort of beanbag game set up. People stood around it, talking and laughing.

Liam waited in silence for me to make up my mind, and I could already feel his judgment if I said no. But I couldn't bring myself to say yes either.

"It's not the right image," I said finally.

He didn't argue, just put the truck into gear and drove off. For some reason, his silence made me feel defensive.

"The investor is going to be studying us. I can't give the impression I—"

"The impression you what? Like to have fun?"

I cut him a look, but he just stared straight ahead at the sea of red taillights in front of us. "CEOs don't go to clubs like that," I said shortly.

"Maybe they should," he muttered.

"What is that supposed to mean?"

He opened his mouth, clearly about to say something, but then took one look at me and promptly closed it again. "Nothing."

"You're a lot grumpier than the rumors in high school suggested," I said finally.

He looked over. "I guess you just bring it out of me."

"Oh, I make you an ass?"

"An ass, an eardrum." He shrugged. "Looks like you're responsible for a lot of my key parts."

I shook my head and stared out the window. Deep down, though, I had to admit that I was kind of enjoying this. I'd shared something really personal with Liam and he wasn't treating me like I was breakable for it. If anything, he was being harder on me.

"What? No quick reply for that one?"

I swiveled to glare at him. He was baiting me. I knew it, but I also couldn't just let him have the last word. "I'm used to being the responsible one, what can I say?"

He frowned like that hadn't been the answer he'd expected and when he spoke again, his temper had drained away. "You don't ever punch out, do you?" It was a sincere enough question, but he'd pushed me too far. I hated how defensive I felt around him, but I couldn't seem to shake it off.

"Just because I don't burn it down every night after work doesn't mean I don't know how to unwind."

"Uh-huh. Name one recent thing you did to relax."

I shot him a glance and then looked away. His smugness was evident as he said, "I thought so."

"I can't go out and get drunk all the time," I said, frustrated.

"Who said anything about drinking? I just meant pleasure.

It could be something as simple as…" I jumped as his fingertips brushed over the back of my hand. "I rest my case."

"You're talking about sex."

"I'm talking about pleasure," he insisted again, but if anything, it only made me think about sex more. I swallowed hard, thinking of all my failed attempts to do exactly as he'd just suggested. If he only knew.

"I tried. It didn't work," I said quietly.

He pulled over and turned to look at me. In the dark cab of the truck, his eyes glinted with desire that felt suddenly dangerous to acknowledge or accept. "You're not trying it with the right people then."

I licked my lips, and he growled—a low rumbling in his throat that made my stomach tighten. He scooted closer so that his chest strained against his seat belt. I backed away, my head bumping the window behind me.

"You don't have to be afraid of me. I won't hurt you," he said quietly.

I lifted my chin. "I'm not afraid of you." Lie.

"I can't stop thinking about you," he admitted.

I blinked, completely at a loss.

"I think about you too," I heard myself saying.

He leaned closer so that his warm breath washed over me when he spoke again. "Let me touch you, Cassie."

His voice was rough with need and even from here I could sense how tense he was. Holding himself back. Going slow—for me. It scared me, but I couldn't explain that to him now. Besides, I didn't want this moment to end, and I knew, the moment I admitted how terrified I was, and why, he'd stop. "I thought you said this wasn't about sex."

"It's not. I just want to give you pleasure. No sex. I swear."

Not yet. The unspoken words hung in the air between us: a

clear line drawn in the sand. He was leaving it up to me. I could say no. But I didn't want to. For once, I wanted this. Maybe it would prove I wasn't as frigid as they all said.

"All right," I whispered back.

Slowly, he reached for me, using a single finger to trace the shape of my face. He let it trail from my forehead to chin before dropping low to skim over my throat and down my chest. With his dark eyes locked on mine, he dipped his finger between my cleavage, tracing a line along the edge of my dress and then trailing up again to tangle in my hair. Everywhere his finger touched left a fire burning in its wake.

That, more than anything, was a shock.

I didn't speak; too afraid to break the spell.

We were both breathing heavily, and I noted the fogged windows while somehow not taking my eyes from his. It was exquisite, this kind of contact. No pressure for whatever should come next. And no thoughts either. My mind was the quietest it had been in forever. All it could think about was this moment. And Liam's hands on my skin.

I tried to remember the last time I'd been touched. Or the last time I'd enjoyed it this much. But I couldn't and I didn't want to. All I wanted was Liam. More of Liam.

"Don't stop," I whispered, my eyes meeting his and my skin humming with the feel of him.

His finger found my chest again. Slowly, it dragged lower, over the thin fabric of my dress, and lower still, until it reached the hemline and grazed my bare thigh. I sucked in a breath, but he didn't stop there, sliding his finger underneath my dress and up my thigh, higher and higher, painfully slow.

I watched him, too caught up in the sensation of his skin against my own to talk or even breathe.

"Does that feel good?" he asked.

I nodded wordlessly, my lip caught between by teeth.

His mouth inched toward mine in the darkness.

My lips parted as I stared back at him, wondering for the hundredth time what it would feel like if he kissed me. Would my body respond at all? Would it feel as good as it did when he touched my face? My gaze dropped to his mouth and I couldn't help but imagine it on my own. Or on other parts of my body.

As if he'd read my mind, he changed direction. Instead of kissing my lips, he veered sideways and pressed a kiss against my cheek. His breath tickled my ear, and I shuddered. His finger slid along the edge of my panties.

"Liam," I whispered, no idea what I was even trying to convey.

"Shh. Just focus on the pleasure." He leaned closer, kissing a trail down my throat to my chest, his lips skimming the neckline of my dress. I jumped when his finger slid inside the edge of my panties and brushed over my clit. My eyes closed while he explored, and I felt myself practically melting against his touch, every one of my fingers and toes going liquidy and tingly at the same time.

Was this what it was supposed to feel like to be kissed?

Was this what the rest of the world experienced when they were intimate?

"I want it," I whispered, realizing too late that my words sounded like a direct invitation to skip straight to the part where we got naked. "But just—" I winced, stiffening at the thought of taking this that far right now, and Liam drew away.

"Just not with me," he finished, the words sounding like a question and an accusation at the same time. I knew the moment had ended when he pulled his hand away.

"It's not that. I—"

"Don't worry about it," he said, his voice tired. I let it go, watching with tense muscles as he slid back into his seat and put the truck in gear. "Just let me take you home."

Neither of us spoke again as he pulled a quick U-turn and headed back toward my house. My thoughts were a jumbled mess, too disjointed to form any kind of response as he pulled up in front of my house and parked. He made no move to walk me to my door.

"I'll call you to set up our next date," I said, feeling awkward to be the one in charge now.

"Sounds good." His voice was neutral. Almost cold.

Just before I got out, I spared a glance at him, but he didn't meet my eyes.

Finally, without a word, I climbed out of the truck and walked away.

Behind me, the truck revved into reverse and pulled out of my driveway, the exhaust filling the empty street in its wake. I didn't turn to watch him go and instead concentrated on fitting my key into the lock and then getting inside. In the foyer, I was shocked to realize my blurred vision had nothing to do with the darkness outside and more to do with the tears filling my eyes.

I blinked them back and shut my front door behind me with a hard click. Wine. I needed wine and lots of it to make sense of Liam Porter. Because something either awful or amazing had just happened between us; but I had no idea which it was.

CHAPTER NINE

LIAM

GETTING blown up notwithstanding, Cassie was going to be the death of me. The more time I spent with her, the more I wanted her. The look on her face when I'd touched her in the truck last night, the way her body had practically hummed underneath my touch as I ran my fingers over her skin had been more erotic than anything I'd ever done—and we hadn't even kissed. I'd come home and taken a cold shower, but even that hadn't diminished the ache. When I'd finally fallen asleep, I'd dreamt about her eyes again, but this time, the ice in them had melted, replaced with a heat like liquid fire. I'd woken harder than I'd been in a long fucking time. Even after I'd taken care of myself, all I wanted was her.

In the light of day, though, all I could think about was what she'd been about to say when she'd put the brakes on. I'd shut down, thinking at first it was personal, but that had been knee-jerk. And mostly it had been about my own feelings getting too big for me to understand.

I'd freaked out on her. And then she'd freaked out on me.

And now, I had no idea how to come back from it without sounding like a lovesick high schooler all over again. All I could do was wait for her to call me. I had a feeling after the way I'd acted it wasn't going to be anytime soon. In the meantime, I had the worst case of blue balls I could remember.

Today was going to be a long day. And tonight would be even worse.

I needed a distraction.

"Sophie," I called as I finished breakfast.

A door opened upstairs. "Yeah?"

"I'm headed to the shop if you need me."

"Okay. I'm off to work in a few, but I'll see you for dinner?" she called back.

"Uh." I hesitated. "I'll let you know."

There was a pause and then, "Does this have anything to do with Cassie Franklin?"

I smiled to myself and grabbed my coffee. "With any luck it will. Love you!" I didn't wait for an answer before I slipped out the back, adjusting myself as I went.

CHAPTER TEN

CASSIE

I woke the next morning with more regret than my last hangover. And that included skinny dipping in a stranger's pool. I groaned as I fumbled with the alarm and rolled over. It was Saturday. And that meant a full day out of the office with nothing else to do but continue living my own lie. It also meant another day with Liam Porter. I wasn't even sure I still wanted to see him after last night. He'd been pushy and rude and nosy and—

Who was I kidding?

I definitely wanted to see Liam Porter. And if I was being honest, I wanted to touch him too. To pick up right where we'd left off in that truck. Before I'd ruined it all with my second-guessing and Liam had shut down over it. Maybe Jess had a point though. Maybe I liked him better when he didn't talk.

I snickered and got up, heading for the kitchen where I knew my coffee machine had already started my coffee. While I sipped, I checked emails and read the Business section of the local newspaper on my open laptop. Summerville didn't have a lot of business, so it mostly covered Charleston, focusing on anything relating to Summerville's residents. A headline on the sidebar caught my eye, and I clicked on it with a growing sense of dread. Skimming it, I felt my stomach drop to my knees as I read all about the company's tenuous position—and my botched attempts to fix it—through the eyes of a stranger.

"Franklin Industries' Trouble in Paradise: Cassie Franklin's Frozen Heart to Blame for Financial Woes"

I read quickly, and when I got to the part about how I'd hired Liam to be my boyfriend in a sad attempt to appear likeable, I sucked in a breath, shaking my head to try to block out the reality of the words and how many people must have read them already. I shoved the laptop away and lowered my head to the counter, squeezing out a few hot tears before giving in and dropping my forehead against the cool granite.

This could not be happening.

My phone rang. I ignored it and got up from my stool, retrieving the bottle of whiskey and adding a double-shot to my coffee before sitting again.

This time, when my phone rang, I picked it up. "Hello?"

"Miss Franklin? This is Rowena Bennett from the *Summerville Sun*. I'd like to get a statement from you regarding today's story about—"

I hung up.

In the silence, I gulped more spiked coffee and stared at my phone, my anxiety already sending my heart racing. When it continued to ring, I considered going to get a hammer and put the thing out of its misery. My panic and my temper were both at full blast. Nothing reasonable, like shutting the thing off, felt good enough. It had to be destroyed. Just like my life.

When it rang again, I looked down.

The display showed one short word: Dad.

Instead of answering it, I picked it up and chucked it as hard as I could against the far wall. It hit a glass-coated canvas of the Bermuda coastline from my trip there last year. Both the phone and the glass shattered.

I stared at it, finishing off the last of my coffee.

My insides churned as I debated what to do next. There would be no date with Liam now. No deal with the investor. No saving the company. Whoever had leaked—and written—this story had made sure of that.

And how the hell had they known about everything?

It had to be someone on the inside. Someone I knew. But I'd only told one person the entire story.

Liam.

I finished off the coffee and hurried to get dressed. Suddenly, I knew exactly what I was doing next. It started with "M" and rhymed with "Herder." Because if I was going down in flames, I was taking Liam Porter with me.

LIAM'S house made me think of waffles. I'd driven by it countless times over the years on my way to see Jess who lived another two miles down. Every time I did, I thought of waffles or pancakes. Probably because it looked a little like the log cabin on the label of the syrup we'd always bought when I was a kid. Usually the connection gave me warm fuzzies or some twinge of nostalgia for a time when everything felt easier. Happier. Now, though, the sight of it only made me more pissed.

I pulled to a stop, kicking up a cloud of dust thanks to my

speed, and shoved the car into park. Heartbeat thudding in my ears, I stomped over the soft mulch and up the steps, banging hard on the front door. New rocking chairs had been added to the porch, I noted. And a welcome mat that said 'Come In' right side up and 'Get Out' upside down. Cute.

I waited, drumming my fingers on my elbows where I'd crossed my arms over my chest. The rash that had almost disappeared in the last day or so was already itching again, but I ignored it. Finally, the door opened, and I blinked at Sophie, Liam's little sister. The last time I'd seen her was the funeral for Jess' parents. She already looked older than she had then— maybe because she wasn't crying and holding on to her dad this time. Four years behind us, she was what—a freshman in college now? I'd heard she was taking a year off to save up for law school, but she greeted me in a sweatshirt with Charleston University printed across the front.

"Cassie. Hey…" she said, obviously shocked to see me here.

"I need to talk to Liam," I said, working to keep my voice civil.

"He's out in his shop," she said, pointing at a large building to the left of the house. The big bay door was closed, but the small side door stood open. From here, I could just make out the distant whir of a power tool.

"Thanks." I whirled and marched toward it.

Sophie mumbled something and then shut the door behind me.

The power tool shut off, and I picked up the pace, picking my way carefully over the gravel and onto the grass beyond it. A scraping sound reached my ears and grew louder the closer I got to the open door. When I finally stepped inside, my feet landed on a fine layer of sawdust coating the floor, and I stopped, blinking until my eyes adjusted to the darkened space. Several pieces of furniture all half-finished littered the room. A worktable lined the far wall and Liam stood bent over it, shoulders hunched, as he sanded a long, narrow strip of wood.

I narrowed my eyes and stalked over. When he still didn't turn, I tapped him on the shoulder and said, "We need to talk."

He whirled, yanking earbuds from his ears with jerky movements. I jumped back as his eyes widened at the sight of me. He clutched his chest. "Holy shit! Are you trying to stop my heart, woman?"

"Your heart's not my concern," I snapped, my temper returning full force now that he was in front of me. God, I was an idiot. Taken in by a handsome face and a charming smile. Because obviously Liam was still exactly what he used to be. No, scratch that. Now, he was worse.

"I can offer some other suggestions if you are interested in one of my organs," he said.

Heat crept over me and I told myself it was rage. Nothing more. How could I be attracted to him after what he'd just done to me? "You're a real piece of work, you know that."

His smile faltered as he took in my expression. "What's wrong?"

"Oh, nothing. Just my theories about users proven right. Again. You are so lucky you didn't sign that contract, or I'd sue your ass to Hell and back for this."

"Sue me? Cass, what's this about?" He reached for me, and I nearly fell over a sawhorse jumping clear of him. "Whoa," he began, trying again to close the distance and help me regain my balance, but I moved out of his reach, unsteady on my feet but determined not to let him touch me.

"This is about your little stunt with the media. I don't know who you spoke to, but I promise I'll find out, and when I do, that underwater explosion will look like a fucking training exercise compared to what I'll—"

"Okay. Hold on. What the hell happened?" His voice boomed over mine, instantly hardened at my threat. Somewhere in the back of my mind, I felt guilty for using his injury to get him to take me seriously. But I was too pissed to care right now.

My heart was thudding hard enough to shake my shoulders and echo in to my temples. I sucked in a ragged breath, itching everywhere and feeling like my skin was too tight. "I…"

"Take a deep breath," he encouraged, watching me closely.

But my breath was too fast. My head spun—

"Shit." Liam's muttered curse came a split second before I fell.

My knees buckled, and I went down. Liam's arms caught me just in time, barely saving me from crashing to the floor. In one fluid movement, he dropped the sandpaper and scooped me into his arms. His expression as he stared down at me was full of concern and worry—and I hated it.

"Breathe, Cassie," Liam instructed.

Opening my mouth, I tried sucking in a deep breath, attempting to steady myself and end whatever this was. But instead, to my horror, a sob escaped, and I burst into tears.

"Okay, let's take a time out."

He strode out, still carrying me as he headed straight for the house. I wanted to argue, but words were impossible now. My breaths came in short wheezes no matter how hard I tried to even them out.

When he opened the back door, Sophie's voice rang out almost immediately. "What happened?"

I shut my eyes, burying my face in his neck against the onslaught of tears that shook my shoulders and left me even more breathless than before. Worse than losing my shit in front of Liam was losing it in front of his little sister.

"Is she okay?" Sophie demanded when Liam didn't answer quickly enough.

"She's having a panic attack. Can you get her some water? I'm going to take her into the living room."

"I'm on it." I heard footsteps hurry deeper into the house. A second later, the back door slammed shut behind us thanks to Liam's booted heel.

A moment later, he stopped and lowered me gently down to the couch. I clung to him, forcing him to come with me as I landed lightly against the cushions. Liam scooped me up again, this time sitting first and pulling me onto his lap. I clung tight to his neck, too embarrassed now to do anything else but use him as a shield—and a pillow.

"Here." Sophie returned.

"Thanks." Liam paused, and I could tell they were both waiting for me. "Cass, can you sit up?"

I wasn't bawling anymore, but I damn sure wasn't ready to face them. Like a complete coward, I remained silent.

"Soph, can you give us a minute?" Liam asked quietly.

"Sure." Footsteps sounded against the hardwood and then faded.

I tensed, waiting for Liam to say something. But he was quiet, stroking my hair and holding me close, his lips murmuring comforting words as the moment passed. After what felt like an eternity, my breathing returned to normal. My heart rate slowed.

I swiped at my wet cheeks, positive my mascara had painted my face into something scary, and reluctantly sat up. Liam's expression softened at the sight of me. Somehow, that made everything worse. A new round of tears threatened; this time out of self-pity.

"You want to tell me what's going on?" he asked gently.

I sighed, suddenly too exhausted to form the words. "Where's your phone?" I asked.

"Here." He handed it over without question, and I pulled up the article I'd read earlier.

I waited while he read it, watching as his expression shifted from confused to shocked to angry. By the time he looked up at me again, his jaw had hardened and his eyes glinted.

"I didn't do this," he said flatly.

"You're the only one I told, Liam."

He seemed to debate something. "Look, I know what you must think. And I really can't blame you for suspecting me. You don't know me well enough to trust me. But I'm also not going to bend over backward convincing you. It wasn't me."

I climbed off his lap and shoved to my feet, needing to put some distance between us. "How can you say that?" I asked, my voice a whisper to keep from it breaking.

"Look at you, Cassie. You had a panic attack just now over this thing. And your rash isn't any better, I see. You're a mess."

"How do you know about my rash?" I asked.

He gave me a withering look, and I realized he was a lot more perceptive than I'd given him credit for—on a lot of things. I tucked my reddened arm underneath the other one, crossing them awkwardly over my chest. "My rash is none of your business."

"You're right. It's not. But I've seen this kind of stress before. If you don't do something about it now, it's going to get worse. You can't keep this act up forever."

"It's not an act. I'm losing my company. My life—"

"That company isn't your life. And if it is, that's sad."

I fisted my hands, furious all over again. "I can't believe I confided in you."

He snorted. "You didn't tell me shit."

"Of course I did—"

"Facts. You told me facts about your circumstances. The only real thing I know about you is what kind of cookies you like and how you felt about not being able to eat them."

"Well. I don't know shit about you either," I pointed out.

He rose, stalking over to me so that we were close enough for me to smell the sawdust on his skin. It was delicious and sexy, and I hated how much I liked it. Or him. "I dreamt about you when I was overseas," he said and all thoughts of his sawdust-scent evaporated.

"What?"

"When I was in Africa, I dreamt about you. It was mostly just your eyes but still. I couldn't shake them. Always watching me. Judging me. I pretended they wanted me, but it was probably lack of sex and too much sun frying my brain."

"You thought about me that way?" My voice was small, much smaller than the confidence I was always trying to fake. But I couldn't wrap my head around what he was saying *and* pretend I had it all together.

"I've thought about you that way since high school," he admitted.

For a moment, I forgot I was angry. I forgot why. Liam Porter had a crush on me? This was not the way I'd expected this conversation to go. "I..." Before I could form the words to tell him I'd had a crush on him too, his expression went flat.

His dark eyes flashed with irritation and regret as he looked from my face back down to my rashy arm. "But after the last few days, getting to know you, I see now that you're not any different than you were then. And it's catching up with you."

"I don't know who else to be," I admitted, and the words were so unlike me, I almost didn't recognize my own voice as I said them.

Admitting I didn't know something, especially something as simple as my own identity was—

"Go out with me."

"What?"

Liam grimaced. "Not the best timing," he muttered. "Or delivery. But go out with me."

"But the article—"

"That's my point. You don't have to do this anymore. The article proves that. Go out with me because you want to, Cassie. Let me see you. Not the person you want me to see but the real you."

"They'll talk about you," I warned. "The article will only make it worse. They'll take our pictures. Spread gossip. Ask you personal questions that you don't want to answer."

"I don't care."

I bit my lip, trying in vain to think of some other reason we shouldn't do this. But in the end, I couldn't. Just the idea of telling him no made me feel like a prisoner. I'd been trying to be who they wanted for so long now and Liam was right. It was catching up.

"I'm scared," I admitted, hating how it felt to say that out loud.

But Liam didn't look surprised. "Of what?" he asked and in those two words, I heard the challenge. What could Cassie Franklin possibly be afraid of?

"Of everything," I yelled, losing it and letting the words just tumble out. "Of being seen, being judged, being disliked, being liked. Of getting close. Getting hurt. I could go on."

Liam reached for my hand. "Cassie—"

But I wasn't done. There was one more thing I had to say. "I've never had an orgasm."

Liam blinked, stunned. So was I. It wasn't the "real me" I'd ever intended on sharing. Not with anyone and certainly not with Liam Porter. Now that it was out there, I was pretty sure I was going to have another panic attack.

Liam's lips twitched. I tensed. If he laughed at me over this, I'd never forgive him. There would be no more dates. God, I'd have to move. Or change my name. Or my face.

But he didn't laugh.

My breath caught as Liam's gaze heated and he stepped closer, his dark brown eyes lowering to my mouth.

I licked my lips—a reflex reaction.

His gaze sharpened.

I gasped as his mouth crashed over mine.

CHAPTER ELEVEN

LIAM

CASSIE tasted like whiskey and coffee. Somewhere in the back of my mind, I wondered about that, but for now, it was too much. Sensory overload. Cassie Franklin was in my arms, and I was kissing her. And she was kissing me. That was everything. It was also a reminder that I wasn't dead after all. An erection like I hadn't had in a very long damned time pressed painfully against the fabric of my jeans.

Cassie's lips were hot and swollen from her crying. Her cheeks were wet as I cupped her face with my hands. And her breath was like a drug that knocked me off balance as I inhaled it into my still-fragile lung.

I still wasn't sure how to respond to her words a moment ago. *Never had an orgasm.* What did that mean? For a split second, I'd wondered if she was a virgin, but I'd quickly dismissed it. Cassie wasn't someone who minced words. If she was a virgin, she would have said so. But never had an orgasm? That was just sad.

And suddenly her behavior in the truck last night made

sense. She'd been trying to tell me this when I'd pushed her about experiencing pleasure. Her hesitation wasn't personal to me after all. If anything, I seemed to be the exception to the rule. I wasn't entirely sure I could do it for her, but I damn sure wanted every chance to try. Making Cassie Franklin come when no one else ever had? It was better than any of my fantasies could ever be.

"I've wanted this for way too long," I murmured, struggling for control as my body strained toward hers.

"I…"

I felt the change in her a split second before she yanked away. Her chest heaved with labored breaths, and I wondered if she was going to panic again.

"—can't do this," she finished, her eyes widening and her breaths short.

"Cass…" I began.

But she shook her head, backing away, and looking around like she was just noticing her surroundings for the first time. "I have to go. I have to…" She stumbled for the door. "Go," she finished as she disappeared around the corner.

A second later, I heard the front door open and close.

Sophie appeared from the kitchen, her eyes wide. "What was that?"

I sighed, running a hand through my hair and then over the thick stubble covering my jawline. "That was inevitable," I said at last.

CHAPTER TWELVE

CASSIE

I kissed Liam Porter. No, Liam Porter kissed me. No, I kissed Liam Porter. Holy shit, what was I even doing anymore? I drove aimlessly, winding around the back roads of Summerville, and trying to make sense of what had happened—and what I wanted. I ended up in the city following the lazy weekend flow of brunchers and shoppers as the sun rose higher and higher then dipped lower and lower. It was the most peace and quiet I'd had in months. Maybe years. My phone was still lying broken on my floor at home. The radio was off. It was only my head that screamed like a thousand crazed voices. And all of them wanted me to turn around and drive back to Liam's. To finish what we'd started. But what was the point?

In the end, it wouldn't change a damned thing. My father was right: I was too cold. And if that was true—if I tried and failed with Liam Porter—it was hopeless. I was broken. The problem wasn't them. It was me.

Sure, last night in the truck had shown me I could enjoy a man touching me. But that didn't change the fact that I'd had sexual experiences and none of them had left me satisfied. Liam seemed different but the idea of testing that theory, and being wrong, was too terrifying to consider.

So I kept driving.

Afternoon slid toward evening and I pulled into my driveway with my stomach grumbling. I had no idea what to do about the investment deal, or the article, or worse than any of that, what my father was going to say—but before I could deal with any of it, I needed food.

I got out and immediately regretted my decision to come home when I heard my name. "Cassie! God, there you are." Evan appeared, and I realized belatedly he'd parked down the street. Probably to avoid me noticing his car.

I did a double take when I saw he was with my father.

"Evan? Dad?" I looked back and forth between them.

"We tried to call you but you weren't answering," Dad said in a voice that made it impossible to tell how pissed he was.

"I went for a drive," I said.

Dad's brow shot up. "I've been calling you since this morning."

"Well, I'm here now. Let's go inside." I unlocked the front door and pushed it open, going straight to the whiskey still sitting out. I poured two fingers' worth into my empty coffee mug from earlier and left it sitting there before facing my father again.

"What's going on?" I asked, my heart rate already racing along. I willed it to calm down after the episode I'd had at Liam's this morning. I did not need a repeat of that. Not now.

"I was thinking you could tell me," Dad said and there was an edge to his voice that grated on my already raw nerves. I sighed, unsure where to begin about why I hadn't answered my phone all day. But Dad wasn't waiting. "You tried to hire a fake lover? Are you out of your damn mind?"

I winced. Apparently, we were skipping the inquisition about how I'd spent my day. "I was trying to save our company."

"Well, congratulations on failing miserably. Nichimoto pulled out of the deal the moment he saw this." Dad dropped a newspaper on the table between us, and I jumped. Plastered across the Entertainment section was Janice's photo of Liam and I at the fundraiser the other night. His lips weren't touching mine, but they were too close to be anything but a kiss.

"You want to explain to me how you thought it would be a good idea to hire a goddamned gigolo while we were in the middle of the deal of our lives?" Dad demanded.

I kept my voice level as I tried to reason with him. "Liam isn't a gigolo. And I didn't know it was him when I offered."

"So you admit you were trying to hire a prostitute?"

"What? No." My gaze flicked to Evan who was listening to our exchange with a tight expression. "You told me I needed to show Nichimoto I was headed to the altar, and we both know that's not the reality."

"Well, it could be," Evan said, offering me a pointed look.

I ignored him and focused on my father whose face was a deep shade of crimson and only getting darker the longer this went on. "Dad, listen. I didn't mean to make things worse. I was only trying to—"

"Of course you made it worse! God, Cassie. This article makes you look pathetic and desperate."

I sucked in a sharp breath, the words stinging like a slap. Hot tears stung my eyelids. "I'm sorry," I said. "I don't know who leaked—"

"Doesn't matter," Dad said, dismissing the whole thing way too easily as he blew out a heavy breath.

"Why not?" I asked, on edge even more now that he'd so easily moved on. What was really going on here?

"Evan's managed to get Nichimoto back to the table."

My gaze swung to Evan who was picking my broken phone out of the glass on the floor. He carried it over to me and set it carefully on the table, clearing his throat. "Nichimoto understands that the press was misled by the charitable dinner you had with Liam."

"It wasn't charity," I began but Evan waved me off.

"He also understands whoever claimed you were hiring a fake boyfriend was just trying to stir up a bidding war. I explained everything, and he's willing to come back to negotiations. He'd like to speak with you first, but it's just a formality, of course."

"You explained everything," I said slowly.

Evan nodded.

Dad avoided my gaze and a sick feeling settled in my gut. Since when did Evan have the right—or the reach—to explain anything on behalf of Franklin Industries? My father hadn't even extended that kind of authority to me and I was his daughter, the future CEO.

Suddenly, I was no longer hungry. Or in the mood to apologize for my crazy idea that had gone haywire. "You said you explained everything. What does that mean exactly?" I asked.

Evan shrugged. "I told him you and I had called things off for a while so I could get treatment for my stress-induced anger issues, and now that everything's under control, we're picking up where we left off. His concerns about a single woman running a multi-million dollar company are unfounded."

"Are you serious?" I looked from him to my father. Evan beamed and Dad looked away, grabbing the whiskey from me and pouring a shot of his own into a glass hanging from the bar. I covered the glass with my hand before he could raise it to his lips. "His concerns are unfounded? But not because I'm capable as a single woman. Because I am not a single woman at all."

Evan sighed but said nothing.

I glared at my father. "You can't be on board with this."

He looked up at me, his eyes accusing. "It's just until the deal goes through."

I blinked, stunned.

The pain was like a knife sliding right in between my ribs. My back literally ached from it. I looked away, back to Evan, my eyes blurring with tears. God, what was happening to me that I couldn't even get worked up to a proper temper without blubbering everywhere?

"Get out," I said quietly.

Dad didn't answer, but Evan took a step toward me. "Cassie, just listen—"

This time, I screamed, "Get out!" I picked up the coffee mug and hurled it at Evan. It missed, hitting the wall behind him before shattering into the same pile as the glass I'd broken earlier. The whiskey inside splattered along the wall in large brown droplets.

Dad's chest puffed up with a deep breath. After a beat, he looked at Evan and said, "Come on. Let's go."

Dad marched out, his shoulders stiff, and Evan followed.

I waited until the door slammed shut behind them. When I was alone, I downed my father's untouched shot, completely and utterly at a loss.

A moment passed, and I focused only on how delicious the heat from the whiskey felt as it ran the length of my throat and into my stomach. When the burn began to fade, I picked up the bottle and took a swig directly from it. The heat seared me, mixing with the adrenaline still racing through me.

I couldn't believe what had just happened.

Not just them. Me.

I'd thrown my dad and Evan out—and in doing so, I felt freer than I ever had. Lighter. More in control. Not less.

It was heady, more intoxicating than the whiskey in my hand.

But it wasn't enough. I wanted more. I wanted to keep this feeling going. And I already knew exactly how I wanted to do it. Swigging more whiskey, I stepped carefully over to my phone. It was definitely shattered, and the screen was only half-responsive as I called up a number in my contacts. A number I never actually expected to use again. I dialed, keeping it on speaker phone as it connected the call. The pixelated screen didn't even register when he'd picked up.

"Hello?"

"It's Cassie."

"Hey."

"Hey."

"You okay?"

"I wanted to apologize for the way I left things earlier."

I could hear the surprise in Liam's voice as he reassured me. Clearly, he hadn't expected me to call him again either. "No need. I should have—"

"Can you come over?"

There was a pause and then. "Now?"

I tried not to be too disappointed. Or pushy. "If you're busy, we can—"

"I can come now."

"Good. Door's open. Let yourself in."

"Okay." He drew out the word, clearly confused about my change of heart. But it wasn't something I wanted to explain with words. Or at all.

"See you soon," I said and then ended the call, tossing the phone back into the pile of glass and grabbing the whiskey before heading upstairs.

It was time to slip into something less like the girl I'd been and more like the girl I was suddenly determined to become.

CHAPTER THIRTEEN

LIAM

CASSIE was in trouble. I'd known it that first day when she'd tried to hire me to be her fake boyfriend, and I knew it now that she'd called and asked me to come over. Something had happened. Something besides our kiss earlier and her crazy admission before that. I'd thought of calling, but every time I remembered how scared she'd looked as she'd run out of my house, I'd decided against it. I could recognize panic—and when a person just needed space. But her voice when she'd called me back just now had been closer to the edge than I'd ever heard it. No, that wasn't right. She'd gone over the edge. I just couldn't figure out why.

The article this morning had been pretty harsh. Whoever the source was, they didn't like Cassie very much. I couldn't blame her for the panic attack. The details the article shared were about more than just a bad business deal. They attacked her as a person. According to the rest of the world, Cassie wasn't the ice princess anymore. She'd graduated. Now, she was the ice queen.

I couldn't blame her for being so upset. But she'd seemed to pull it together—and then our kiss happened. Not my best timing, obviously. But the call had been about more than that. Something told me things were bad.

When the stoplight turned green, I pressed my foot harder on the gas and sped across town toward Cassie's place.

The street lights were on by the time I pulled up, with twilight casting shadows thanks to the trees lining the street. I parked in the driveway behind Cassie's car and glanced around uneasily, not even sure what I was looking for. Another reporter maybe? And why the hell did I care who saw us?

That would mean Cassie Franklin's reputation mattered to me.

Fucking A. Maybe it did. Or, maybe for once, I gave a shit about my own.

I kept my head down and ducked around the hedge, glad that it shielded the front door from the street. I hesitated, my hand on the knob. I'd never let myself into someone else's house before. Except Jamie's. And even then, I hadn't done it often. It felt strange and sort of alien. But she'd said it was open.

I cracked the door just enough and slipped inside, letting it click softly shut behind me. In the dark hallway, I blinked, letting my eyes adjust to the bright white bulbs in the chandelier over the dining room table. For a split second, I swayed, thrown off balance by the sudden change in lighting. My hand came out, bracing on the wall for support. The room spun. My breath caught.

When it passed, I exhaled slowly and reminded myself to take it easy. Recovery was a process, and I wasn't the most patient when it came to my own body's limitations. When I felt steady enough, I took a step and felt the crunch of broken glass underneath my boots. I bent low and found Cassie's phone on the hardwood among shards of broken glass. I sniffed, my nose wrinkling as the scent of whiskey hit me. A second later, I spotted the stains on the wall.

What the hell?

My chest tightened and adrenaline flooded me as I shot to my feet, my thoughts racing. An unlocked door after that article had come out, broken glass, and no sign of Cassie. Had something awful happened?

I started to call her name and then stopped. Instead, I scanned the room, suddenly on full alert. Nothing else was broken or seemed to be out of place. My breathing turned shallow, and I forced myself to take deep, slow breaths, willing everything to stop spinning. Recovery had gone pretty well overall, but I still hadn't fully regained my balance. Dizziness would come and go, according to the doctors, during the weeks that my body adjusted to the implants.

Panic was definitely on the list of things to avoid for at least another four weeks. But Cassie's phone was in a heap of broken glass by the door and the house was dark and quiet.

Too quiet.

Again, I bit back the urge to call out. My training was too ingrained to consider yelling. If someone else was here, better not to spook them until I was ready. I considered going back out to the truck for my gun but decided against it. Now that I was inside, it was too risky to leave. If there was an intruder, I didn't want to give them the chance to slip out the back without hearing them—or worse, lock me out entirely.

I kept my footsteps silent as I made my way through the downstairs, room by room, listening intently for some sign that she was here. Her car had been in the driveway, I remembered. And the door hadn't shown signs of forced entry, but then why would it if she'd left it unlocked.

Fuck.

Had some angry reader or pissed ex seen the article? Had that Evan guy gotten furious that she was dating someone else and come to confront her?

The first floor was empty. I doubled back to the kitchen and grabbed one of the knives from the block.

Moving slowly and silently, I made my way upstairs.

At the landing, I stopped and inhaled.

Perfume.

Cassie's perfume.

Holding my breath again, I listened to the soft sounds of the bedsheet being pulled back followed by the floor creaking lightly against someone's weight.

So she was here.

But possibly not alone, I told myself with a sick feeling roiling in my gut.

I slid around to the edge of the doorway, my heart pounding like a fucking jackhammer, a dull roaring in my ears drowning out the silence. I counted to three, adjusting the knife in my hand, and then spun into the room, shoulders heaving with exertion.

What I saw stopped me short.

Cassie stood before me, her blonde hair hanging in mussed waves over her shoulders that were only barely covered by the thin black straps of her lingerie. Black lace clung to her ass and breasts, showing more skin than it covered, before giving way to garters and stockings and the highest black heels I'd ever seen. It was breathtaking.

At the sight of me brandishing a knife, Cassie screamed, and I quickly lowered the weapon. I blinked, realizing belatedly I was supposed to be looking for a threat of some kind.

"What's going on?" I asked. "Are you alone?"

"Of course I'm alone. What are you doing with a knife?" she shrieked.

My shoulders sagged. "Your phone was lying in a pile of broken glass. I thought…" I trailed off, completely speechless at the sight of her. Whatever fantasies I'd had about Cassie Franklin had just been overridden; the reality was far better than anything I could dream up.

I licked my lips, my mouth suddenly dry as I took a second look at her. My gaze swept from her face to her toes and back up, lingering where the lace left almost nothing to the imagination along her thighs and then again where it just barely hid her nipples.

When I reached her face again, I saw her eyes were still wide with surprise, though the fear had thankfully dimmed as she glared at the knife hanging limp in my hand. Now, more than anything, she looked pissed. "You could have killed me."

"No. I was going to kill whoever was hurting you," I pointed out.

She frowned, and I wasn't sure my admission had actually helped matters. "No one is hurting me," she said. "I just wanted to see you. And I wanted you to see me," she added, gesturing to the lingerie she wore.

"You look…" Even after another full sweep of the garters and stockings and black lace that only barely covered her full breasts, I still didn't know how to finish it.

She glanced down, her cheeks flushing. "God, I can't believe you thought … I am such an idiot." She spun, heading for the walk-in closet that stood open between here and the bathroom.

I set the knife aside and ran to stop her. "Wait." I grabbed her arm, spinning her around to face me and nearly lost myself in her blue eyes. I'd been right. She was in trouble, but that didn't matter nearly as much as making sure she knew how fucking hot she was. "You look amazing. No, that's not enough. You look so fucking sexy and delicious right now that it's taking every ounce of my willpower not to rip this off of you and bend you over the dresser. But you dressing like this for me, calling me. It's unexpected, especially after earlier, so I'm at a loss. I just need a minute to let it sink in. To find the words I need to describe the thoughts I'm having about you right now."

Her smile was slow and just shy enough to make me groan with need. "Thank you."

It took everything in me not to devour her right then and there. I didn't even know why I held back. But between her panic attack earlier and the strange call and broken glass, I knew better than to accept what she was so clearly offering or believe it wouldn't have repercussions. Cassie didn't strike me as the type to offer herself up this way. I couldn't help but feel privileged that she'd chosen me.

"Maybe you could show me what you're thinking," she said.

Fuck me sideways. The way she looked up at me through those thick lashes nearly brought me to my knees.

Focus, Liam. Do not fuck this up.

I took her chin in my hand, forcing her eyes to mine. "Tell me what happened first."

She shook her head, lifting her chin out of my grasp in defiance. But when she faced me again on her own, every ounce of temper was gone. It its place was desperation. Pleading. "Not yet."

It was the one version of her I couldn't refuse. So I nodded slowly, still searching her face for what I'd missed. For what had made her decide to do something so out of character for her. Or, least out of the character I knew. "All right. Tell me what you want, Cassie," I said quietly.

She hesitated.

We both knew full well what she wanted. With an outfit like hers, there was no mistaking it. But goddamn, I wanted to hear her say it.

"I want you, Liam. It's why I called you here. But—" She bit her lip. "I have to tell you something."

"What is it?" My cock throbbed against the fabric of my pants at the mere idea of what she was asking for. It was exactly what I'd wanted from her and I had to force myself to concentrate on what she was saying next.

"I wasn't lying this morning when I told you I've never had an orgasm."

"I didn't think you were lying," I told her honestly. "I just don't care."

Her eyes widened in surprise.

"Are you a virgin?" I asked.

"No," she said quickly and my shoulders sagged in relief.

"Well, then." I shrugged. "So what?"

She stepped back and ran a hand through her hair. "So it's a big deal. I thought at first that I'd just picked the wrong partner." Her lips twitched in that hint of a smile that I knew was the closest thing she had to one. "I thought I was gay for a while, so I experimented just to see."

Now it was my turn to stare with wide eyes. "You slept with girls?"

"Calm down, I am definitely straight and that is not the point."

"Uh-huh. We're definitely coming back to that part," I said. She rolled her eyes. "So you've never gotten off? Not once?"

She shook her head. "I think I'm broken that way. And I wanted to tell you up front so that you weren't disappointed or think that maybe you'd done something wrong when I don't get there."

"Get there?" I laughed before I could stop it and her eyes narrowed. Shit. This girl was serious. "Okay. Right." I swallowed my smile and nodded gravely. "Thank you for telling me."

She cleared her throat, looking away awkwardly. "What I mean is that I really want to try having one with you, but if I don't, that's okay too. Either way, I'm sure it'll be great."

I stared at her, brows raised. *I'm sure it'll be great?* "Wow." I rubbed a hand over the back of my head. "I appreciate your honesty." It came out like a question and Cassie grimaced.

"I know. It's not a sexy conversation," she admitted. "But I needed you to know what you were getting into."

I sighed. "Okay, look. Obviously, I could say something really douchey about how you've clearly been doing it with the wrong people. Or they've been doing it wrong with you. But I won't."

"Thanks," she said sarcastically.

I winked. "Don't thank me yet. What I want to tell you is that I'm fine with all of this. I just want to make you feel good. No pressure about anything else."

"Thanks," she said again, looking a little relieved now.

I watched her, fascinated at the myriad of emotions that passed over her face one after the other in such quick succession. I was sure if I blinked, I'd miss something important.

Finally, she made a face against the silence that had fallen between us. "Ugh. Can we just forget about everything I just said and take our clothes off?"

That got my attention. "I thought you'd never ask." I stepped close, sliding my hand into her hair to cup her neck.

"Where should we start?" she asked softly.

I breathed her in and whispered, "Do you want me, Cassie?"

She nodded, her eyes wide and trusting and so intense. "I do."

"And do you trust me?"

She nodded again, this time a little less certain. I appreciated the honesty in that and something about it made me want to work harder to convince her I was worth it.

"Then starting right now, I want you to forget everything. Forget the past. Forget what you just told me. Forget who you are and what you think you should do or how you think this all works. Just focus on my hands on your body." I slid my other hand up and over her hip, my fingers skimming over the lacy fabric that only barely covered her perfectly shaped ass. "Can you do that?"

"Yes," she whispered.

"Good." I leaned in, skimming my mouth over her jawline and felt her jump against me. She was tense as hell, every nerve ending standing on edge. No wonder she'd never had an orgasm. She was wound tighter than a virgin monk.

This girl *needed* an orgasm. And even though I knew it was more about her than me, I wanted to be the first one to give it to her. I wanted it bad.

Kissing a trail along her chin, my mouth found hers. Softly at first, but when she responded so willingly, I couldn't hold it back. My arms tightened around her, pulling her in close as my lips pressed hot and hard against hers. Cassie's reaction was instant. Her arms came up and around my neck, her fingers grabbing at my hair as she pressed her body flush against mine. Through the thin layer of her lingerie and my shirt, I was hyper-aware of her breasts rubbing against me and I wanted more.

I wanted to feel every inch of her.

To make her feel every inch of me.

And then I wanted to make her come.

I had a feeling it was going to be a challenge I'd enjoy more than anything else I'd ever done.

Deepening the kiss, my tongue slid over her mouth until she parted her lips for me on a soft moan. I grew harder the instant my tongue entered her mouth. Just like this morning, she tasted like whiskey. And unlike this morning, she wasn't shutting me down. My hands moved on their own now, exploring and running the length of her from shoulders to thighs. Underneath the whiskey and the scent of her perfume was a taste specific to Cassie and I couldn't get enough.

"Liam." The sound of my name from her lips was like magic.

I didn't give her a chance to finish before I scooped her up and carried her to the bed. She looked up at me from where she lay on her back, her blue eyes warmed to a steamy stare that froze me in place. "Will you touch me? Like you did in the truck?"

"Fuck," I groaned softly, my hands already coming up to cup her breasts. "God, you are so sexy when you look at me like that and tell me what to do with you." Her lip curled, and I shook my head. "I plan to touch you everywhere, Cassie. Brace yourself."

Just like in the truck, I sat back and used one single finger, tracing lazily over her skin. But unlike before, I didn't start innocently with her cheeks. That lacy top was calling my fucking name, and I wasn't going to pretend I didn't hear it.

She sighed as my hand dipped inside the fabric of her bra, pulling it aside and running the pad of my thumb over her nipple. She inhaled sharply, and I rubbed until it hardened against my skin. When I moved my hand aside and bent low, closing my mouth over it, she jumped.

I held on tighter and a soft sigh escaped her lips.

I kissed and sucked at her until she was pushing her hips against me, all the while lost in the way her body responded to mine. This was not a girl incapable of pleasure. This was a ticking time bomb of release. And I'd walked in at the exact moment of detonation. We were barely five minutes in, and I already knew she was going to come for me. I wasn't going to waste a single second of it.

"Tell me how that feels," I said, releasing her taut nipple and letting my hands tug at the rest of the lace she wore. She moaned as I rubbed my way down her abdomen and over her hips. "Tell me," I repeated, my hand dipping in between her thighs and brushing feathery light over her clit.

"God, Liam, that feels so damn good." She was breathless, every word punctuated with feeling.

I looked up at her from where I'd slid down, my mouth level with her hips. Her blue eyes were on fire now, begging, pleading silently for more. My lips curled into a slow smile. "More?" I asked, letting my fingers dip just inside the lace panties barely covering her.

I didn't want for an answer before I pressed a kiss to the exposed skin along the crease of her thigh.

She leaned in to my touch, her hips jutting forward to meet me. "More," she breathed, the single word sexier than any outfit she could have chosen to wear for me.

I sat up suddenly and Cassie's eyes flew open. "What are you—"

"This has to come off." I reached for the snaps on her garter belt.

Cassie didn't pull away, but she bit her lip, unsure. "I

thought you'd want to leave it on."

"No way. I want to see you. All of you."

"I—" She broke off, frowning as she complied with my nudges, raising her hips so I could shimmy the belt and straps off her body. I tossed them aside, undressing her in silence.

When she was naked, I stood over her, just looking.

She didn't move or speak but by the time my gaze reached hers, I could see the nerves casting worry lines across her forehead. When I had her full attention, I peeled off my own shirt and then pulled off my pants. Cassie's expression heated as she watched and I tried to remember if getting naked had ever felt quite this erotic.

When we were both naked, I crawled in and lowered myself over her, brushing her hair away from her face and letting my fingers trail over her face and neck. "You're beautiful," I whispered.

And I felt her relax.

"So fucking beautiful," I repeated, and she sank lower into the mattress, her muscles loosening a little more.

"Gorgeous."

Her arms came around me, her fingers shoving into my hair.

I smiled, caught in the spell of her blue eyes all over again. "Flawless," I added, pressing a kiss to her mouth. "Perfect." Another kiss. "Fucking amazing."

When I pulled back, she was smiling—almost. "I get the point."

"Do you? Because I don't think you know how utterly sexy you are." I ground my hips lightly against hers, letting her feel my erection. My voice dropped low against her ear. "How hard you make me."

"Mmm." She relaxed some more, her legs parting, and I

knew I had her.

"Just enjoy me touching you," I whispered before lowering my mouth to hers and running my tongue over her top lip.

Without breaking the kiss, I ran my hand down the length of her, dragging it lazily over her bare skin. She shivered underneath me, her own hands sending tingles along my spine as they roamed my back. I slowed and dipped a finger between her legs, slipping it between her folds. Her muscles tightened, her hips rising ever so slightly to meet me. I sucked in a breath, groaning at how wet she was for me.

She tensed, but this time I knew it wasn't nerves that had her muscles bunching and coiling. The moment I slid a finger inside her, she tightened her grip on my shoulders, moaning softly against my ear.

My cock strained at the sound and the feel of her, aching to be inside her. But I concentrated on Cassie and on the way her hips rose to meet me as I slid a finger in and out of her wetness. I could feel her, the way her walls tensed against me with every stroke. And I knew. She was close. This was happening.

And I felt somehow honored by it all. Even in the middle of my own aching and the desire that felt bigger than anything I'd felt before, I felt awed by it. By her. I slid my finger free and felt her disappointment as she nearly collapsed back onto the mattress.

When I positioned myself at her entrance, and met her eyes, there was absolutely no resistance in her expression. Everything about her was telling me yes. I slid inside her, my lips crashing down over hers as I filled her. Both of us inhaled sharply, and I went still, my legs already shaking with the beginnings of an orgasm. But I wasn't the only one, I realized as I began moving in and out of her in a slow rhythm that had Cassie clutching at my shoulders and breathing hard against my lips.

Her legs wrapped around my hips, locking, and I knew. Cassie Franklin was about to come.

My cock throbbed in response to the pressure as she squeezed against me. Tight. So fucking tight. And tense. But as she rode closer to her own climax, the tension drained away, and in its place was pure, raw pleasure—more intense than I'd ever seen on any one person.

Her lips parted, and she lifted a hand, running it through her hair and then letting it fall again to clutch at my arm. Her neck arched, and she threw her head back, writhing against the sheets as I slid into her over and over. She was entirely wrapped up in her own sensations and completely unaware of how utterly sexy she was in this moment. Every inch of her expression was complete abandon. I couldn't breathe watching her. She was more gorgeous than anything I'd ever seen, more incredible than I could have possibly imagined. But she was still teetering on the edge and I wanted to see her go all the way over.

I broke the kiss long enough to whisper against her mouth.

"Let go," I said, not sure which of us I was even talking to anymore.

In the end, it didn't matter, because where Cassie went, I gladly followed. And I knew, after today, sex would never be the same.

CHAPTER FOURTEEN

CASSIE

LIAM'S body was the key to a locked door I'd been looking for my whole life. On the other side was freedom. I knew the moment he touched me that this time would be different, but nothing could have prepared me for the reality of the pleasure that came next. When his hands cupped my breasts, it was nothing like the other men I'd been with. It wasn't rough, but it wasn't nice either. It felt like he could read my mind. Like he knew the exact amount of pressure I needed in order to make me crave more. And his hands…

I'd never been so broken apart by someone's hands on me before. The way he stared down at me, holding my gaze while sliding his finger in and out of me was the most erotic moment of my life.

I could feel it building in me—a pressure that promised a release I'd never had and wasn't sure I was ready for now. I held back, happy to toe the line right along the edge of it for as long as Liam would let me.

But just like before, he read me perfectly. And he wasn't

going to let me hold back for very long. I lost myself in the sensations of him; his kisses and the way he whispered encouragement into my ear to enjoy myself. The way he filled me so perfectly, stretching me until I couldn't move without my nerve endings going crazy over the feeling of him touching me so deeply.

And I could feel my insides tightening. The pressure built higher. I threw my head back, arching my neck and losing myself in the way his body made me forget everything else but this moment. Him. Us.

He leaned over, still thrusting in exact time to the pulse of my own need, and whispered, "Let go." And that was all it took to shove me over the edge of my own orgasm.

I screamed, a half-moan of pleasure and a half-yell from the terror of it all. I'd never, not once in my life, let go this way. I'd also never had anyone convince me I could. But without even understanding it, I knew being with Liam, letting myself go like this with him, was safe. He'd meant what he said. He wouldn't hurt me, and he wouldn't take more than I wanted to give.

Suddenly, I wanted to offer everything I had.

I flung myself into that free fall, and something inside me clicked open. A blinding explosion went off behind my eyelids. I bucked and rose to meet it, not concerned in the slightest that it stole my breath and paralyzed my muscles.

For a split second, it was as if the rest of the universe ceased to exist. There was only this: pleasure and Liam and the wave we were riding together. Vaguely, I was aware that I was calling his name. Loudly. But I didn't care. Our bodies, slick with sweat, fit together so perfectly. Everywhere his hands touched, my body tingled. It was magic. Pure fucking magic. I had no idea if it was thanks to Liam or just the timing of it all, but I never, ever wanted it to end.

I came down from the high slowly.

My muscles felt like Jell-O. My skin exposed and raw. Nerve endings I didn't know I had tingled deliciously.

"Holy shit," I managed to say, my voice hushed with shock and awe. It was stupid, but I felt proud somehow. My body had finally given me the one thing I'd never thought it could. An orgasm. No, not my body, I realized as Liam finally fell still over me and then gently rolled to the side. Liam's. Liam Porter had given me an orgasm.

My own sense of pride diminished. It its place was a desperate yearning to convince Liam to never leave this room. Toying with the idea of chaining him to the bedpost, I lay back, dazed and tingling. Every nerve ending was on alert and trained on Liam where he lay beside me. I looked over and caught him already smiling at me. My skin heated all over again at the knowing grin he shot me.

There was an intimacy between us even now that I hadn't expected. "That was…"

"A fucking miracle?" he guessed.

Part of me wanted to contradict his words, to keep his ego from swelling, but I couldn't do anything but sigh and melt further into the mattress. "Yeah."

And then, completely against my own will, my eyes teared up and emotion clogged my throat. "Holy shit," I said again.

Liam raised his head, using his elbow to prop himself up. "You okay?"

I tried rolling away, mortified that the best sex of my entire life was about to end in tears. Who the hell cried after great sex? "I'm fine," I said, my voice muffled where my face was pressed against the mattress.

"Cass," Liam said, tugging me back so he could look down at me.

His eyes were light but not laughing. Just happy. Satisfied. When he saw the tears brimming in my eyes, his lips pressed together and I knew he was hiding a smile.

"Do not laugh at me," I warned.

"I am not laughing, I swear. Just… I can't lie. Moving you to tears because of my sexual prowess is a pretty big achievement. My ego's enjoying the moment."

I tried to laugh, but it came out like a hiccup. A tear fell, running down my cheek, but Liam caught it with his finger. "I'm kidding," he said gently. "And this is understandable."

I didn't answer. I couldn't trust my own voice. Not yet. Not when my insides were still swirling with the delicious sensation of release and my emotions were apparently under the impression that applied to them too.

"That was seriously your first orgasm ever, wasn't it?"

"Was it that obvious?"

"No. I mean yeah. I mean it was amazing. *You* were amazing."

Our gazes met, and I couldn't tear myself away from the intensity in his stare. He leaned down to kiss me, a slow, lingering kiss that lasted long enough I was already considering round two by the time he pulled away. But then he sat up and handed me the bottle of water beside the bed. I took it gratefully.

"Ugh." I sat up, running a hand through my tangled hair. What must I look like now with bed hair and flushed skin? Self-conscious, I grabbed for the blanket and yanked it over my body.

"Beautiful." I looked over and found Liam watching me. I made a face, but he shook his head and grabbed my chin in his hands, forcing my gaze to his. "I mean that. You are gorgeous. More now than earlier because you've let your guard down and that's sexy and kind of addicting."

"Addicting, huh? After just one time?"

He arched a brow. "You trying to tell me you're not feeling that?"

"Okay, I see your point." Actually, what was addicting was Liam. All of him. Not just the sex, but his smile and his hands and his compliments and all of it. But thinking about all of it only reminded me of how we'd gotten here. My good mood darkened a little, and I sighed.

"I guess this is the part where I tell you why I called you here," I said, the reality of all that had happened today finally crashing down around me. My breath became short again, and I concentrated on that, determined to remain calm.

"You don't have to tell me anything you don't want to."

When I cast him a grateful glance, he grabbed my hand and squeezed. "I mean it. If you need some more time to process things, I get it. Orgasms can be emotional."

Apparently. "Thanks," I said. "But you deserve an explanation. Especially after my behavior today." And I found myself actually wanting to tell him. And trusting him enough to feel safe with sharing it. That was a new one.

"All right."

"Well." I cleared my throat. "After I left your house, I just drove all day. I guess I needed time to think and time away from everything. My father was waiting for me when I came home. He saw the news article and apparently so did Nichimoto."

"The guy you're trying to make the deal with."

I nodded, staring down at our joined hands. I wasn't sure what was stranger: that he was still holding my hand or that I was letting him. "Nichimoto pulled out of the deal when he saw I'd hired …. Anyway, my dad came here with Evan to tell me the deal was being fixed."

Liam's eyes narrowed, and he sat up. I tried not to get distracted by his body still on display, but the sight of his broad shoulders and chest made my mouth go dry all over again. "Fixed how?"

I looked away, focusing on the story I was telling rather than what the sight of his abs did to me. "Um. Evan took the liberty of contacting Nichimoto to tell him that the article was the media's mistake, that he and I are dating again. Nichimoto agreed to the deal again, but only on the assumption that Evan and I are basically on our way to the altar."

"What the …? But you're not."

"No." I shook my head. "When I told my father that, it didn't end well. I lost my temper. Threw my phone at the wall."

"The broken glass was you?"

"Yes."

"Damn." He whistled.

My brows shot up. "Are you impressed?"

"Damn straight. There's more heat in you than I realized."

For some reason, his words made me feel better. Hopeful. Not to mention the orgasmic sex. The combination inspired a bravery in me that I hadn't expected.

"You know what? You're right." I hopped off the bed and started for the door before I remembered my phone was fully broken now. I doubled back to Liam. "Can I borrow your phone?"

"Sure." He jumped up and pulled his phone from the pocket of his discarded pants. "Who are you texting?"

I bit my lip, typing fast and hitting send before I could second-guess myself. Then I handed it back to him, letting him read it for himself. He scanned it and then looked back at me, brows raised. "Vacation, huh?"

I shrugged. "I have days saved up."

"Uh-huh. And what do you plan to do for this vacation?"

I crept closer, winding my arms around his neck. "I was thinking I'd make it more of a *stay*cation."

His lips curved. "I like the sound of that."

"Good." I brushed a kiss over his jawline, his stubble scratching against my lips. "Because you're my plus one."

"And when does this staycation begin?" he asked, his voice low and sexy against my ear.

I shivered, pulling him closer. "Right now."

CHAPTER FIFTEEN

LIAM

CASSIE was insatiable; a word I'd never in my wildest dreams imagined would fit the girl I thought I knew in high school. I spent the night at her place—not that either one of us got a wink of sleep. By the time we'd had breakfast and then two more rounds of mind-blowing sex—all of which ended in orgasms for both of us—I was exhausted.

Cassie, on the other hand, only seemed more energized. It was insane.

"Are you sure you have to go?" she asked, clearly pouting and hoping it would work to get me to stay.

I bent low and kissed her throat and then her lips before answering. "Woman, you have no idea how much I wish I didn't have to go. But I promised Sophie I'd have lunch with her today since our welcome home dinner was interrupted last week."

"Fine. That's an excuse I can't argue with. A solitary staycation it is."

I pulled back to study her, noting the bright eyes and too

innocent expression. "You okay?"

"Yeah." She blew out a breath. "I'm just not sure I'm ready to face reality yet."

I couldn't help raising a brow over that. "I'm not real?"

"Of course you're real. I know because I keep pinching myself to be sure. Besides, those orgasms weren't something I could deny."

"Damn right they weren't." I grinned. "Although, if you begin to doubt, you could always ask your neighbors. I'm sure they heard you scream."

"Very funny. I mean that you're fun. And without you, the harsh reality of Cassie Franklin, ice queen, is all I have left. That is not fun."

I frowned. Fun? Why did it sound like she had just called me a one-night stand? "Can I call you later?" I asked, if only to prove last night had been more than just a fling.

"Please do."

My own relief was like a warning bell inside my head. Since when did I give that many shits about whether a girl let me call her after sex?

Since Cassie Franklin came no less than seven times in one night, obviously.

I sighed. Either way, it wasn't a feeling I was used to. "Does this mean you're taking me up on my offer from yesterday?" I asked.

"What question?"

"You'll go out with me?"

"Liam, that article lets you off the hook. We don't need to keep up the charade anymore."

"Good, because my offer has nothing to do with any of that. No more fake boyfriend deals. No more strings. Just you and me."

She cocked her head. "Does that mean you've accepted the spotlight that puts you in?"

"I already told you—"

"I know what you told me. I also know that every time someone recognizes you or calls you a war hero, you look ready to commit murder."

I sighed. "Guilty. But also worth it." I winked.

She bit her lip. "Okay."

"Okay?"

"Okay."

My grin at her simple answer felt stupid even to me. Between the shit-eating grin and the fact that I'd started repeating her words back to her, it was definitely time to get the hell out of here.

"I'll call you." I pressed a final quick kiss to her cheek and then headed for the door. With my hand on the knob, I stopped and looked back. Cassie stood in the kitchen, the t-shirt she'd thrown on earlier only barely skimming the top of her creamy thighs. Her blonde hair was messy with that just-been-fucked look, and it was enough to make me hard all over again.

But what I really noticed were her eyes. Bottomless blue pools with no trace of ice or chill as she stared back at me, half a smile still hanging from her full lips. If the ice princess she'd been before had been gorgeous, this new version was fucking breathtaking. Hot, passionate, and with the sexiest O face I'd ever seen, this girl was enough to make me believe I'd died after all—and woken up in Heaven.

CHAPTER SIXTEEN

CASSIE

I'D lied to Liam. Maybe he was real, but he was also too good to be true. Liam Porter's new reputation as war hero didn't cancel out the old one: Liam Porter, ladies' man. According to the rumors in high school, he'd always been a serial dater. And after the way he'd run out of here this morning, it looked like not much had changed there.

Part of me wanted to feel embarrassed or ashamed for how I'd offered myself up to him—seven times if I was counting correctly—between last night and this morning. But the other part of me, the completely relaxed and finally orgasm-capable part of me, didn't give a shit about how desperate I might have seemed. Or how quickly Liam might move on now.

Every ounce of me felt lighter. Freer. Happier.

Is this what an orgasm did?

If so, why wasn't I doing that instead of popping Xanax like they were Tic-Tacs? Obviously, I was doing this whole "anti-stress" thing all wrong.

I finished cleaning the kitchen and headed upstairs for a

shower. When I caught sight of my reflection, I did a double take. Despite the mussed hair and lips still swollen from kissing, I looked more relaxed and sated than I had in a long time. The rash on my arm and chest was gone. And despite the lack of sleep, my eyes were clear of the shadows that had plagued me for months now.

I looked good.

"Girl, you were overdue," I told myself, thinking of what Jess would say.

Jess. She would lose her shit if she knew what happened last night. I was halfway to the stairs, intent on calling her, before I remembered how dead my phone was.

Shower first. Then I'd tackle the phone issue.

When I was clean and dressed, I headed downstairs in search of the mess I still hadn't cleaned up from yesterday. The coffee mug and glass were still in pieces on the floor. In the middle of it all was my broken phone. A new one was going to require a trip out into public. A trip I was not ready for.

In fact, without work as an excuse, there wasn't a single thing outside the walls of this house that felt important enough to brave the public eye. For a split second, the downtime was a relief—until I looked around my sparsely furnished living room and realized there wasn't a thing to do in here either. Hobbies hadn't exactly been a priority until now.

What did one do on a staycation?

Ready or not, it was time to find out.

⁓

DISTANT banging caught my attention, yanking me out of the deep concentration I'd fallen into as my paint roller swept over the wall of my bedroom. I frowned as the banging came again, shocked to see how much time had passed since I'd begun the project that had been on my to-do list for over a year now. I set the roller aside and ran for the front door.

When had it gotten so late?

I threw the door open, breathless, and stopped short at the sight of my father standing on the front steps. "Dad?"

He exhaled, his shoulders sagging. But not in relief. In irritation. "Finally. I was beginning to wonder if you'd—" His eyes landed on my painted fingers and then darted to the broken glass in the hall over my shoulder. "You haven't even cleaned up the mess you made? What have you been doing all day?"

I held up my hands, wiggling my fingers. "Painting." I wasn't going to try to explain I'd left the glass there to remind me what was so important about my impromptu vacation.

"Why the hell would you want to do that?"

"Because I can do whatever I want. I'm on vacation."

He frowned, souring even more. "Yes, I got your text. Can I come in or does yesterday's order still stand?"

I pulled the door wide and stepped back, the lightness I'd felt all day instantly evaporating. "By all means."

I followed Dad into the kitchen and folded my arms. If he was pissed I didn't offer him a drink or a chair he didn't comment. When he turned back to me, his expression was tight, and I braced myself for whatever lecture he was about to deliver. At least Evan hadn't come with him this time.

Then again, that wasn't a good thing if it meant he was going to use the visit to berate me for my many shortcomings. My father had never laid a finger on me. He didn't have to; his words always found their mark.

"Look, I know yesterday wasn't ideal. Emotions were high. That article—"

"The article had nothing to do with it," I said as calmly as I could.

"You can't just take a vacation," he snapped.

"I am an employee entitled to an employee's benefits. Nothing more. I should know. You've told me so enough times."

"This deal is our entire fortune!"

I blinked, collecting myself before answering very quietly. "I know that."

"And yet, you're doing everything you can to throw it away."

My temper was like ice water being splashed over my head. One minute it was absent and the next I was drenched by it. I flinched at his words and balled my hands into fists. Even before I could get the words out, my arm began to itch. "Last time I checked, it still said your name next to CEO. A fact you point out every chance you get. Which means I am not the one responsible for making—or losing—our fortune."

Dad glared, and I was surprised to find I held his stare. Normally, when he looked at me like that, with the weight of his condescension bearing down so heavily, I gave in. But today, I just stood there, watching him and waiting for whatever he was going to pull next. "You are the future of this company," he began carefully. "Without it—"

"What, Dad? I have nothing?" I rolled my eyes. "Sorry. You've told me that one so often it doesn't sting anymore. What else you got?"

His cheeks reddened, and I knew I was pushing too far, but I couldn't help it. Not after the last twenty-four hours I'd had. "You're being selfish."

That blow landed—just enough to make me hesitate. Guilt pricked at me, and I lowered my head, hating that his manipulations still worked on me even after so many years.

When I raised my eyes to his, I saw his triumph just before he masked it. It was enough to snap me out of it. "Dad, we both know your debts are what got us here. Not my selfishness. Yours. You've risked and gambled and pissed away every good decision this company ever made. You are the reason investors run away after one deal. You are the reason we've had to expand our horizons to foreign relations. And you are the reason we will lose everything if the deal doesn't work."

"You have no right to speak to me that way!"

I took a step forward, and he nearly shrank back, eyes wide. "You're wrong," I said quietly. "I have every right. And it's about damn time I spoke this way."

The shock was understandable; in twenty-two years I'd never once stood up to him this way. Who knew a good orgasm was all it took for me to find my backbone? "I'm not going to keep letting you use me to clean up your mistakes and all the while listening to you tell me how much you don't need my help and I'm too cold, single, or unqualified to possibly run things better than you. I'm sick of hearing everything I do wrong. You're the one who invested badly. Not me. And I'm not going to lie for you anymore either. Not even if it means losing the company. I'm sorry, but the next time the board asks what happened, I will tell them."

"You're sentencing us to destitution if you don't help me."

The pleading in his voice was worse than the accusations and nearly broke me. I hated seeing him reduced to basically begging. But I couldn't do what he was asking. And I couldn't listen to his dramatics either. "We would hardly be destitute."

"We would be out on the street. No longer a good name—"

"That is not my fault. I offered to take over two years ago, but you refused me. You've always treated me like I wasn't good enough, and I've practically killed myself to prove to you that I am. But I'm done doing that. You created the mess. You can clean it up." I pointed at the pile of broken glass. "I've got my own messes to tend to."

Dad's eyes flashed. "Your mother would be so disappointed that you're turning your back on your family."

Any other time, the words would have broken me. Instead, I lifted my chin and shook my head. "Mom would have been ashamed of you and so am I."

He blinked and his expression shuttered until I couldn't see a trace of temper or caring. Without a word, he turned for the door and left.

In the quiet, I stared after him, numb.

What had I just done?

I had never spoken to my father that way. And even if some of it was deserved, and all of it was true, I'd never brought my mother into it. That had been low. Even for me. I had a feeling my dad wouldn't be speaking to me any time soon, and I tried hard to decide whether that bothered me.

In a daze, I made my way back to my bedroom and studied my own handiwork. The color I'd chosen was green and warm and held no trace of the coldness inside me now. The feelings warred with each other inside me, feeling like a juxtaposition that couldn't possibly co-exist. Warm or cold? Paint or work? Live for me or for them? I couldn't have both, I realized as my arm itched. Ignoring it, I picked up the paint roller, deliberate and determined, closing the bedroom door and returning to my own priorities.

I was finally going to do all the things I'd put off in favor of seeking my father's impossible approval. From now on, the only person I had to please was me…and hopefully Liam Porter.

CHAPTER SEVENTEEN

LIAM

I parked in the grass in front of Jamie's house and got out, crossing the yard to the front porch, lost in thoughts of last night. I'd gone home to shower and change, but I could still smell Cassie on me and that made it hard to concentrate on anything else. Thankfully, Sophie had already been gone when I got home so I hadn't had to explain where I'd been—though I'd ignored her texts asking me that very thing so I knew there'd be hell to pay when I saw her for lunch.

Even Jamie had left a voicemail last night and again this morning about the wood he'd offered to let me confiscate from his dad's work shed before they cleaned it out once and for all. When I'd called him back, he'd drilled me on my whereabouts last night. In the end, I'd given up the idea of working on my latest piece and driven here instead. Now, at the sight of Jess' car parked beside mine, I wondered if I shouldn't have just invited Jamie to my place instead. I had a feeling she might be less than thrilled when she found out what I'd done to *help* Cassie Franklin with her troubles.

I raised my hand to ring the bell, but the door flew open before I could make it that far. Jamie grinned back at me through the screen. "He's alive!"

My lips twitched as I pulled the screen door open. "You know, I fought wars without you worrying this much."

He stepped back to let me enter. "Clearly, you underestimate the hidden dangers of Summerville."

"Clearly," I agreed and followed him back to the kitchen.

The house was almost exactly like I remembered; the trinkets and décor still nearly the same as when his parents had been alive. They'd passed away in a car accident last year while I'd been in Japan and getting back for the funeral had been impossible.

My mom had written me and said the service was sad but beautiful. I'd ached for Jamie, but he'd had Jess and my parents. Sophie said the twins seemed to be leaning on each other pretty well ever since. I'd told myself it was okay that I'd had to miss it, but seeing the reminders of what my friend had to go through without me hurt. I looked away from the framed photos of the four of them still hanging in the hall, keeping my eyes straight ahead until we reached the kitchen.

The scent of bacon hung in the air and the curtains were new. I kept my attention on these things instead of all the reminders of what was missing. Jamie's mom had been like a second mom to me for a long time, and if I missed her this much, I could only imagine how he felt living in a house surrounded by his parents' furniture.

"It's weird, right?"

Jamie's words caught me off guard. I looked up and found him watching me, a sad dip to his expression. His gaze flicked to the kitchen table where we'd spent a lot of time as kids with his mom feeding us. "I miss her," I admitted quietly. "I'm sorry

I didn't make it back for the service."

Jamie shook his head. "Don't apologize for shit. You have a damned good reason. And she wouldn't have wanted you to feel bad about it."

"Sophie says you've been great about checking in with her since our folks moved to Florida," I told him. "I owe you for that and I feel like I haven't repaid you well."

He shoved his hands into his pockets, not meeting my gaze. "It's the least I could do. What you did matters, Liam. For our country."

I snorted, hating that line more and more every time I heard it. The recognition was bullshit. "I am not a hero. I'm just a guy. Like a thousand others out there doing the same damn thing right now."

"Fine. It matters for your family then," he said instead.

I didn't answer. He was right about that. But I still didn't want to attach the word hero to any of it. Sophie was my sister. I'd do it again in a heartbeat. "She's top of her class already." I couldn't help but brag a little.

Jamie chuckled. "I didn't doubt it for a second. She's going to make the teachers look bad. I can't believe she didn't get a full ride to begin with."

I shrugged. "What they offered combined with my GI Bill money is enough. That's all that matters."

"You think she'll remember us when she's a Supreme Court justice?"

"Sure. She'll be the one to have you committed when your crazy gets to be too much," I shot back.

He snickered, but his smile faded and he looked at me. "You did a great thing putting her through school."

"She's family. I did what anyone would have done."

"Liam, we both know with your ears, it's a lot more

complicated than that."

"I don't want to talk about it."

My ears. What he meant was my medical discharge and the fact I'd gotten a parting settlement large enough to live like a king. Instead, I'd put it toward the house and Sophie's education.

He frowned but didn't press it. I knew he wanted to ask how I was feeling, and I was grateful when he didn't. Instead, he cleared his throat, and I knew the topic wasn't completely forgotten, but he was giving me a pass for now. I'd take it.

"So," he said. "Where were you last night? I called you like four times."

"I was out with a friend."

Jamie's eyes narrowed. "A friend," he repeated knowingly. "Does this friend have a name?"

"She does."

"*She.* Uh-huh. Anyone I know?" He sounded way too damn pleased about the whole thing.

I knew he assumed I'd come right back home and fall into my old habits. For some reason that bothered me. Not that I'd corrected his assumptions up until now. How could I explain to someone who hadn't seen what I'd seen—who hadn't almost died—that everything felt different now? Life itself—the act of breathing—felt different. I could never go back to the way I was. And I didn't want to. But I couldn't bring myself to say it out loud. Not to someone who hadn't experienced it. He would probably laugh and tell me I was crazy or that I needed to get drunk then laid. I knew because four years ago that's what I would have said to me too.

"Sort of," I said at last.

"Fine. We can do vague. Just tell me her measurements. I'll guess from there."

I shook my head, laughing. "You're disgusting."

He snorted. "Please. Like you're any better."

That got me. My smile disappeared, and I opened my mouth, not even sure how to respond. On the one hand, I wanted to tell him I wasn't the same Liam Porter I'd been before. But on the other—I *had* just spent the night making Cassie Franklin come for me.

Jess walked in, grunting at us on her way to the fridge.

"Morning sunshine," Jamie said.

"Go to hell."

I snorted. Clearly, her morning demeanor was just as cheery as it had been in high school.

Jess stood with the fridge door open and drank straight from the juice carton. When she was done, she wiped her mouth and looked at me. "Have you heard from Cassie?"

"I have, actually," I said slowly, choosing my words carefully and shooting glances at Jamie.

But Jess wasn't picking up my cues. Or didn't care. "And?" she prompted. "Did you talk to her?"

"Yes?" I winced, knowing I was being way too obvious.

Jess put the carton away and slammed the fridge. "What's going on? Why are you being cagey? It's too damn early and I haven't had coffee yet so I can't decipher what you're not saying. Did you find anything out or not?"

"Wait a second." Jamie's eyes widened. He stared at me, no longer trying to pull Jess back. "Cassie Franklin is your friend from last night? The reason you didn't call me back? Holy shit, bro! That's—"

His smile died as he caught sight of Jess glaring at him now. Instead, his mouth twisted into a deliberate frown and he shook his head at me. "That's no bueno."

"Oh my God, Jamie, stay out of it. This is not one of your

little conquests. This is between Liam and me."

"You mean Liam and Cassie," he corrected.

Jess narrowed her eyes. "It's too damn early to argue with you." She thrust the bag of coffee grounds at him. "You make the coffee and I'll work on not letting my head spin all the way around. Deal?"

"Deal." Jamie went to work making the coffee.

I took a step back from both of them, giving them both plenty of space. Jess looked at me, clearly waiting for an explanation. "Look. She came by yesterday morning. She was a mess over the article that ran about her trying to hire me to be her boyfriend in order to save her business deal."

"A bunch of fucking vultures. It's horse shit," Jess muttered, folding her arms over her chest.

"Actually, it's true," I said and her eyes snapped up to mine.

Jamie's jaw dropped. "No shit? You're a gigolo now?"

"No, I'm not a—" I took a deep breath and started over, my gaze on Jess who clearly needed an explanation before she decided to murder me in her own kitchen. "Did you know she has panic attacks?"

Jess blinked. "No."

"Well, she had one yesterday. And she has a rash. Hives. It's a stress thing. I think she's taking pills which actually only makes it worse." I sighed. "You were right. She was in trouble."

Jess bit her lip.

"That article really blasted her," Jamie said. "It was cold even for the ice princess." He winced as Jess shot him a look. "Well, she is," he added.

Jess rolled her eyes and looked back at me. "She was that upset?"

I nodded. "She was pretty bent up."

"It's embarrassing, I'm sure," Jess murmured.

I kept my mouth shut as I realized Jess knew nothing of the company's precarious financial situation.

"Is she okay now?" Jess asked a moment later.

I took a deep breath, remembering how worried I'd been all day yesterday before she'd called me back. "She left pretty quickly, and I wasn't sure. She drove around after that, but then she called me back again last night. Asked me to come over."

Jamie looked much more interested now. "And?"

"She sounded strange on the phone and when I got there, the door was unlocked and there was broken glass in the hall. I thought…" I swallowed hard, remembering what I'd thought. "Anyway, she apparently had a big fight with her dad and Evan."

Jess frowned at that. "Evan's a real fucking creep," she said.

I didn't disagree.

"Who's Evan?" Jamie asked.

We both ignored him.

"Anyway, she's finally decided to step out from under her father's iron fist, I think."

"What do you mean?" Jess asked.

"She threw them both out of her house. Threw a glass at Evan when he didn't get out fast enough. Then she called me and I've been there since." I explained.

Jess looked at me, her eyes widening as my words sank in. "Wait. Are you saying—?" Jess stopped and started again. "Please tell me you're saying what I think you're saying."

"What do you think he's saying?" Jamie asked, darting glances back and forth between us.

I folded my arms to match Jess, my expression hardening. "I'm not saying anything because it's none of your business. But if I were saying it, I'd tell you that Cassie initiated everything. Nothing happened that she didn't ask for, and she was very satisfied with the outcome."

Jess gasped, and I braced myself for more fury and finger-pointing. But then, shockingly, her expression transformed once more, and she looked...happy?

"I thought you'd be pissed at me," I said, cautious as I studied her.

"Of course I'm pissed at you. You've made all of her problems worse. But you also might have made everything better."

"I don't understand."

"I need to call Cassie," she said and abruptly turned on her heel, hurrying out, her phone clutched in her hand. "Keep doing what you're doing, Liam Porter, war hero," she called over her shoulder.

A moment later, a door upstairs slammed.

The house went quiet.

"Damn. I think my sister just gave you permission to bang her best friend."

I didn't answer.

"Earth to Liam," Jamie called a moment later.

Slowly, I turned back to find him rubbing his jaw thoughtfully. His eyes gleamed in a way I didn't trust. "Interesting turn," he said.

"What is?" I demanded.

"You like her."

"I like the challenge," I corrected.

"I thought you just completed the challenge," he shot back.

I knew what he meant. The sex. And I thought I'd agree but now... "There's more there. She's passionate. Fun. Free." I stopped, realizing how sappy I sounded. "She's totally different without the cameras pointed at her."

Jamie winked. "When she's not people-pleasing, she's

Liam-pleasing, huh?"

"Shut up." I turned my back on him and went to the fridge, yanking it open and pulling out a beer. It was only eleven in the morning, but right now, I didn't care. Having the twins both interrogate me was worse than any debrief I'd done in the military.

"Holy shit, bro. You fucking like the ice princess," Jamie said. I glanced at him over the can I was currently chugging. His eyes were lit with the kind of glee that only came from discovering one of my secrets.

I lowered the can, now half-empty. "Don't you have a firewall to breach or something?"

Jamie snorted. "Holy shit. It's like a damned Nicholas Sparks movie or something."

"Book," I said.

"What?"

"Book. Nicholas Sparks writes books. The movies came after. And no it's not. Wait. How do you even know who Nicholas Sparks is?"

He shrugged. "Janie Foster made me watch one of his flicks last month. I don't know anything about a book."

I snorted. "Clearly. Wait. You dated Janie Foster?"

"Uh, 'dated' is a strong word."

I rolled my eyes.

"It doesn't get any more tragic, you know."

"Janie Foster?"

"Very funny. The player from high school comes home a war hero and finally catches the attention of the one girl he could never have."

"What the hell's so tragic about that?"

"Just wait."

"Wait for what? You sound like an idiot."

"All I'm saying is that an alligator doesn't change its stripes."

I stared at him, waiting for the nonsensical words to somehow make sense. Finally, I shook my head and said the only thing that would end this inane conversation. "Dude, you are way too wise for me."

He grinned and snagged a beer of his own. "I always was." He cracked the can and smacked me on the shoulder. "Come on. Let's go see if I have anything in the garage you can sand into a masterpiece."

I followed him out, wondering about Jamie's cryptic comment long after I probably should have. Did he mean me or Cassie when he talked about one's true colors remaining the same? And what the hell was Jess saying to Cassie now? What was Cassie saying to Jess? And why did I care so much about any of it? All I'd wanted was to make her come—to see her O face. But suddenly Jamie's words were ringing in my ears, and I wondered if there was more to it.

The idea of wanting something real with Cassie Franklin—or anyone, for that matter—felt foreign. I'd never had a real relationship before. From the sounds of it, she hadn't had many either. Just the idea of it made my palms sweat. But the more I thought about it, the more I wondered if Cassie wasn't exactly what I'd swore to myself I'd find when that bomb had nearly killed me. After my surgery, I'd made a promise to myself to find and hold onto the things that really mattered to me. To live—and to love. To enjoy the life I had left. And right now, I couldn't imagine anything more enjoyable than Cassie.

CHAPTER EIGHTEEN

CASSIE

A rap at the door made me jump, nearly dropping my toast. I hesitated before I remembered my new phone delivery I'd scheduled for first thing this morning. Jumping up, I went to sign for the package, careful to keep my robe pulled tight in front of the delivery man. Back inside, I booted the phone up and reloaded all of my accounts, waiting for my contacts to sync. Halfway through checking my email, I remembered none of it mattered, anyway. Not with me on vacation. Because there wasn't a single message there that didn't involve Franklin business. Nothing personal. No friends. Not even a hobby. I set it aside and was still trying to figure out what to do with my day when the phone rang.

The number on the screen wasn't programmed, so I answered cautiously. "Hello?"

"You look delicious right now."

My lips curved at the sound of Liam's voice. I shuddered, remembering how those words had sounded when he'd said them into my ear yesterday morning—and all night before that.

"How do you know what I look like right now?"

"Call it the law of averages. You've never not looked delicious."

My insides warmed, and I set my toast aside. "Well, I am wearing that robe you liked and not much else."

"Such a tease."

"Not at all. Come over and I'll follow through."

"That's exactly why I'm calling. If I come over, I don't stand a chance against you."

"What's so wrong with that?"

"Not a damned thing. But we're doing this right."

"What do you—?"

"Tonight," he cut in. "You. Me. A real date. I pick the place. Wear something scandalous that is not appropriate for a five-star restaurant."

"Okay," I said slowly, unable to ignore the butterflies batting wildly against my stomach right now. Everything felt scandalous with Liam and it was starting to scare the hell out of me. "Where are we going?" I asked.

"You'll see."

I hedged. "I'm not sure I like surprises."

"Do you like me?" he shot back.

"Yes," I admitted without a single second's hesitation.

"Do you trust me?"

The question was innocent enough, but my heart pounded so loudly, it drowned out my ability to think. Did I trust him? This felt big and much more important than one mystery date. "Yes," I said finally, a lot quieter than before.

Liam paused. "I'm not going to hurt you," he said finally.

I let out a breath. "Okay."

"Okay," he repeated, sounding just as nervous but a lot more sure than I felt. "See you tonight, gorgeous."

"See you tonight."

⟶

IN my kitchen, I patted gently at the fresh ink on my forearm and then pulled the gauze away to admire the tattoo all over again. Jess came up beside me, a drink in each hand. I took one of them and sipped the chilled cocktail, glad for something cold. The tattoo shop had been smoky with incense although the artist had been surprisingly not terrifying compared to what I'd expected from the movies I'd seen: a fact I'd mentioned to Jess much to her entertainment.

Now, back home, Jess cocked her head as she studied the symbol I'd chosen. "I still can't believe you went through with it," she said before tossing back half her drink.

"Me either," I admitted. "But I'm glad I did it."

"No regrets, huh?"

"The new Cassie doesn't do regret," I said firmly.

"Well then, I'm a fan of her."

Jess met my eyes in the mirror and we exchanged a look. Not a smile per se—Jess and I didn't do warm and fuzzy—but something close to it. "I'm glad you came with me," I said quietly.

She squeezed my shoulder and then backed off. "I'm glad you called," she said. "I've missed you."

"I know. I'm sorry," I began but Jess held up a hand.

"Stop apologizing. I told you, I understand. I was just worried."

"Yeah." I sighed, replacing the gauze and pressing the tape back into place before readjusting the waistband of my sweatpants.

Sweatpants.

Another anomaly for me.

When Jess had shown up earlier, she'd taken one look at my clothing and almost fainted. According to her, the sweatpants alone meant I was going "off the rails." But when I'd told her the full story, including how my father had tried to sell off my personal life in exchange for saving his own fortune, she'd stopped ragging me about my clothes and started offering to put a hit out on anyone I wanted, starting with Evan. I'd waved it off and made her promise not to talk about it anymore, at least for today. I didn't want to focus on all the bad. I wanted to look forward and choose things that made me happy for once.

Hence, the tattoo. An idea Jess fully supported.

"So what's next for Miss Rebel With A Cause?" Jess asked me now. "A tongue piercing? Or maybe a clit piercing?" She wiggled her brows, the ice in her empty glass clinking as she twirled it.

"No, to both of those things." I shuddered. "Especially the latter."

"I thought you were living dangerously."

"Dangerous is fine. Pain is not. Besides, I don't have time for any more rebellious body art today. You've gotta go and I've gotta get ready."

She lowered her glass, her eyes widening in a pout that was all too familiar for Jess. "You're kicking me out? Happy hour hasn't finished yet."

I shook my head. "You're going to have to find a way to be happy without me. I have plans."

Her pout turned to a full-blown scowl for only a split second before her face lit up. "Wait. Are you talking about Liam Porter?" Her voice dropped to a whisper despite the fact that we were completely alone. "Is it a date? Are you guys going to...ya know?" She wiggled her eyebrows.

I held back a smile. "None of your business." I shooed her toward the door so she was forced to grab her bag and scramble ahead of me.

"Oh Cassie Franklin's first O face most certainly *is* my business," she hooted. "Do you know how long I've waited for you to... Wait. Why do you look like that?"

I'd kept a lid on this all day since we'd spent it in the presence of a total stranger while he inked me. But now, I could finally admit it. "It's not my first," I admitted.

"Wait. The other night...?" At my tiny nod, she whooped. "I knew it! I fucking knew it! I can't believe you didn't call me immediately."

"Sorry about that."

"Whatever. I told Liam—" She broke off abruptly and fell silent.

My eyes narrowed. "You told Liam what?"

"Uh." Jess cringed, suddenly much more silent than was characteristic for her.

"Jess," I said, my tone a warning.

"I saw him yesterday when he stopped by to see Jamie." She spoke slowly as if choosing her words carefully.

"And?"

"And he said he'd spent the night with you. I was just hoping." She shrugged, and I knew there was more to it, but she wasn't spilling, and I didn't have time for an inquisition before Liam showed up.

I glared at her. "This isn't over," I said.

Jess nodded and grabbed the doorknob, all too happy to leave all of a sudden. "Sure. Call me tomorrow and let me know how it goes," she sang before slipping out.

When the door clicked shut behind her, I leaned on the wall and exhaled. So Liam was telling people he'd slept over.

Interesting. He'd never been a bragger in high school. His reputation had grown purely on the talk of the females. But time had changed a lot of things. Apparently that too.

Good thing I no longer cared what my father or his company or anyone else thought of me, I reminded myself, and went to get changed.

I raced for the front door and made it down the stairs by the third chime of the bell. I'd gotten sidetracked trying on nearly every piece of lingerie I owned—which wasn't much—but I'd also never worn any of them for another person. That black lace two nights ago had been the first. Mirrors had been moved and selfies had been taken, all so I could figure out which one I had the guts to wear underneath my dress tonight. And now, Liam was clearly getting impatient.

The bell rang a fourth time just as I reached the hall. "Coming," I called out.

I threw open the door, breathless.

At the sight of me, Liam's expression transformed into shock and then pleasure. "Not yet. But you will," he promised.

Glancing down at the red slice of fabric I'd decided to let pass for a dress, heat crept up from my toes and curled into my stomach. I grabbed his wrist and pulled him inside, slamming the door behind him. "Get in here."

In the back of my mind, I wondered at this new confidence that had me initiating everything, but then I closed the distance between us and pressed my lips to his—shutting off all thoughts for the moment.

"What did I do to deserve this kind of greeting?" he asked, his lips still brushing over mine as he spoke.

I tipped my head back when his mouth dipped lower, clinging to his shoulders as he kissed a trail down my throat to my collarbone. "That fourth doorbell ring," I teased, my breath coming in short gasps as he dipped lower to the cleavage already amply displayed by my dress.

"Is that right? Four rings is the siren call?"

"Yep," I managed as his tongue dipped between my breasts.

My body jerked against him and he lifted his head so that we were eye to eye. His grin made my stomach flop. "Liam," I began, already ready for round one. Or eight if we were still counting the last thirty-six hours.

"Dinner first," he said. "Then dessert."

I'd never appreciated Jess and her pouty face nearly as much as I did in this moment. My lower lip jutted out with what I prayed was sultry disappointment.

Liam chuckled. "Good Lord, that look has probably brought lesser men to their knees." He kissed me before I could admit I'd never used it on anyone but him. That stoic chill I'd used as a mask on everyone around me was an expression I seemed to use less and less when Liam was around.

He took my hand, leading me out the front door. "Come on, gorgeous. There's some place I want to show you."

"Is it your bedroom?" I asked, snagging my purse and coat as I followed him out.

He laughed.

In the truck, I stared out the window as the town flew by. My tattoo itched, and I ran my finger over the gauze lightly. Just knowing it was there felt liberating. I couldn't hide it. Not in a board room and not in a ball gown—and that's exactly why I'd chosen that spot. Getting it in plain sight had been just as important as the artwork. For what it all represented. A new version of Cassie Franklin. Like being reborn. Or reinvented.

"What is that?" Liam asked. "Is your rash worse?"

I looked over and found him studying my hand where I rubbed absently at the bandage on my arm. "No, it's... How do you know about my rash, anyway? I've been wearing long sleeves for weeks to cover it up."

"It was hard to miss that first day in your office," he admitted, coming to a stop at a red light. "And when you came to my house the other day about the article."

"Right." I grimaced, remembering the panic attack. "I'm sorry you had to see me like that."

We hadn't had a chance to talk about it since, and I didn't want to start now. Not after the great day I'd had.

But he simply reached across the bench seat and took my hand, squeezing it as he accelerated through the intersection. "Don't apologize. I'm glad I was there. Though, I'll admit, I prefer seeing you like this." His eyes ran over me in a quick but hungry inspection. "Where the hell did you get that dress, anyway? It's practically painted on."

"Is it too much?" I asked, looking worriedly down at myself.

"Hell no," he said firmly. "It's exactly fucking right, babe. You look delicious as usual."

My insides warmed at that. When was the last time I was complimented on anything? "Thanks, I bought it at a boutique in Bermuda last year while I was on vacation."

His hand came up to cover his chest, and he looked stricken with shock. "You actually took a vacation?"

"Hilarious. I take a vacation every year, actually. This year I went to New Orleans."

"The French Quarter is a blast. Who did you go with?"

I hesitated only a split-second. "Myself."

He glanced sharply over at me, one brow cocked. "You took a vacation alone?"

I shrugged, but it felt defensive. "Why not? I don't need anyone else to have fun. Besides, when you grow up as an only child, you learn to enjoy your own company."

"Nothing wrong with that," he agreed quietly, still glancing at me.

He went back to watching the road, and I gritted my teeth in the silence that followed. I braced myself, waiting for him to make some pitying comment about how I didn't have enough friends or something, but he didn't mention it.

Instead, he glanced at me sideways, his eyes narrowed mischievously. "You never did tell me the story about how you figured out you weren't gay."

"Probably because the truth isn't nearly as interesting as whatever you're imagining right now."

He wiggled his eyebrows. "Try me."

I shook my head. "I was in college. At a party." He feigned shock again, and I rolled my eyes. "Yes, I went to parties. Anyway, my roommate and I were talking to these frat guys all night, and we wound up with a dare: every time my roommate and I kissed, they'd take off an item of clothing. I'd had enough to drink that I was feeling adventurous, so I agreed."

"And?" he prompted when I fell silent.

"By the end of the night, they were naked, and I was positive I was straight."

He shot me a glance. "And the guys?"

I shrugged. "I don't know. Once the dare was done, it didn't seem as fun anymore so we went home."

He blinked, waiting a beat, then he threw his head back and laughed. "You are way more fun than they give you credit for."

"I always figured it proved what a bitch I was."

"For not having sex when you don't want it? No way."

"Huh. I never thought of it that way."

He squeezed my hand. "You're too hard on yourself," he said quietly.

I didn't answer. Maybe he was right, but I'd never been able to see myself without looking through the eyes of someone else. It felt strange to start now.

A second later, we pulled up to an old, worn-looking building that I knew all too well in Summerville. Liam cut the engine, and I shot him a look. "This is what you wanted to show me? Letty's Place?"

"To be honest, I thought about taking you to a nice dinner at this place I found on the water when I was driving around the other night. But I think you need this more." He unbuckled and motioned for me to get out. "Come on."

I climbed out slowly, unwilling to move even a step closer to the dive bar across the lot. The brick had long since faded and was scarred with the evidence of serving what was not exactly an upscale crowd in Summerville.

Back in high school, it had offered a teen night where they'd shut the bar down other than soda and brought in a bunch of pool tables and dart boards. But those nights had been more of a "bring a date" scene. As such, I'd never actually stepped foot inside. Considering my dress tonight—and my date—I wasn't sure I wanted to change that now.

"Liam," I began when he tried leading me toward the entrance. Two other couples passed us on their way inside. One of the girls eyed Liam openly, and I felt a streak of hot irritation whip through me. "Maybe we should check out that restaurant you mentioned instead."

"Look, I know it's not a place you would normally choose, but considering you and me, and that dress you're wearing, I'm betting you don't want to go anywhere normal."

He had a point.

Hadn't I just taken an impromptu vacation? Hadn't I walked away from my father and told him to figure it out on his own? Hadn't I sworn to look for—and find—the real Cassie Franklin underneath all the "shoulds" and "have to's?"

I bit my lip, staring up at the wood-planked facade that rose two stories above me into the night. The entrance was bathed in an orange glow thanks to the one working streetlight in the parking lot. Beyond that, dim shadows disappeared into utter darkness on both sides of the building. Even though I'd never come here in high school, I knew full well what went on sometimes in those darkened corners of the parking lot after teen night had ended.

"Isn't this place a hangout for high school kids during the week?" I asked.

"Not anymore. I think Letty got tired of boy band music. That and all bathrooms she had to clean thanks to the smuggled alcohol." He paused and then added, "But I will tell you that Jamie says a lot of kids we knew back in school still come here." His brows dipped together in a show of concern. "Is that all right?"

I looked up at Liam in the darkness, debating. The look on his face made it clear that this moment right here was my opportunity to say "Hell, no" and get back in the truck. Walking in there was the complete opposite of the Cassie Franklin this town knew. Hell, it was the opposite of the Cassie *I* knew. Walking in there would change everything on a level I couldn't even quite wrap my head around.

The prudent thing would have been to walk away. To let Liam take me to a quiet, five-star restaurant on the opposite side of town and then take me home. Even smarter would have been to let him leave after that. To stop letting myself fall harder and harder for the biggest player this town had ever known.

Instead what came out of my mouth, like it had a mind of its own was, "Sure. Why the hell not? I missed out on all this in high school. Might as well make up for it tonight."

Liam grinned, a slow spread of his curving lips that stole the oxygen from my lungs and told me everything that came next would be worth it if he would just smile at me like that some more. And if his hands were on me while he smiled, all the better. God, I was a fucking mess. But I was also having the time of my life. I just hoped whatever Liam left of me when he was done was recognizable.

"Let's do it, sunshine." He grabbed my hand and led me inside.

CHAPTER NINETEEN

LIAM

CASSIE was a firecracker. Somewhere between the third and fourth shot, she'd shaken loose of the tight, tense girl I knew and transformed into someone completely alien. I stood against the bar, catching my breath after four dances in a row, nursing a beer to cool me off. Cassie had wandered off to find the bathroom, and I was hoping to talk her into eating something when she came back. I wasn't sure if she'd always been a lightweight or if she just had an empty stomach, but food couldn't hurt.

The music twanged and thumped through the speakers and the familiar scent of fried food still hung in the air. Letty, the woman who'd run what I remembered as a family-friendly pool hall and arcade most weeknights, ran the place now and was currently tending bar for a full crowd of Summerville locals.

She smiled at me from the other end of the bar and I raised my beer in silent hello. We'd catch up later. For now, I needed to breathe before both lungs squeezed their way out of my chest. It was smoky as hell in here and the speakers were loud enough to screw with my balance, the way they vibrated the floor with their bass—not a great combination for my insides.

"Yo, dude. Long time no see."

I looked up and did my best to hide a grimace as I recognized the guy in front of me. "Mark Williams," I said, taking his hand after only a slight hesitation. It wasn't personal—Mark and I had been friends before—I just didn't want to hear what came next.

"Liam Porter. War hero." Mark grinned.

I ran my tongue over my teeth. "Something like that."

I'd known when I'd picked this place that I'd be recognized, that I'd have to field the million questions that came with "catching up" and I'd opted to do it anyway. Rip the Band-Aid off, Sophie would say.

"You back for good?" Mark asked.

His eyes followed mine as I did a quick glance toward the bathrooms.

"Yeah, I bought the house from my parents so they could retire. Been spending some time in Dad's workshop."

"No shit? That's awesome. I guess you need a creative outlet after wasting so many terrorists, right?"

I turned back to him slowly, half-wondering if I could just pretend I hadn't heard him. A flash of blonde hair stopped me from laying Mark out like a new floor rug right here and now. Cassie slid in close, winding her arm around my back and kissed my cheek, and I knew she was purposely ruining the moment. Or saving Mark's nose. "Hey you," she said.

"Hey." I took another swig of my beer.

"Cassie Franklin." Mark looked back and forth between us and I realized too late this was why he'd come over. No one else had approached us yet. Not even people I'd known personally four years ago. I'd assumed Cassie had scared them off which was fine by me, but Mark was just enough of an asshat to corner me alone and not leave when he'd clearly overstayed his welcome.

"That's me," she said. "And you are?"

"Mark Williams. We had World History together." He said it like that was going to click something personal into place.

Cassie just shrugged, a polite smile pasted on. "Right. Sure. Good to see you." Her blue eyes shone warm and bright from the alcohol. Mark clearly took that as an invitation to linger. But Cassie had already moved on, swaying to the beat of the song that had just switched from something slow to a fast one.

"You want to dance?" I asked.

She nodded, her expression lighting up at my offer, and I sent Mark a nod as we both headed for the dance floor. I felt Mark's stare trained on us as we went and made sure to lead us as far from him as I could. With any luck, we wouldn't run into him again. His idiotic comment on the other hand… I couldn't shake that nearly as easily. The pulse of my temper thumped in time to the music.

Shoving it aside, I concentrated on Cassie. On moving my body and appreciating the way she moved hers. For a moment, she was lost in it, her head tossed back, her hips swaying to the bass, and the sight of her like that stole my breath. She was fucking gorgeous on a normal day, but like this? With her inhibitions lowered and her body feeling into the music like nothing else mattered and no one else existed beyond the pleasure of the movement.

I had to touch her—to be a part of that—so I grabbed her wrist, yanking her against me as our bodies moved in tandem now.

"You can dance?" she said after only a couple of minutes. The surprise was clear, but she continued before I could comment. "I guess I shouldn't be surprised. I'll bet you made it your business to be good at anything involving joining your body with another female's."

"What's that supposed to mean?"

She shrugged. "Exactly what I said. Everyone knows how you were in high school."

"That was high school," I pointed out, not sure I liked what she was implying.

She shrugged again. "Nothing wrong with enjoying each other's bodies now either."

I frowned and when she tried to go back to the dance, I leaned in. "Yours is the only body I wanted to enjoy," I said against her ear.

Instead of melting against me, her shoulders stiffened and she pulled back, her expression full of apology. "Sorry. I didn't mean—"

"I know what I used to be, Cassie. But that's not me anymore. I don't want anyone else but you."

She nodded, but her mouth was pressed tightly together, like she hadn't quite convinced herself of that yet. The fear in her eyes was subtle, but it was there. And I realized her resistance had more to do with her own shit and the people in her life that had hurt her than it did me. Without pressing the issue, I pulled her in close again.

If I couldn't tell her with words, I'd show her.

We went back to dancing, slower this time, and I held her in a way that I hoped made it clear I'd meant my words. After a few minutes, I felt her relax.

"I'm not very good at this," she said, surprising me with her honesty.

I didn't pull away, too afraid I'd spook her again. "Me either."

"My table for two at that restaurant we went to that first night? I eat there alone a lot," she said.

"Why are you telling me this now?"

"I could see the way you looked at me," she explained. "Like you assumed I brought dates there. I haven't had a date except for Evan in two years. No real boyfriends. Between work and school, there wasn't time. And there wasn't anyone worth it, I guess."

I tightened my arms around her, appreciating how much of herself she'd just shared with me. It was easier this way. On a crowded dance floor. Surrounded by people and music so loud you could hardly hear your own doubts much less each other's secrets. It was safer somehow. "I'm kind of starting to hate your dad," I admitted.

"He wasn't this bad before my mom died."

"What happened?"

"Breast cancer. We didn't know until it was too late. After that, my dad changed. It made him harder. And he worked more. Took more risks. Pissed off more people. Like he realized how fragile his own life was and then it was like he…"

"Went in the opposite direction of valuing it?" I guessed.

"Exactly."

"I guess I understand. I mean, when that bomb went off and then I woke up without my hearing, I realized how lucky I was. My lung collapsed and my guys re-inflated it, saving my ass with their training and quick thinking. But the reality was that I'd nearly died. And I was damned lucky to get this second chance. It's a crossroads, I'm told, when something like that happens. Like you can see the fork. One direction is to grab hold of life and appreciate the shit out of it. The other option is to throw it all away even harder and faster than before."

"You chose the first."

"For me, it was never a question. Maybe it's a personality thing. I don't know. But it was always automatic for me. I want to appreciate it all. Find things I care about and hold onto them." My arms tightened around her as I said the last part.

"I didn't almost die or anything," she said slowly, "But I think I want to live like that too."

I hugged her close, inhaling her scent and just letting the moment hang there. Cassie clung to me and I felt my chest cracking open, letting a little more of her in—and my feelings out. Somewhere during that exchange, I'd fallen for her. I wasn't sure what that meant for us. But there was no denying it now.

Cassie stiffened in my arms, yanking me out of my thoughts. I released her and the moment I did, she went perfectly still. No more swaying hips. No more bedroom eyes. In fact, the chill that had surrounded her when we'd first met had returned. Whatever—or whoever—she was looking at was not a welcome sight.

"What's wrong?" I followed the direction of her stare and found what had made her go frigid. "Is that—?"

"Evan." Her voice was tight. Barely controlled and not anywhere in the vicinity of friendly. I couldn't blame her if things had ended between them as badly as she'd said.

She marched off the dance floor and over to Evan. I followed, wondering if I should just hang back and leave them alone. But something about the way he was watching her made me stick close. It was just like the photo I'd seen in her office. Evan had a glint in his eyes that put me on edge.

"What are you doing here?" Cassie asked without preamble. The flush of anger on her skin covered her cheeks and chest.

"It's nice to see you too." Evan smiled, but it was too much teeth and struck me as predatory rather than friendly. His gaze flicked to me, giving me a once-over that made me inch even closer to Cassie for some reason. "And you are?"

"Liam Porter." I stuck my hand out, and when he took it, I squeezed until he flinched.

"Evan Swindell." He retracted his hand, and I swallowed the self-satisfied smirk I wanted to give him. Beside me, Cassie was uncharacteristically quiet.

"You two on a date then?" he asked.

"None of your business," Cassie said icily.

Evan looked at me, and I answered smoothly. "Yep."

Evan's interest grew and he let his gaze wander the length of Cassie. I tightened my hold on her waist, my jaw tensing as I watched him.

"Interesting," he said.

"What are you doing here, Evan?" Cassie's voice was flat, but I could feel the irritation rolling off her.

"Enjoying my evening," he said simply. "With a friend." He gestured toward the bar where a familiar face watched our exchange with uncertainty.

"Bev?" Cassie demanded, whipping back around to stare accusingly at Evan. "Are you serious right now?"

Evan's eyes narrowed fractionally. "I don't see how it's any of your—"

"We had an agreement," she said, her voice dropping low. She spoke through clenched teeth. "You leave me and my staff alone and I keep quiet about what happened at your last job."

Evan's jaw tightened.

I tensed. *What happened?*

"You're on vacation. Technically, Bev isn't your staff right now," he said.

Cassie rolled her eyes. "I can't deal with you right now." She glanced at me. "I'm going to get a drink and talk some sense into my assistant. I'll be back."

I offered her a tight smile—and a kiss on the cheek, just to prove my point. "I'll be here, baby."

She walked off without a glance back.

When we were alone, I faced Evan. "So what exactly did happen at your last job?"

"Liam Porter. War hero." He drew out the words way too long, ignoring my question completely. My hands balled into fists, but I kept my expression blank. Evan grinned as if he knew exactly where my buttons were and how to push them. "I never got to thank you for your speech. You brought in some serious cash for us that night."

"You work with Cassie?" I asked, trying to keep my cool at least long enough to figure out this guy's game. The fact that he'd just ruined Cassie's good mood so quickly put him right at the top of my shit list. His slippery smile and backhanded insults weren't helping matters.

"VP of Investor Relations." He said it like he wanted me to be impressed.

"Uh-huh. And how many investors have you had relations with exactly?"

The smile shifted. Now, it was more of a sneer. "I've known Cassie and her family nearly all my life. A lot longer than you have. Cassie and I are going through some things together, but I wouldn't get too comfortable with her, friend."

I bristled. "And why is that?"

"She's spoken for."

The way he said it, the way he watched her and treated her like a damned possession, was really starting to piss me off. "Funny. Cassie doesn't strike me as the type to let anyone speak for her. Speaking of which, she says you have your mental health to deal with. Sounds like you have your hands full.

Friend."

Across the space, I watched as Cassie finished up with Bev and headed back this way, a drink in each hand. She stepped carefully, making sure not to spill either one. Bev, on the other hand, remained at the bar, watching us carefully.

I looked back at Evan just in time to watch his eyes narrow, all of his attention aimed at me now. "You know, sooner or later, Cassie will get tired of you. And then she'll come back to me and get it for free."

He winked, and my fist swung out before I even knew I'd told it what to do.

It connected with the side of Evan's face, and he went down.

Cassie gasped, jumping back so he wouldn't land on her shoes. Alcohol sloshed over the edge of her glass and splattered across Evan's shirt. I stood there, torn between regret and the urge to do it again. The people around us scrambled back to give us space. When I didn't move to continue the fight, they slowly closed in again, trying to get a front row seat to the drama.

"What the fuck, dude?" Evan got to his feet, spitting blood into his cupped hand.

Out of the corner of my eye, I could see Letty coming toward us from around the bar followed closely by Bev who looked terrified of the whole scene.

"Instinct. I'm trained to take down the assholes," I said with a shrug and backed away so the others could crowd around him, asking if he was all right.

Letty shook her head at me, her lips pressed tightly together. "Sorry," I mouthed. She rolled her eyes and barked at one of the bartenders to bring her some ice.

In the middle of the chaos, Cassie's hand slid into mine and pulled. Before I knew it, we were standing by the entrance. No one stopped us or even called us back. Everyone's attention was on Evan over by the bar. Vaguely, I was aware of Cassie calling my name, but all I could see was Evan. His lip was split, but the urge to do more than that was making it hard to concentrate on anything else.

"Liam!"

I blinked and found Cassie's hands cupping my cheeks. Her eyes were on mine, searching for something I knew she wasn't going to find right now. My chest felt tight. My breath short. And my balance teetering.

"Are you all right?" Cassie asked.

"I'm fine." I swayed, propping my hand on the wall beside me for support. "We should go."

She nodded, and I let her lead me out.

Instead of heading straight for the truck, I veered right, taking us both into the thick shadows that clung to the side of the building. It was cooler here and in the thick darkness, it felt almost removed from the rest of the world. I led us both far enough back that we were completely hidden from sight if someone came outside.

"What the hell happened?" Cassie asked.

"Mark's comment earlier got to me and then Evan was being a dick about you and me and…shit. I don't know." I took a deep breath, willing the adrenaline to ease and my breathing to calm down.

Finally, Cassie giggled.

"What's so funny?" I asked.

"I really thought the worst thing that could happen tonight was someone calling me ice princess or stuck-up bitch. You punching Evan Swindell was not a possibility in my mind."

I couldn't disagree. "That guy's a douche. I don't like the

way he looks at you."

"Is that why you hit him?"

"That. And he called me a hooker."

She gasped. "He didn't."

"He definitely did."

"I'm really sorry, Liam."

"You are not the one who should be apologizing."

"I know. But I feel like our perfect night is ruined."

I hesitated. The adrenaline had waned and now that it was quiet and dark, I couldn't help but notice how close we were. Suddenly, every inch of my body was aware of hers. This close, with no one else around, I couldn't think of anything else.

Cassie seemed to notice it too. She fell silent, her eyes locked on mine in the darkness. I reached for her, my hands gripping her waist—softly at first and then harder. More insistent. She pressed herself against me, offering silent permission for whatever this was. In an instant, every rational thought left my head, and I pulled Cassie against me and kissed her. Hard.

She moaned against me, immediately responsive, and I pressed harder, aligning our bodies so that my erection pressed into her. I ravaged her mouth, cupping her face and her throat in my hands, and unleashing all the tension inside me on her lips and tongue. It felt hot and harsh and punishing, but I didn't let up. I barely breathed, and when I did, it was with my tongue against hers, until my head swam with the taste and scent of her.

My hands, one of them still tangled in her hair, no longer shook, but I didn't want to stop. I couldn't. Not yet. "I need to feel you," I said, my voice ragged and foreign to my own ears.

Cassie leaned in again, her lips brushing lightly over mine. Her hands tightened around my neck, sending need into every single nerve ending I had. "Do it, Liam. I'm here."

On a thick exhale, I kissed her again. My hands explored, my fingers not gentle as I shoved her dress up her thighs, shimmying it to her waist, and cupped her ass, lifting her so that I could feel her right where I wanted her against me.

With one hand holding her in place against the wall, I used the other to feel my way down to the heat between her legs. The silky fabric between us was already wet, and I groaned at how ridiculously sexy it was to realize she'd been wearing something this hot underneath that dress all night.

"What are you wearing?" I demanded.

"Lingerie. It was going to be a surprise," she answered, breathless.

"You can show me later," I promised.

She murmured an agreement, already reaching for me again, but for some reason, I hesitated. The full reality of what we were doing crashed over me, and I blinked my way back to some semblance of control. I looked over toward the parking lot that was thankfully empty. Anyone could come out at any time. Was I really going to screw Cassie Franklin of all people behind Letty's? In high school that might have been a wet dream come true, but now it felt wrong—for a lot of reasons.

I pulled back. "Cass, I can't—I mean, if you don't want to do this right now, we can go back to—"

"I don't want to go anywhere. Please. Don't stop."

Her whispered words were fervent and her hands latched onto my shirt, urging me closer, a clear sign she wanted this. Still, I hesitated.

"I should tell you that I've never had sex in public or even outside," she admitted, her voice dropping even more, making her sound shy in a way that made my balls ache. "And we both know I've never had an orgasm this way either. Please?"

With that, all of my remaining sense drained away. I shoved

her slick panties aside and slid a finger inside her, swallowing her moan with another kiss. "In that case," I said softly, working my finger in and out of her wetness, "We're definitely doing this."

Her sigh was both relief and ecstasy. At the sound of it, I knew I wasn't stopping, not for anything.

My lips trailed a line of kisses until I reached her ear, letting my breath tickle as I spoke low, "First rule of public sex: you can't get caught. That means no screaming."

"Fuck," she managed and I could feel her walls already tensing. My cock hardened just from knowing I was turning her on this much. God, the orgasms had been more of a game the first time. A challenge. A way to see if I could do what no guy had ever done for her. That and I had to see what her face looked like as she came for me. And it had been so fucking arousing and amazing watching it all. But feeling it. Hearing it. Having only these limited senses to experience her; it was just as good.

As her tight walls tensed around my finger, I slid it nearly free. She whimpered and my lips curved upward as I slowly slid two fingers inside, moving more deliberately now as I felt her orgasm building. She thrust her hips forward to meet me, eager for more, and suddenly I didn't mind the risky location. And I damn sure didn't mind decking Evan Swindell if it landed me here.

"Liam," Cassie said, panting now as I worked two fingers in and out of her, my other hand still holding her up between me and the wall. Faster and faster I went until I felt her getting close. Then I slowed. "Liam, I'm going to come."

Her breath tickled my ear, and I grinned knowing how much control it had taken her to whisper those words rather than yell them. "I know you are, baby. That's exactly what I want from you."

Her breaths were short, her hips rocking back and forth against me in a rhythm that was just begging me to go faster. I kept my movements slow and steady, finding the top of her dress with my mouth and dragging it down with my teeth.

In the darkness, I found her breasts. No bra. Fan-fucking-tastic. My tongue found her already hardened nipple. I did a slow circle that had her bucking against me, and then I pulled the hardened tip into my mouth, sucking until she buried her face in my shoulder and moaned softly, finally coming apart.

Her orgasm shook her entire body, and I slowed my rhythm until, finally, she shuddered once and fell still against me. For a long, quiet moment, we didn't move.

My cock throbbed inside my jeans, and I was fully aware that Cassie's tight walls still pulsed at every small twitch of the fingers I still had buried inside her. But for a moment, I just stood there, enjoying her like this. Enjoying that no one else had ever had her this way. God, she felt good in my arms. Coming or not.

When the door to Letty's opened, Cassie's head came up and we both turned to watch Evan leaving with Bev, an ice pack held to his bottom lip. We were silent as they both got into his car and drove off.

My cock strained against the zipper of my jeans, reminding me only one of us had gotten off. But I had a feeling it might not be the best timing to try to continue. Instead, I started to ease Cassie down to her feet.

She grabbed at me, resisting my efforts. "What are you doing?"

"Putting you down."

"Don't tell me fighting for your honor didn't turn you on as much as it did me." I chuckled, but before I could answer, her hand slid down to cup my cock. She squeezed and then rubbed up and down against it with her palm. Even through the fabric of my jeans, the friction of her touch made my dick twitch. My balls tightened and she purred, "I thought so. Now, don't put me down until you come too."

She didn't have to tell me twice.

I lifted her up and once again arranged our bodies so that my erection pressed into her wet center. She rocked her hips to meet me, and I muffled a groan as her hands came down to fumble with the button of my jeans. I nuzzled against her neck, inhaling the scent of her shampoo and aching to be inside her now.

Her hand slipped inside my pants, wrapping around my length and pulling it free. She ran her hand up and down the length of it in lazy strokes. I sucked in a sharp breath, bracing a hand on the wall behind her.

Straining with the effort it took to control myself, I guided my cock to her entrance and pushed inside her slowly. Both of us shuddered then, clinging to each other in silent need as I set the rhythm.

Around the corner, the door to Letty's opened. Bass and guitar strained flowed out, along with the laughter and chatter of a group of people headed for their cars. I slowed, holding my breath as I strained to hear if they were coming this way. A car door opened and closed. Still, I waited, barely moving against her—just enough to keep her muscles pulled taut and her thighs squeezing my hips.

"Don't stop," Cassie whimpered. Her arms tightened around my hips, urging me onward. I gave her what she wanted, upping the tempo. Once again, I pumped faster and faster as I slid in and out of her, both of us slick and breathless as the pressure built between us.

Somewhere in the lot, a car turned over, the engine humming to life. The headlights flicked on a moment later and the beam nearly found us as the car backed out and then headed through the lot for the street beyond it.

I barely registered when we were alone again, lost in the sensations and in Cassie's nearly silent moans. Her lips pressed against my ear, her arms tight around me, her hips bucking and pulsing in time to my thrusts. Over and over, I slammed into her, driving her against the wall at her back.

"Come for me, Cassie," I encouraged when the moaning fell silent and I knew she was holding her breath in an effort to keep quiet. "Let go."

Her legs twitched and then tensed and then finally relaxed against me.

When I heard her moaning as she came, my mouth crashed over hers, swallowing the sound just as my own orgasm rocked through me, driving me into a frenzy before I was spent and suddenly exhausted.

When it was over, I leaned my forehead against hers, enjoying the feel of our breath mingling together. My knuckles ached, but I ignored it, happy to be here in this moment, with this girl where life felt ridiculously simple and free.

We stood that way for a long moment. Finally, I kissed her and eased her down so I could drive her home.

"Hey, Cass." I grabbed her arm, stopping her before she could climb into the truck.

"What's up?" she asked, turning back to blink up at me.

My fingers brushed over the bandage I'd seen earlier, momentarily distracting me. "What happened here? You never told me."

"Oh." She blinked as if she'd forgotten about it. Slowly, she picked at the edge of the bandage and then peeled it away. "I got a tattoo."

"You got a tattoo? When?"

"Earlier." She shrugged like it was no big deal. I could only stare at her.

"What are you thinking right now?" she asked, cocking her head. "I mean, it's crazy right?"

"Insane," I agreed, smiling at the idea of Cassie Franklin gracing the doorway of a tattoo parlor.

"Good. That's what I was going for. Although, it was a lot less biker bar-ish than I expected. The guy who inked me is a vegan health studies student at the community college."

I chuckled. "Of course, he is. Damn, I am really sorry I missed that conversation." I looked again at the black ink, studying the shape. "A sword?"

"Damn right." She wiggled her brows. "It means I can fight my own battles now."

My laughter was instant and loud as I thought back to what I'd just done in the bar. "Noted," I said pointedly.

She grinned and for a second, I couldn't breathe. I braced a hand on the door of the truck, still hanging open. This time, the dizziness that swept over me had nothing to do with my healing eardrums. "You should do that more often," I said quietly.

"What?"

"Smile."

"And laugh." I'd almost missed her giggle earlier, too distracted by the feel of her. "Your laugh is my new favorite sound."

She lowered her lashes. "Noted."

Something curled in my gut at her innocent happiness. Not lust. Something else. Bigger. More solid. Whatever it was, it made me want to crush her against me or drop to one knee or something. All of it felt slightly crazy, but I couldn't stop myself from blurting my next words. "I want to date you," I said, feeling ridiculous as soon as the words were out.

She raised a brow. "I thought that's what we were doing right now."

"I know that. I mean that I like you." Fucking shit. So smooth. This was what I got for never having a real girlfriend before.

But Cassie's lips quirked like she was more amused than anything else at my awkwardness. "I like you too." She gave that same hint of a smile I'd come to love.

Love?

I blinked, startled at my own thought.

Fuck that.

I liked her. But love? The thought of it was enough to startle me out of whatever post-sex coma I'd just been in.

"Good. Just making sure we're on the same page." I gestured to the open door behind her.

She gave me one last look that made it clear I was being weird and then climbed inside. I shut the door behind her, taking my time rounding the hood and climbing inside. In the cab of the truck, I shoved the key into the ignition and held my breath, positive she was going to grill me the moment my door closed. But she didn't push me on it, and I realized she was probably just as content to let it go as I was.

Fun. Dating. Sex. These were the things I was good at.

Feelings? Sharing them? Love? Not so much.

And neither was she.

I wondered if it was a doomed match anyway. If I should have just let it go. Enjoyed whatever this was. Live in the moment. But as I looked over at Cassie, my gaze catching on the way her blonde hair nearly glowed in the streetlights, casting a halo around her face, I knew it was only a matter of time.

Maybe not tonight, maybe not tomorrow, but one day soon, I wouldn't be able to pretend anymore. This wasn't just about sex. Or fun. Or dating. This was about all those things I wasn't good at—this was about making Cassie Franklin mine. For good. Because if I was being honest, I didn't just want to make her come. I wanted to make her stay.

CHAPTER TWENTY

CASSIE

I stood in the center of Liam's garage, my jaw hanging open. How had I missed all this the first time I'd been here? Oh. Right. Anxiety and rage had blinded me. Still, I couldn't believe I hadn't noticed the beautiful pieces Liam had created. I should have put it together when I saw the brand new rocking chairs on his front porch that day. But seeing it up close now, I realized his creativity and talent went beyond simple furniture making. The precise lines and the careful sloping of the accents he'd routed into the edges in various pieces were amazing. It was art.

In fact, all the beautiful creations filling the space made it hard to argue: Liam Porter had great hands—on a lot of levels.

"What do you think?" Liam's words brought me crashing back to the moment, the memory of our date two nights ago fading. For now. But I was looking forward to a repeat today if possible.

I turned back to him, letting my admiration show in my

expression and words as I gestured to the various handmade items surrounding me. "Liam, all of it is beautiful. The lines are incredible and the quality is just amazing. Where did you learn how to do this?"

He shrugged, but I could see how much he appreciated my words. "My dad's a carpenter. He taught me a bit and the rest I picked up just hanging with him out here as a kid."

"Right. He builds houses. I remember."

Liam eyed me, surprise registering as he cocked his head playfully. "I didn't realize you knew so much about me."

I paused to run my fingers over the smoothed edge of a cedar nightstand. "Obviously, I didn't," I said, gesturing around the workshop at all the furniture. "At least not the real you."

He tugged me back to face him, his expression gentle. Slowly, he reached a hand up and tucked my hair behind my ear. I caught his hand in mine and held it closer, inspecting his knuckles. "The swelling's better today," I said.

Liam grunted, never taking his eyes off me. Clearly, he didn't want to talk about the incident at the bar the other night. The look he gave me sent tingles all the way to my toes, and suddenly, I didn't want to talk about it either. "I didn't know the real you, either. But I'm glad to know you now, Cassie Franklin."

I shivered and stepped back, mostly to regain some semblance of control. Sexy, horny, playful Liam was one thing. I understood that version of him. But sweet, sensitive, deep Liam was a different creature, and I wasn't sure I trusted myself with this side of him. Maybe I'd lied to Jess when I told her I wanted to live dangerously, because letting myself get sucked into Liam's soft gaze felt way too risky.

"Well, I don't know much about woodworking, but your creations are incredible," I told him when I could think straight.

"You're really talented."

"Thanks." He was still watching me, but he didn't call me out on ruining the moment. If anything, he seemed patient. Somehow, that only made me more nervous. "Seriously," I went on, knowing full well I was babbling mostly to fill the silence. "You should do something with all this. You can't just let it sit around in here collecting dust. These pieces deserve homes."

"Yeah, I've been thinking the same thing. I've had a couple of custom orders for friends since I've been back. But the deliveries are getting to be a lot."

I nodded. We hadn't seen each other in three days, mostly because Liam had an order to finish and deliveries to make. "You need a place people can come and see you," I said.

"I have a meeting next week with a property management group about a shop space open in town."

My head came up and I met his gaze, surprised he'd already thought it through. "You're going to open a store? Wow. Liam, that's great!"

"Hold your horses," he said, holding up a hand. "It's just a conversation. I don't know if I'm ready to make it official or anything—"

"You have to do it," I insisted, coming closer again, my excitement taking over. "Your stuff is one of a kind. People here would go nuts over it. If you want me to come with you, I could help negotiate—"

"I'm good, but thanks."

I frowned, backing off again. The sharpness had been unexpected, but it was also a clear message. He didn't want my help. "Sure. Well, if there's anything I can do..."

He grabbed my hand, tugging me closer. "You're already doing it. Besides, I want you to focus on enjoying your time off.

You need it."

I bristled at that, not even sure why since he was right. Still, I didn't like hearing it, like someone pointing out my flaws. "Yeah. Of course."

I hadn't heard anything from Evan since that night at the bar and still no word from my father either. With each passing day, I felt freer. But it was a scary sort of freedom; a void I didn't know yet how to fill except with Liam—and the more I saw of him, the more I wanted this to be something meaningful. And wanting that was far more terrifying than freedom. Something I hadn't yet admitted out loud.

Time for a subject change. I pointed at the headboard with intricate leaf carvings done along the rim. "You did all of that too?"

"My dad had a router lying around that he never used so when I'd come in here to hang with him, he always let me play around with it." Liam shrugged. "I got good at it, I guess."

"You're amazing at it," I corrected, wandering closer to study the lines. "I bet your dad is proud." When he didn't answer, I straightened and turned back to find Liam standing with one hand pressed against the wall, his face pale.

"Are you okay?"

I hurried over, but he took a deep breath and then nodded, his hand dropping away. He smiled tightly. "Fine."

"What's wrong? Are you having a panic attack?"

He chuckled, but it was strained. "Not exactly. That new cochlear implant you gave me takes some getting used to. Sometimes it likes to remind me of the fact."

"What do you mean? Like you can't hear? I thought the implant fixed everything."

"I can hear just fine although some of our louder encounters leave a buzz in the background for a while afterward. My balance isn't a hundred percent just yet, I'm afraid."

"So, you're…"

"Dizzy," he supplied. "Sort of like vertigo."

I frowned, my stomach clenching with worry as I noted how pale he still looked. "Maybe we should get you to a hospital or call your doctor—"

"I'm good," he assured me and his color did look better now, but I watched him warily.

"Okay, but please get it checked out sometime soon, all right?"

"Don't worry. I'm not going to keel over and give your product any bad press."

It was a joke. I knew that. But for some reason, I felt the stab of what he was implying like a direct cut. His smile died away as he took in my expression. "I was just teasing you, Cass."

"I know." I tried to force a smile, but it wouldn't come, and I knew my sensitivity was just that. The old, easily offended, and way too serious Cassie was hard to let go of. I took a deep breath and let it out again. "I wish I'd had the courage to know you in high school."

He blinked. "Really? Why is that?"

"You're so…easy."

The moment the words were out, I could feel the heat rush to my throat and face. Liam smirked, one brow raised.

"That's not what I meant," I rushed to add.

"Uh-huh. It's cool. I know what you really think of me now." He teased, but I shook my head.

"I'm serious. You're just easy to talk to and easy about life. Problems, hard situations, don't affect you like they do other people."

His brow rose even higher. "You do remember the part where I decked a guy for calling me a hooker two nights ago, don't you?"

My lips twitched. "Yes. But that's what I mean. I wouldn't have had the balls to actually punch him."

He cast a look at the ceiling. "Thank God for that. There are enough balls in this relationship already, thank you."

"Very funny. I mean it. You could have taught me a lot about rolling with the punches."

"Oh, now who's the comedian?"

I giggled, and Liam stopped dead in his tracks, staring at me like he'd seen a ghost. "What?" I demanded, looking behind me but the shop was still empty except for us. "Why are you looking at me like that?"

"You just laughed."

I exhaled. "Yeah. So?"

"So that's twice in two days, and I was a little too distracted to fully appreciate it before. I want to enjoy it this time."

"You're so ridiculous. I laugh all the time."

He folded his arms over his chest. "When was the last time you laughed?"

"I... It was... Shit, I don't know, but I must have done it." Liam didn't answer, and finally my shoulders sagged. "Wow. It's true. I am the ice princess."

Liam snorted. "Were," he corrected. "And if anyone doubts it, you just wave your sword at them and they'll back off, I'm sure." He tapped my still healing tattoo.

I pursed my lips. "Maybe next time I can be the one to defend your honor."

Liam hooted. "That is a sight I would pay to see."

"Ugh." I groaned. "No more jokes about taking money from each other."

But that only made him laugh harder. "Deal," he said. He stepped closer, his arm coming around my waist as he pressed a kiss to my cheek. "I'm really glad you offered me that job, though. I'm enjoying the position of boyfriend."

"Is that the official title?" I asked, my throat strangely tight. The idea of Liam being my boyfriend was thrilling—and terrifying.

"It is," he whispered, his breath tickling my ear.

"Good to know. I'll have to alert the masses the position's been filled." My eyes glazed over and my head fell back as his lips kissed a trail from my jaw to my collarbone.

"Actions speak louder. Pretty sure my fist made it clear the other night," he said and I smiled. He continued, his lips making their way lower and lower until I was lost in the feeling of him. Until Liam was right and we no longer needed words anyway.

BY one week into my self-imposed exile, I was bored out of my damned mind. Liam had sequestered himself in his shop in order to finish a dresser he'd promised to a friend on deadline and Jess was away for work until the end of the weekend. I'd finished repainting nearly every room in my house and my fingers were stained with the evidence. My toes were freshly manicured, my whiskey and wine were both gone, and thanks to the rain that hadn't let up in two days, my entire stack of "I'll read it when I get time" books were actually finished.

On top of that, all I could think about were the projects I'd left open and undone at work. I needed to do something constructive. So, wearing my best suit and don't-fuck-with-me heels, I put on enough lipstick to do battle with my father and drove myself to the office.

It rained steadily the entire way. By the time I'd parked and made my way upstairs, my hair dripped at the ends, leaving wet marks all over the lapel of my suit jacket. I shrugged it off just outside my father's door, nodded at his receptionist who whispered back that I could enter, and shoved the door wide as I waltzed inside.

"Cassandra." Dad stood abruptly, his paperwork forgotten as he tore off his reading glasses and stared at me across the room.

His office was large and the furniture was oversized to match. It used to make me feel small. Maybe even insignificant. Today, though, I ignored it all, including his utter surprise at the sight of me. Drowned rat wasn't my best look. Whatever.

"Hi, Dad," I said, sitting in one of the leather chairs across from him without waiting for an invitation. I crossed my legs and folded my hands in my lap. I was in charge here, I reminded myself. In control. I just had to act like it.

"What are you doing here? And why are you dripping wet?" Dad's frown wasn't encouraging, so I ignored that too.

"I've decided to end my vacation early." I pointed to the window behind him. "And it's raining outside."

He barely glanced at the window, the blinds obscuring the view outside, as usual, before he looked back at me. "I see." He sat slowly, tossing his glasses onto the pile of folders.

I raised my chin, refusing to be bowed by his condescending tone. It was meant to make me question myself. It was a trick that used to work. "I wanted to check in with you before heading to my office," I went on. "To let you know that I'm more than happy to rejoin the negotiation with Nichimoto."

"I don't see how that's possible now," he began.

"Especially after that stunt at the bar the other night."

Damn. Evan was such a fucking tattletale. But it didn't have to change anything for me. I plowed through, ignoring his words. "I would think it's more than possible," I said. "It's ideal." His brows crinkled, and he shook his head, clearly ready to argue that point, but I shoved onward. "I don't like your terms for me in this, but the reality is that I wouldn't have to lie about my relationship status since I'm seeing someone now. And while I don't agree with the sexist mentality, I can't deny Liam's local celebrity status and his military career would go a long way in impressing someone like—"

"Cassie, stop," my father interrupted and something about his tone silenced me. A pit formed in my stomach as I took in the drooping expression he wore. Beaten—that's what he looked like. And my father never looked beaten.

"What's wrong?"

He sighed. "You can't help with the deal."

His hesitation only made me more nervous. "If this is about our fight last week, I'm sorry," I said, hating the feeling of the words on my lips. But if that's what it took—

"It's not about the fight."

"Then what—?"

The door opened behind me, and I twisted in my chair as Evan walked in. The pit in my stomach turned to a boulder. Bile rose in my throat at the sight of his placating expression. Even the sight of his still fading bruise that covered the entire center of his face didn't quite console me. Not with his eyes so coldly calculating.

He didn't apologize for the intrusion, either. Instead, he strolled right in and stood behind the empty chair next to me. "Cassie, what a surprise."

He didn't sound nearly as pleased to see me as I'd expected, which was fine by me. The feeling was mutual. I glared up at him so he knew it. "Evan. What the hell are you doing barging in here? This is a private meeting."

"Cassandra," my father admonished. "Don't be rude."

"Sir, it's fine. I'm sure this transition can't be easy for her."

"What transition?" I blinked at that and turned slowly back to my father, glaring as something unspoken passed between them. "What's going on?" My heart thudded and my breathing turned shallow. If this was some ambush about Evan and I being a couple again, I was going to start throwing things for sure.

Evan's gaze flicked to my father. "You haven't told her yet?"

"She just got here."

"Tell me what?" I demanded, my voice rising.

"Cass, when you quit, you left your father in quite the bind," Evan began.

"I didn't quit. I took a vacation," I said.

"Of course. But your absence came at a very sensitive time. Without the Nichimoto deal, the company was in a precarious financial position."

I spoke through gritted teeth, pushing to my feet so I could properly glare at Evan. "I know what kind of position *my* company is in."

Evan didn't miss a beat. "Well then you'll understand why we had to act quickly. We didn't have time to wait for your tantrum—"

"I didn't quit and I wasn't having a tantrum. Dad, please tell me what the hell is going on." I rubbed my temples, but I didn't miss my father's wince before he finally answered me.

"The fact of the matter is that Nichimoto left the table and there was no bringing him back. Not after your behavior," Dad said. I bit my lip to keep from spewing every curse word I could think of. I couldn't believe they were still acting like this was my fault when my father was the one trying to sell me down the river. First to an investor's backwoods sense of sexism and then to Evan as some sort of dowry bride.

My stomach churned as he went on. "Evan's offer wasn't one I could refuse considering the extenuating circumstances."

"Wait. What offer? What are you saying?" I forced my fury aside and concentrated on reading between the lines.

I took in Evan's suit, sans jacket, and the stack of files he carried tucked in one hand. Not to mention how he'd known to show up as soon as I'd walked in. And wasn't his office two floors down? So how had that happened?

My dad was still talking in circles trying to cushion the blow. "He's paying more than a fair price for his shares. Much more than we would have gotten from Nichimoto or anywhere else for that matter."

I whirled on Evan. "You're buying a share of the company?" I asked, knowing damn well there wouldn't be this much excitement over one measly share.

"Not just one," Evan said, looking way too smug.

"How many?" I demanded, my voice weirdly shrill. Even for me.

"Fifty-two percent," Evan said with pride—as if he fully expected me to high-five him for his accomplishment.

"Well, I object," I said, and Evan's expression instantly darkened.

"Unfortunately for you, it's a little late for that."

"It is not late. I serve on the board, and that gives me—"

Evan cut me off, clearly reciting from the company handbook as he sang, "If a board member takes an unauthorized absence of any kind, they wave their right to a vote or voice including but not limited to share purchases or sales, mergers, updating bylaws, or invoking—"

"I'm here, asshole," I hissed, unable to listen to any more of this. "My vacation is over. And the first thing I'm going to do is stop this insanity."

But Evan answered smoothly, "I think you misunderstood. The deal was finalized yesterday."

"Holy fucking shit." My knees buckled, and I slid back into the chair that was still wet from earlier.

"Cassandra, language," Dad said again, but it lacked any real bite. It sounded more like a plea than anything. He was begging me to go quietly.

"What does this mean?" I asked dully, my entire energy focused on my father now—and on not trying to claw Evan's eyes out.

My father's expression tightened. "In light of the new ownership, there are changes being made to personnel including some executive positions."

My palms went clammy. "What changes?"

"Your position is obsolete, Cassie," Evan put in.

At his words, everything stopped. My brain, my ability to move, maybe even my heart. I turned slowly to look at Evan, fully expecting fake sympathy or maybe even outright enjoyment, but he seemed to stare right through me now. And I knew: this was what he'd been after the entire time. Not me. Not our relationship. My father's company. I was just a status symbol for him. A way to get what he really wanted. And now that he had it he no longer needed me.

"But my projects," I heard myself saying.

"Were nearly all philanthropic," Dad said. "And that's a luxury we don't have while we restructure."

"Restructure," I repeated.

"I assumed you'd be happy about this," Evan said. "It'll give you more time to focus on your personal life. After that article, I can only imagine how strained things must be for you."

"That article. You were the one who leaked the information?" I couldn't believe it—mostly because of the negative light it shone on the company. But Evan was far less concerned with this place than I ever thought.

Still, with my father standing there, he painted on an innocent look and said, "I don't know what you're talking about."

"You little—" I began but he cut me off.

"If you want a position once we've re-stabilized," Evan said, "I'm sure we could find something for you. I'd be willing to negotiate your hiring package myself to include the full scope of our benefits and retirement plans."

I didn't bother to look at him. Instead, I stared at my father. He didn't meet my eyes, but he also didn't contradict Evan's words. And he clearly still clung to his denial over what a creep Evan really was. My own father had just sold me out. To the only guy in the world who had less integrity than he did.

I couldn't believe it, but then I also sort of could believe it.

My entire life had been a series of obeying my father's commands and trying to live up to his expectations, always just barely clinging to his approval by a thread. In the back of my mind whispered a voice, a remembered echo of something I'd heard my father say once: but I'd wanted a son.

I'd ignored it. Tried harder. Buried the pain when nothing I did mattered. Turned cold. And this was where it had gotten me. Thrown out like a minimum wage nobody. Clearly, my father wanted me to go quietly. Evan, on the other hand, wanted me to beg. I could feel it radiating from them both.

But I was going to do neither.

I took a deep breath and stood, making sure to use every ounce of ice I could muster as I looked at my father. "You're going to regret what you're doing to me," I said quietly.

Dad had the decency not to argue.

"Both of you," I added, casting a cold glance at Evan.

He was unmoved, but I wasn't going to stick around and wait for him to agree. I had a life to live. A new Cassie to meet. Tattoos were just the beginning.

"Where are you going?" Dad called as I marched out.

"I don't know," I called back without turning. "But wherever it is, it'll be my choice." I paused, one hand on the knob and turned back. "Also, I quit."

CHAPTER TWENTY-ONE

LIAM

I felt like an idiot with my feet dangling where I sat perched on the high table in the exam room. The doc was a decent guy, laid back and not nearly as impressed with "Liam Porter, war hero" as everyone else. Thank God for that. He read my chart and then listened to my heart and lungs. When he was satisfied there, he walked me through a series of balancing exercises and ended by looking into my ears. His frown deepened the longer he looked. That probably wasn't good, but I waited quietly while he finished his exam. When he was done, he wrapped the stethoscope around his neck and stepped back, leaning on the counter across from me.

"Well?" I asked. "What's the damage, doc?"

"According to your file, it's not nearly as bad as it could have been. You obviously took care of yourself and took your recovery seriously. A lot of guys don't."

"A lot of guys didn't have enough fluid in their ear canal to drown a cat."

"Good point." He sighed, clearly still too distracted by what he'd found to show amusement at my joke.

"But," I prompted.

"But the ears aren't as healed as I'd like," he admitted.

"More fluid?" I guessed.

He nodded. "It's affecting your balance on both sides. Although, the left is worse."

"But that's the cochlear implant."

"Which is why I'm concerned. Look, I know you've already come a long way but the first few months after a procedure like this are critical. You're still well within that window which means taking extra caution and remaining watchful."

"I'm committed to healing," I assured him. "What can I do?"

"I'm glad to hear that." He handed me a script. "Use these drops twice a day to dry up that fluid."

"Will do. And if the fluid doesn't resolve on its own?"

"We'll have to go in and drain it, which, for a new implant, can be a little traumatic. If it comes to that, I'll want to consult with the donor company and its representatives on the tech—"

"It won't come to that," I assured him.

Fucking A, the last thing I wanted to do was have to ask Franklin Industries for more help. Especially after the way Cassie's father had treated her and what I knew about him now. Not to mention Evan.

"All right then. Use those drops and check back in with me in a week."

I shook the doc's hand, promising him I would do everything he said. On the way out, I checked my phone. It lit up and buzzed with several new texts.

One from Jamie: *Bro, Katelynn Hooper says she wants your "wood." Hehe.*

Something about a custom banister. Call me.

And one from Cassie: *At Summerville Country Club. Would love to see you in a bathing suit. Or your birthday suit. Also—I think I drank myself under the table. It's a celebration, bitches!!*

I shot Jamie a quick response, promising to call him later—and ignoring his crude innuendo. I reread Cassie's text and hesitated. Part of me wanted to ignore it because Summerville Country Club seemed like a prime location for my ridiculous celebrity status to be exploited, and I couldn't afford to punch anyone else right now. My knuckles needed to be in full working order if I was going to make a banister.

But Cassie sounded pretty buzzed, and I couldn't bear the idea of leaving her to drive herself home. Besides, I hadn't seen her in a couple of days now thanks to all the furniture orders I'd had. Word spread fast in a town like this one, and I had a feeling those words came specifically from Jamie bragging about me to all his lady friends. Still, I'd take it where I could get it. The idea of a shop was seriously growing on me.

In the end, my manners won out and I started up the truck, heading for the club despite my reservations.

***

I'D barely made it through the club's lobby before three different women had stopped me and fawned over "the war hero back home again." I'd even been cornered by one gentleman whose hair looked slick enough to drift tires on. He'd tried convincing me to shoot a television commercial for his car dealership, complete with me in military uniform and waving a giant American flag for the camera. It had taken everything in me not to tell him to "fuck off" and instead politely assure him I'd think it over.

By the time I found the pool area, and Cassie lying in a

lounge chair at the far end, I was ready to get the hell out of here.

Cassie, however, was not.

She sat up when she saw me, setting her nearly empty drink aside hard enough to send the little umbrella tumbling out onto the concrete deck. The loss went unnoticed by Cassie.

"Liam!" she called loud enough to turn heads.

I grimaced and hurried to close the distance. "Hey. What's the occasion?"

She patted the deck chair beside her. "Celebrating life," she said except that it sounded like "celubratin luff."

"I see."

She studied me with glassy eyes. "You don't look like a celebration."

"I think your definition of celebrating and mine are a little different."

Her bottom lip poked out, and she offered me what was left of her drink. "You should catch up to me."

"Nah. I'm good. Can I drive you home?"

"Later," she said, waving her hand. Her eyes lit up as a server walked by. "Miss," she called, which sounded like "mish." "Can I get another drink?"

The server eyed Cassie and then glanced at me. I shook my head once. A subtle no. "Surrre," she said, walking off. I watched as she went straight to the juice dispenser and poured a glass of that instead.

"I usually hate this place," Cassie said, leaning back against her chair.

"Why did you come here then?" I asked, because honestly, I didn't disagree with her. Everywhere I looked, golfers and trophy wives were strutting around each other like preening peacocks. Across the pool, a group of women sat locked in conversation, their dark glasses making it impossible to know what they were so hushed about—until one of them pointed at me. I looked away, pretending I hadn't noticed, but my knee bounced in impatience, my keys clutched tight in my hand.

"Because," Cassie answered, "I don't think I'll be back after this, and I wanted one last day to feel like I was somebody."

That got my attention. I waited until the server had delivered Cassie's juice, complete with a little umbrella and a slice of pineapple. She sipped and seemed oblivious to the lack of alcohol. "Cass, you are somebody."

She shook her head. "Maybe, but I'm not a Franklin."

"Of course, you are."

"No. My daddy made Evan a Franklin instead. He gets everything, and I don't even have a job anymore."

I stared at her, trying to make sense of the words. She was drunk and definitely slurring, but she didn't seem confused. "You really lost your job?"

She shrugged. "I quit. Screw them. I'm not going to let Evan win. And I'm damn sure not going to let him be my boss. I'll figure something out." Her eyes lit up. "Maybe I'll paint."

"You paint?"

"I painted my bedroom. And all the other rooms. Maybe I can paint rooms on canvases," she said—except it came out canvushez.

"Sure," I said. "I bet you'd be great."

"Oh. I have a better idea." She leaned forward, grabbing my shirt and nearly missing before she caught a handful of it in her fist. She yanked me closer, so we were eye to eye. Now, I could really feel everyone's eyes on us.

"Cass," I began, grabbing her wrist and drawing her away.

"Maybe we could paint each other," she whispered.

Or tried to whisper. It came out louder than anything else

193

she'd said. Some of the conversations around us died.

"Cass, let me take you home," I said and she nodded, clearly taking that for my agreement to her brilliant idea. Not that it was horrible, but considering how drunk she was, it wasn't happening today.

She let me help her up, and I dropped a few bills onto the table beside her chair. "You don't have to do that. I have a tab," she said.

"Well then it can be a tip," I said, nodding to the server watching us from across the deck. She looked relieved to see us leaving.

"This is going to be so much fun," Cassie said.

"Huh?" It took me a minute to realize she was still talking about body paints. "Oh, right. Yep. Fun."

She stopped walking and turned to glare at me suspiciously. "You don't sound very into it."

"I think the painting idea would work better another time," I said carefully.

"Whoa." Her eyes widened. "What is even happening right now? Is Liam Porter turning down sex?"

I frowned, very aware of how many people could hear us right now. "I think we should talk in the truck," I said quietly.

"I don't want to talk," she pouted. "And I can't believe you do either."

My shoulders stiffened at that. "What's that supposed to mean?"

She rolled her eyes as if the answer were obvious. "Please. You know what I mean."

"Tell me anyway."

She scoffed. "You don't *talk*, Liam. Everyone knows that. Your talents lie in other areas." She winked—or tried to—but it looked like an awkward blink.

I had to work hard to remind myself she was just drunk. But it was really starting to grate on me, the assumptions she kept making. "Let's just go," I said finally, suddenly exhausted in ways I couldn't even describe right now.

Cassie yawned abruptly. "Okay," she agreed easily, oblivious to the tension between us. Or to the stares we'd drawn during our exchange.

I grabbed her elbow, and we started walking again.

No one stopped us on our way back through the lobby, and I suspected Cassie's drunken chatter kept them away. At least it had one perk. Because while I did enjoy getting to know her and watching her come out of her duty-imposed shell, I was not a fan of drunken Cassie.

In fact, the more I saw of her, the more I couldn't deny that while Cassie had clearly changed in the last few weeks, so had I. One night stands and casual sex no longer sounded as good as it once had. Neither did day drinking for that matter.

Now, I wanted a real life and a real partner to share it with. And when I imagined who that partner might be, I couldn't deny the fact that it was Cassie's face I saw when I closed my eyes, albeit a much more sober version of that face. But it seemed like the more serious I got—about us or just life in general—the farther away she drifted. Like we were on opposite· courses, intersecting every now and then, and veering off and away when the exchange was over.

I wondered if maybe we were just too different. Or if it was bad timing. Or if maybe karma was playing a cruel joke on me. I'd nearly died to realize exactly how I wanted to live. And now that I knew, it seemed the universe was determined not to let me have it.

It was still strange, all these changes in how I saw my life, my future. That bomb hadn't been my first encounter with

195

danger. I'd spent four years diffusing and detonating bombs. I'd dove in shark-infested waters. I'd jumped out of helicopters when I hadn't been sure what was below me. But even after all of it that explosion had done something to me. Gotten my attention. Made me think. If defying death over and over again these last four years had taught me anything, it was this: you could only avoid fate for so long before she got your ass in the end. And fate, apparently, had a twisted sense of humor.

CHAPTER TWENTY-TWO

CASSIE

THE sunlight threatened to burn holes in my retinas. My head pounded in what was quite possibly the worst hangover anyone had ever had in the history of hangovers. And to top it off, I couldn't find my phone. I made a mental note: "New Cassie" was still a lightweight when it came to mixed drinks.

After a shower, an attempt to eat toast, and a thorough search of my house, I still hadn't overcome any of the issues plaguing me. The sunlight, even through the closed blinds, hurt like hell—but not as bad as my head.

And I still couldn't find my phone.

I sighed, hesitating at the bottom of the stairs as I thought back to when I'd last seen it. I remembered drinking by the pool at the club yesterday and using my phone to text Jess who had been stuck at her job—a thing I no longer had. And then texting Liam an invitation to come join me.

"Ugh." I groaned as I remembered how drunk I'd been when Liam had shown up. God, I must have been a hot mess.

I barely remembered a word I'd said to him and the last

thing I remembered before I'd passed out was him tucking me into my bed. Despite how sweet that sounded, I knew instinctively that it wasn't. When he'd walked out, he hadn't seemed happy, and he hadn't made a single move to sleep with me. Not even after I'd stripped down in front of him while nearly tripping on my swimsuit bottoms. Not my finest hour.

Hell, maybe he'd seen enough and run for the hills.

I couldn't blame him after that.

But the idea of Liam moving on bothered me. A lot more than I wanted it to. I told myself that was ridiculous. No matter what happened between us from here on, hadn't it been the best sex of my life?

I should be grateful for it.

So why did I feel so empty at the thought that it might be over soon—if not already?

Dragging my feet and nursing a sadness I didn't understand, I climbed the stairs slowly and crawled back into bed. I didn't have a job. Or my phone. What I had was a dark room and a blinding hangover. So I did the only thing I could with both of those: I slept.

THE music was loud but thankfully my head was no longer pounding. Instead, I held my bottled water and sipped slowly as I bobbed my head to the beat of the band onstage. A two-day recovery from my poolside debacle wasn't nearly enough to make me want to drink again so soon. Or be here for that matter. But I needed to get out and stop feeling sorry for myself. At least that's what Jess had told me when she'd shown up on my doorstep earlier. I wasn't yet convinced, but I had agreed to put in a solid hour before giving up and going home to sulk.

Across the dance floor, Jess was locked in what looked like a serious conversation with the band's manager. I might have been fooled into thinking she was flirting if the guy hadn't been someone I remembered from high school. And the fact that I'd never, ever seen Jess date anyone I knew. She pursed her lips and said something that earned a loud laugh from the guy, and I wondered if maybe I wasn't the only trying new things these days.

Someone tapped me on the shoulder, and I whirled, already dreading whatever conversation I'd be trapped into with whatever acquaintance had spotted me here. "Oh." I blinked. "Liam. What are you—?"

I stopped short at the sight of a girl beside him, but I relaxed instantly when I recognized Sophie, his little sister. The jealousy that had reared up dissolved again, and I pretended it hadn't been irrationally possessive for the split second I'd recognized it.

He hadn't called me since the pool incident. I knew that because I'd had to pick up my phone from the club's front desk the following day. And as the events of the day had already started to trickle back that was a walk of shame I didn't care to repeat. Not with the club and not with Liam though I definitely owed him an apology at the least. Part of me was ashamed of my behavior, but the other part was trying to accept that maybe it was all doomed from the start anyway.

"Hey, Sophie," I said, forcing my voice light as I ignored Liam. One look. One look at him was all it would take for me to lose whatever small sense of dignity I'd mustered to come out here tonight.

"Hey," she said. "How are you?"

Her expression looked genuinely concerned, and for a split

second I panicked, assuming Liam had told her the gory details about my day drinking episode. But then I remembered the last time I'd seen her, I'd been in the throes of a panic attack. Still not a moment I wanted to relive. "Good," I said too brightly. "Just enjoying the music."

Just enjoying the music?

God, I was lame.

"You?" I added.

"Same." She was nodding to the same beat I'd been bobbing to earlier. "School kicked my ass this week. I need a break," she added.

"I didn't know you were in school."

Liam was still standing there, still not saying a word, and I was still pretending to ignore him. Sophie, at least, wasn't awkward about it as she nodded. "I just started this semester. Pre-law at Charleston University."

"Oh my God, that's incredible." Now, my enthusiasm was genuine.

Sophie blushed. "Thanks. I was accepted last year but couldn't swing the tuition. Liam gifted me his GI Bill so between that and the grants he helped me find, it's covered."

"Wow." Finally, I looked over at Liam, surprised and touched. "That's really thoughtful of you."

His dark eyes met mine and there was no possible way I could ignore him any longer. A thousand unspoken things passed between us and none of them had anything to do with the current conversation.

Sophie looked back and forth between us, finally catching on to the tension she'd missed before. "Yeah, I keep telling him he's my new favorite brother," she joked. Neither of us answered and she added, "Obviously he's my only brother."

She cleared her throat.

"O" FACE

Finally, Liam shrugged, his hands stuffed into his pockets. He was still staring at me and when he spoke, I wondered if he'd even heard Sophie's words at all. "It was no big deal. Anyone else would have done the same."

When his words finally registered, I shook my head slowly. "No. Not anyone," I said, thinking of my father and the nights I'd dragged myself to school so I could be what he needed during the day.

Sympathy flashed in his eyes, and I knew he'd guessed what I was thinking.

"Well," Sophie said, cutting into the silence. "I'm going to get a drink. You two crazy kids have fun."

Liam's gaze was still locked on mine as she moved away through the sea of people. "You want to get out of here?"

I exhaled. "I thought you'd never ask."

He took my hand, leading me through the crowd and out the door into the twilight. The air was chillier than it had been an hour ago, and I breathed it in, appreciating the smell of autumn in Summerville. All the while, I braced myself for whatever Liam said next. But he didn't say a word as he led me to the picnic tables set up next to the taco truck parked at the curb.

We sat together on the bench seat, the silence dragging on, and I realized it would have to be me. He wasn't going to bring it up.

I sighed. "Liam, I'm really sorry about the other day."

When he didn't answer, I pushed on. "I'd had the worst day, and I wanted to blow off some steam. Do something I normally wouldn't. I shouldn't have been such a mess when you came to get me. I shouldn't have asked you to come in the first place. It won't happen again."

His hand slid free of mine, his expression tightening. I

201

looked at him, alarmed. Had I said something wrong? "That's what you're sorry for? Calling me to come get you?"

"Well. Yeah. I was a mess and it was probably really embarrassing for you. And I heard Leon Foster asked you to be in his car commercials." I made a face. "I know how much you hate the publicity stuff. Not to mention the fact that Leon's a piece of work."

"Cassie, I'm glad you called me."

"You are?"

"Always. Being the one you called was actually my favorite part of that entire day."

"Oh. Well then, I guess we're good?" I asked, although that didn't explain why he hadn't called me in two days.

His brows slanted as he studied me. "Do you remember anything you said to me the other day?"

"Of course." I sagged. "Well. Most of it."

He exhaled and ran a hand through his hair. It was longer now than when we'd met. Shaggier. And he'd grown his beard out too. I wanted to tell him I loved it and that he was ridiculously sexy with all that hair, but I knew better right now. When he looked that serious, distracting him wasn't going to work.

"Look, I get that you're trying to figure things out right now," he said in a tight voice. "But just because you wouldn't normally have done something before you decided to change doesn't automatically make it a good idea now. I mean, you didn't commit murder before, but I'm pretty sure that won't turn out well for you now, either."

I sat back, shocked and defensive. Whatever I'd been expecting from him, this wasn't it. "I know that. I never said—"

"You keep going out of your way to remind yourself that you're this new version of Cassie Franklin, but it all looks kind of the same to me."

A rush of heat ran through me as my temper flared. "What's that supposed to mean?"

He shook his head, backing off. "Nothing. Forget it."

But I couldn't. Not now. "Look, you don't know what it's like to be labeled as one thing for your whole life. To lose your identity in the labels they give you."

His lip curled into a humorless smile. "You're kidding right? War hero? Player? Ladies' man? Ring any bells?"

"Oh." I winced. "Right."

He grabbed my legs pulling me in close so that we were nearly nose to nose. My temper warred with the desire to let him touch me. "Cassie, if there's anyone in the world who understands what you're going through right now, it's me. And all I'm asking is that you give me the same room to be different that you're giving yourself."

"What do you—?"

"The other day when I came to pick you up, you brought up my past. Accused me of being with you for just sex."

"Oh." The conversation came back to me in bits and pieces. Guilt weighed on me until my shoulders hunched with it. "I'm sorry."

"I like you," he said. "For me, this is about more than just sex."

"I know that. I was just scared," I said, but even as I said it, I realized my skepticism had been the exact thing that made me a hypocrite all along. And now his point made sense. "God, okay. I'm an asshole."

His lips twitched. "See? Same old Cassie Franklin."

I punched him in the arm and he laughed. The tension, and what was left of my temper, faded. In its wake, the fear still lingered, gnawing at me and making it hard to push past the blocks that were still between us. "Liam, I've never had a boyfriend. Not someone I really care about. Truth is, you terrify me," I admitted.

"That makes two of us. But I'm pushing past the fear because I think this is worth it. I wasn't completely honest with you about what happened to me."

"What do you mean?"

"When that bomb went off… and then the aftermath… I downplay it. I know that. But the truth is that it's all I think about. Well, besides you. I mean, waking up from that, surviving it and realizing how lucky I'd been, it made me question everything. Re-evaluate everything I thought was important."

"I can understand that," I said.

"I know you can. I think it's one of the things that drew me to you in the first place. The thing is, those evaluations about my life changed what was important to me."

"And what's important to you?" I asked, heart pounding because I already knew what he was going to say.

"You."

It sounded so simple, and yet the fear only grew at his easy answer.

I stared into his eyes, noting the sincerity in his expression. But that wasn't what held me rooted. It was the clarity. It was how much I could see he meant his words. I mattered to him. And he mattered to me. And that meant I had a lot to lose here.

The pit in my stomach, usually tight with lust or attraction, felt heavier now, and I realized it wasn't straight-up lust anymore. This was feeling. Dangerous, lovely, terrifying feeling. And I wondered if maybe my promise to keep an open mind wasn't also a promise that involved risking my heart. Or maybe it was already too late for that anyway.

Liam's expression shifted, and I knew he'd seen my fear.

He cleared his throat, but instead of calling it out and demanding I let go, he asked, "Hungry?"

I blinked up at him, distracted. "What?"

"Tacos," he said simply, pointing at the truck. "I think this conversation deserves food before we go any farther."

"Starved," I answered, following him over.

Two tacos and a bottle of water later, both of us finally relaxed. Whatever tension had been between us was gone for the moment. The fear that had nearly paralyzed me earlier had dialed back—and Liam was laughing at me. "How is it possible that you've never eaten from a food truck?" he asked.

"Uh probably because it has the words 'food' and 'truck' in the same sentence," I told him.

His brows rose in challenge. "Prejudging is never okay. Besides, I believe it's fair to say that you stand corrected."

"True. I've obviously been missing out."

His eyes twinkled. "You just needed me to show you."

My stomach flipped as I thought about all the other things I'd needed him to show me. Liam's lips curved, and I knew he was thinking the same thing. I held my breath, hoping he was about to offer an invitation for another round of "showing me things," but he surprised me and said instead, "I looked at a shop space yesterday."

I set my napkin aside and leaned in. "You did? That's amazing! Are you going to rent it?"

"We'll see. But I've gotten a lot of inquiries about stock, and I definitely don't want to start handing out my home address. I think it could be cool."

"It could be more than cool." I cocked my head. "You're putting Sophie through school. You bought your parents' house so they could retire to Florida. You're opening a business. If I didn't know any better, I'd say there's a new Liam Porter in town."

"I told you, you're not the only one who's trying new things."

My shoulders fell a little as I realized the difference between us: when Liam tried something new, it worked. When I tried something new, it failed miserably. And what did that say about our chances together?

"Cassie?" Liam prompted.

I blinked, realizing I'd been quiet too long. "Yeah." I shook it off, but even so, the fear was back, and this time, it wasn't budging. I played it off. "The new Cassie still can't hold her liquor. That was the worst hangover ever."

"Nah. I'm pretty sure day drinking is a prerequisite for the upper-class unemployed." When I didn't answer, he reached out and covered my hand with his. "Sorry. I didn't mean—"

"No, it's fine. I don't regret quitting. I didn't really want go back there anyway. But I can't believe my dad actually cut me out of the company."

"Did he really hire Evan instead?" he asked quietly.

My eyes burned with hot tears, and I blinked at them before they could fall. "He didn't have a choice. Evan owns more than half the company now. Evan can hire himself."

"That's shitty, Cass. I'm really sorry."

"Yeah me too. But honestly, I didn't love the job." I snorted. "And don't get me started on the industry. I only went back there because I didn't know what else to do with myself."

"You'll figure it out," he assured me. "Be patient with yourself."

"I know. It's just…"

"Your dad?" he guessed.

I nodded.

Liam played absently with the bracelet on my wrist, his other hand still firmly wrapped around mine. "He'll come around. In the meantime, he doesn't dictate your life anymore. That has to be worth something.

"It's literally everything," I admitted, and my chest tightened with the truth of my words. "In fact, without it—without his influence, his demands—I'm kind of lost."

Except for when I'm with you, I wanted to tell him. But the pit in my stomach held me back. I'd already spilled my guts to him more than anyone else in my life, including Jess. And I'd never, ever been so vulnerable with another person before. I should have been happy Liam and I weren't over after my stupid comments the other day. But all I could think was that I wasn't sure how much more soul baring I could take right now.

He opened his mouth to respond, but another voice cut him off. "Hey, bitches. What am I interrupting?"

Jess sat on the bench across from us, shaking the entire picnic table as she thumped down. "Privacy, for one thing," Liam said and Jess grinned.

Deep down, relief washed over me that our moment was ruined. I needed to breathe—and to calm the raging butterflies in my stomach that were all urging me to hand Liam the master keys to my soul and just let him have free reign of the place.

"Mission accomplished then." She set an open beer in front of her and went to work unwrapping a taco. Liam and I watched her in silence. When she'd taken a bite, she spoke, mouth full of food. "So, are you guys, like, a thing now or what?"

"We're—" Liam began, a deep frown marring his features.

Panic speared through me at what he was about to say. If he said yes, well, I didn't want to deal with Jess's response to that. I could only imagine the dramatics and the attention and the scrutiny that would bring.

I wasn't ready.

Fear and panic sent words tumbling from my lips before I could stop them. "We're just hanging out," I assured her before Liam could answer and felt his heated stare the moment his gaze swung toward me. I kept my eyes trained on Jess.

But Jess was staring Liam down, ignoring me. "Is that true? You guys are just friends?" she pressed.

"Friends with benefits," I joked, but neither of them smiled, and I felt instantly bad for it.

Liam's hand tightened around mine and then slipped away. "Just friends," he repeated, his voice hard enough to make it clear the subject was closed.

"All right, all right," Jess said around another bite. "Inquiring minds wanted to know."

"Well, now you know," I said, my voice full of forced cheer.

Inside, my stomach churned and my palms went clammy but cold. Liam had agreed with her—with me—so why had he pulled his hand away? In fact, he wasn't even paying attention to me anymore. Too busy texting someone on his phone.

My heart sank as he put it away and stood up, gathering our trash. "Listen, I've gotta run, but I'll call you," he said, barely looking at me.

I nodded, numb. "Sure."

All I could think about was how I'd just promised him I'd keep an open mind, and then I'd gone right back to my old fears of being hurt, dismissing what we had the moment Jess had asked. Of course, he was leaving. Of course, he'd pulled away. He'd asked one thing of me, and then I'd sabotaged it with no real idea why. The fear that had been tugging at me since we'd sat down was back full force, curling tightly in my stomach. I watched him walk away, feeling like I'd just lost something important; something I'd never really had to begin with.

CHAPTER TWENTY-THREE

LIAM

AFTER that bullshit interrogation from Jess, the truth was clear: Cassie wanted a fling. Why else would she have been so warm and open with me, sharing personal things and letting me kiss her and touch her—and then deny us in front of her only friend? I told myself over and over I of all people understood that. She'd lived underneath the iron rule of her father and his expectations for years. Now that she was free of it, of course she wanted to cut loose, to avoid being tied down. It was fair. Reasonable, even. It was just sucky timing that I wanted something else. But listening to her tell Jess we were nothing more than friends with benefits had been more than I could handle. I had to get out of there.

When I'd finally called Jamie and told him about it the next morning, he'd been uncharacteristically silent. No weird advice about alligators and stripes this time. No teasing. Not a single innuendo. And I had no idea what to do next, so I'd gone radio silent with Cassie. Again. Instead of facing it—facing her—I'd thrown myself into work. But Jamie had started texting me every hour on the hour to check in which only made my irritation worse.

"What?" I demanded when he called instead of texting two days later.

"Dude. Chill the eff out. I'm just saying hi."

"Hi."

"What are you doing right now?"

"Working."

"What do you want to be doing right now?"

Cassie. "Working."

"Bullshit. You want to come to this art showing with your girl."

I paused long enough to make Jamie nervous.

"Are you still there?"

"What the fuck are you doing at an art show?"

"Lizzie Jeffries has a cousin who just opened at that fancy place downtown. She has some sculptures that look like vacuum cleaners or whatever but it's pretty cool."

"Ahh. Impressing a girl. Now it all makes sense."

"Shut up and come down here. You'd like some of her stuff. There's a fancy bench that she—"

"Jam, I hear you and I appreciate what you're trying to do, but I'm not falling for it."

"Fuck you. There's nothing to fall for. You like Cassie. Cassie likes art. It's not complicated."

I sighed. "Except that it *is* complicated."

"Listen, I don't know how we got to this place where the player is telling the player how to make a chick fall in love with him, but you're really being thick about this. Just tell. Her. How. You. Feel."

"I will," I promised.

"Yeah?" His excitement was overdone.

211

"Yeah. Right after I tell your sister how I feel about her."

Jamie snorted. "You're an asshole."

"I know."

"Did you rent that shop space yet?"

"No."

"Sign the papers already. You lived. Might as well get yourself a life."

"Noted."

"And get the girl," he added and hung up.

I went back to work, but the idea had been planted. I couldn't shake it loose. An hour later, I finished up and showered and made the call, swearing on my life that if Jamie was wrong, I was going to steal his lung in his sleep.

CHAPTER TWENTY-FOUR

CASSIE

FIVE days after what I'd labeled as the "taco truck disaster," my fingers did their best to smudge the concealer over the dark circles underneath my eyes. I wasn't sleeping. And I wasn't in the mood for company, but Jess was not a force I could stop. Not in my current state of mind. It was easier to let her have her way and then end it early. So, I'd put on the first clean thing I could find and attempted some semblance of presentable for a dinner out. By the time I was out the door, I was already running late, but I didn't care.

Jess was already waiting for me at our usual table when I arrived at our favorite sushi place. She took one look at me and whistled in a way that I knew was not a compliment. "Hipster homeless. I've heard that's a new look. I hadn't realized you'd decided to try it out."

"Don't," I said, and when the waiter arrived, I gave in and ordered wine. It had been almost a week since Liam had walked away from me at the taco truck. He'd tried calling twice, but I'd let it go unanswered. Hadn't even listened to the voicemail.

Mostly, I just couldn't bear to hear him officially end things, voicemail or otherwise. Now, though, I wondered if I shouldn't just listen to them. Like ripping off a Band-Aid, just get it over with. But in the back of my mind, I knew why I hadn't. As long as I didn't hear him say the words, I could pretend we were still okay. That I hadn't screwed up the one good thing I'd had.

When the wine arrived, I sipped until I could handle whatever barrage Jess threw at me. "Okay," I said. "Give it to me."

"Give you what?" Jess asked.

"Whatever lecture you're going to lay on me about looking like Cinderella's ugly stepsister or whatever. I have enough alcohol in me to handle it now so go ahead."

"Cass, you're wearing yoga pants. That's hardly slumming it." I raised my brow and she conceded, "Okay, fine. For you, it's a little disturbing, but still. I get it. You're unemployed, unattached, and unable to pick a direction. Yoga pants are more than called for."

"You're not going to lecture me?" I asked, a little stung over the "unattached" part.

"Not about that. Now, about your involvement with Mister War Hero."

"Okay, stop." I reached for my wine again. "I have not had enough to drink yet to talk about that."

Jess just watched me with a look of mild entertainment. "That bad, huh?"

"What do you mean?" Finally, the wine was numbing me from the inside out. I signaled for another glass in case this conversation went south.

"You like him. A lot. Damn." She shook her head. "If I'd known this would happen, I would have asked him to check on you a lot sooner."

"Wait. What did you say?"

"Shit." Jess sat back, looking away as if gathering her thoughts. When she looked back at me, I made sure to glare hard enough that she'd feel it. "I wasn't going to… Ah well, screw it," she said, mostly to herself.

I sat back and folded my arms, waiting.

"Fine. When Liam first got into town, I stopped and had a beer with him, and we got to talking."

"You got to talking," I repeated. "You hate Liam."

"Hate's a strong word. I loathe him. Huge difference."

"Jess," I warned. "Not in the mood."

Ugh. Fine. Whatever. I cornered him and asked him to check on you as a favor."

My voice had turned to ice. "What kind of favor—"

"I was worried about you, Cass." The fear in her voice stopped me from blowing up. I listened as she went on, more quietly now. "You weren't returning my calls. Weren't making time to hang out. I'm not a needy friend, but I do know I'm your only friend. And if you weren't talking to me, I knew you weren't talking to anyone. I saw the anxiety. The rashes. And I knew there was something seriously wrong. I knew you'd see Liam at the press junket for the medtech you guys provided. So I asked him to pry a little, see if he could help you. I never thought—"

"Never thought he'd sleep with me," I finished, my tone twisting with the betrayal of it.

"I never thought you'd actually end your losing streak. Or worse, fall for him," she said and I flinched. "But on the slim chance that you might actually care about him, I let it ride."

"This is not a high stakes poker game, Jess."

"Believe me, I know. It was much more sure." My eyes narrowed, but if anything Jess looked less concerned. She waved a hand as if dismissing the part she'd played in this. "He wasn't your usual type."

"What the hell is that supposed to mean?"

"Cass, Jamie talked about Liam all the time. Even before he got home. When he was in rehab, and I heard them talking on the phone and on video call. Liam's changed. Maybe it was almost dying. I don't know, but he's not a player anymore. So even if something did happen between the two of you, I knew he wouldn't hurt you."

For some reason, hearing her say that made everything worse. "Well, obviously you were wrong," I spat.

"No." Jess shook her head. "I'm not. He likes you."

"Stop." I shoved back in my chair, the legs screeching in the dining room. "Just stop it. I'm not going to listen to this anymore. I have to go."

I grabbed my bag and whirled, my eyes already blurring with tears as I stumbled through the restaurant and out the front door. Jess was right about one thing. Liam was different. He'd stuck around this time, and it had been me who had done the hurting. And in doing so, I'd shattered myself. Now, I was the one in need of a medical miracle. How else did you fix a broken heart?

CHAPTER TWENTY-FIVE

LIAM

I hung up feeling like a punk after leaving a third voicemail. Tossing the phone onto the counter, I refilled my coffee mug and went to stand at the back door. From here, I could see my workshop and the yard beyond that before it gave way to the woods that lined the property. I was still toying with the idea of planting a garden in the open area back there, but that would have to wait for next year now. Maybe Sophie would be into helping me—if she was going to be around. School was only going to get harder for her. Maybe I'd ask Jamie instead. I almost snorted out loud at the thought. Yeah right. Jamie wouldn't garden if it was the zombie apocalypse, and we had to tend our own food to survive.

"You couldn't look any more like Dad if you tried right now."

Sophie's voice startled me, and I sloshed coffee over the rim of my cup. "Shit," I muttered, jumping back as it splashed onto my jeans.

"Sorry," she said. "Didn't mean to scare you."

"You didn't," I lied.

She chuckled and went for the coffeepot, her bag slung over her shoulder. I followed her into the kitchen. "You going somewhere? I thought I'd make you breakfast."

"There's a study group at the library," she said, wincing apologetically. "I could cancel though."

"No, it's fine." I waved her off. "Go study in a group."

"Thanks." She headed for the door, and I called out to her. "Soph."

"Yeah?" She turned back.

"What do you think about moving into the dorms next semester?"

Her eyes widened. "That would be fantastic. The commute sucks. But it's expensive."

"I've got some extra," I said. The words were light, but what they implied was way too heavy to let it be that easy.

Instead of lighting up, her eyes narrowed. "Is it the same 'extra' that you would use to sign the lease on the space downtown and open that furniture store?"

"No, I have enough for both. Wait." I frowned. "How do you know about that?"

"Please." She rolled her eyes. "Jamie won't shut up about it. And you've been moping around like Eeyore over Cassie. The store would force you to move forward—"

"I am not moping—"

"Hard-core moping. Drooping face, saggy cheeks, and your knuckles are nearly dragging on the carpet when you walk by."

I cocked my head. "Pretty sure you're mixing metaphors there."

"Either way, if you don't open up that store, you have a bright future as a professional moper."

I closed my mouth, rethinking further argument. Mostly

because if I pushed back on this, it was only a matter of time before she started in on me about Cassie. And I wasn't sure I wanted to talk about girls with my little sister yet. Or ever. Finally, I sighed. "All right. I'll call them back about the store."

"Great!" She rushed me, nearly spilling more coffee as she threw an arm around my neck. "Then I'll move into the dorms."

I shooed her away, scowling at her easy transition. "You are going to make an excellent attorney."

She pulled back, laughing, and any doubt about whether I'd just been handled vanished. "I'll see you later. Dinner?" she asked.

"Dinner," I agreed, rubbing absently at the ache in my ear that had been getting worse over the last couple of days. I made a mental note to up the dosage on the drops the doc had given me.

For now, I listened as the front door clicked shut and Sophie's car started up out front. A moment later, the engine hummed and grew faint as Sophie drove off. When she was gone, I went back to staring out the back door, imagining a garden—and Cassie out there making it grow. Jamie's words from the other day echoed back at me. He was right about my feelings for Cassie. They were real and bigger than anything I'd ever felt before. And I had no idea what to do about it. Making Cassie come? Not a problem. But how in the hell did you make someone stay?

CHAPTER TWENTY-SIX

CASSIE

I was the first to admit what a bitch I was being about Liam. But I also couldn't seem to stop myself. The fear woke me up at night, drenching me in a cold sweat. The rash was back. And every time I thought about facing him, it felt like I'd had the wind knocked out of me. So, I avoided. It was stupid, but it was all I had.

Jess called me until she wore me down and I forgave her for meddling. In the utter silence that had become my life, painting became a way to escape. It had started with the walls of my house. When those were done, I'd turned to the furniture, re-sanding everything first—but that had reminded me too much of Liam and I'd had to stop.

In the end, I'd driven to the store and bought blank canvas. Within a couple of days, I'd filled every single one, and when I ran out of those, I began a wall mural that covered the accent wall in my spare room. Sweeping hills and lush forests. Abstract became defined lines and I was shocked to realize I wasn't awful. It was no Monet, but it wasn't a kindergarten with finger paints either.

Huh.

With nothing better to do, I kept going with the mural, losing myself in the landscape. Day bled into night—both in the scene of my creation and outside. One wall portrayed a bright sun with cheery hills underneath it. The next featured a silver moon with a howling wolf and dark shadows creeping out from underneath the canopy of trees.

I was shocked after a bathroom break forced me to turn on lights in the pitch-dark hall. I couldn't remember what time it was. Or even what day. But I knew time had passed, and that jolted me more than I expected. Apparently, the world did not, in fact, stop turning just because I'd stepped away from it. I wasn't sure whether that should make me feel better or worse.

But the more time passed, the easier it became to let things go. The company, Dad's betrayal, what I thought would be my future. But not Liam. Losing Liam only got harder.

Because I hadn't lost that. I'd thrown it away. Even if he had only wanted to be with me as a favor to Jess, I'd been the one to ruin it in the end. The beginning was on him. The end was on me.

Through the painting and the clarity that came with it, the fear slowly dissolved. In the end, I was left with the stark realization of everything I'd been too afraid to claim. And now it was too late.

Hours later, I blinked and the mural came into sharper focus. I stared, dazed, at the merman I'd painted underneath the surface of a lake. I stared at his shaggy hair and broad chest until my vision blurred and my knees threatened to buckle under the weight of it all. Too tired of holding it all back, I dropped my brush and sank onto the floor—and let the tears come.

THE doorbell rang, and I sniffled, swiping at my wet cheeks. I debated ignoring it, but it rang again and I climbed to my feet. Maybe it was Jess. Maybe she'd brought food. God knew I didn't have any of that in the house.

But the moment I swung the door open, I realized my mistake. Not Jess.

"Liam."

I blinked hard against the bright sunlight behind him. He squinted at me, taking in my paint-covered shorts and tee—and what was probably a really rough case of bedhead. His eyes caught on the remnants of the rash still covering my arm. I tucked my hand behind my back, and he blinked.

"Can I come in?" he asked. His voice was rough and low and made my heart hurt.

"Of course." I led us into the kitchen, keeping the bar between us when I turned to face him. Space. I needed more space. Room to breathe. And to think. He'd shaved. Why had he shaved? I missed the beard he'd grown out and the way it made him look dangerous and rough. Although, the glint in his eyes still made him both of those things even without it.

That was just Liam. From far away, he was intimidating and unpredictable. Up close, though, I knew better. Inside, he was soft and gorgeous and nothing like what people assumed.

"What's up?" I asked in a strained voice.

My heart thudded erratically. I hoped he couldn't hear it.

But Liam wasn't even looking at me. He was craning his neck around to stare at the walls. "Did you paint in here?" he asked.

"Yes."

I didn't offer more than that and finally he turned back to face me. "I wanted to talk to you."

The heaviness in his tone made me brace myself. Here it came. The official words that would end this for good. And I had only myself to blame.

Again, the fear gnawed at me. Only this time, it was fear of being crushed under the weight of watching him walk away. "Well, I don't want to talk," I said, raising my chin defiantly against the pain I knew was coming.

His expression clouded, but he pressed on almost as if I hadn't spoken. "Cassie, I want you to know that getting to know the real you has been nothing like I expected. *You* are nothing like I expected."

"I…" Neither was he. Too afraid to admit that, I gave in and went with pissed. "Is that why you stuck around so long?"

"What?"

"Jess told me everything. I know I was just a favor to you."

"No." His eyes flashed, first with confusion, and then when recognition dawned, his jaw hardened and his voice turned hard. "She asked me to check on you as a favor. She was worried you were in some kind of trouble. But that was as far as her request went. Because absolutely every interaction we had, every word I spoke, everything we did from the moment I kissed you at that fundraiser—that was all for me. Don't think for one second that it was anything else."

"I don't know what to think," I began.

His expression softened. "Yes, you do. You're just scared."

I cleared my throat, keeping my voice neutral. He wasn't wrong, but I wasn't about to admit that now. Not when he was on his way out. "Is there something else?"

"Yeah." He sighed. "Fuck, this is harder than I thought it would be." He ran a hand through his hair, and suddenly I couldn't take it anymore. This was pointless and only prolonged the pain.

"How about I save us both the trouble then? It's been fun. I'd even say it's been eye-opening. I appreciate everything you did for me. And I wish you the best of luck in your future endeavors." I stuck my hand out in an offer to shake. "No hard feelings. Friends?"

He blinked first at my hand and then at me. "What? No, I—"

"Fine. Not friends then. I get it." I retracted my hand, the sting of his refusal sharp enough to feel all the way to my toes.

"Cassie, that's not what I meant. Listen, I'm trying to tell you that I care about you. That you aren't just sex. It's what I've been saying all along. But you're too stubborn and too scared to admit you like me too. And unless you can do that, I don't know how this is going to work out. So I need you to do that. It's why I came here even after what you said to Jess."

I stared at him, not even sure what to say next. This wasn't what I'd expected. And while it was everything I wanted to hear, I'd been so convinced he'd moved on, it took a minute to sink in. "You're not breaking up with me?"

"Of course not. I know all of this is partly my fault too. I told you I've never had a girlfriend. Clearly, communication is not my strength, but I'm working on it. That's why I came over. To show you I want this."

"When you didn't call, I thought—"

"I did call. Multiple times, actually." He cocked his head at me. "Did you even listen to the messages?"

"No," I admitted. "I didn't want to hear you say the words."

He shook his head. "You're really stubborn, you know that."

I attempted a watery smile. "I'm told that's one of my best qualities. Really puts the 'ice' in 'ice princess.'"

He smirked, and I felt something inside my gut untwist. A weight lifted. But then the reality of what he was offering really hit me, and I felt breathless all over again. Because unlike before, I realized now that I wanted it. I wanted him. For real. Maybe for good. And I wanted it more than I'd ever wanted to be my father's daughter. This was so much bigger than the fear.

"You scare me," I said quietly.

"You scare me too," he admitted.

We'd already admitted that the other day, but now it felt bigger somehow. Because we were really doing this. "I have no idea how to be a girlfriend."

"I have no idea how to be a boyfriend."

I dropped my hands to my sides, trying not to think of all the things that could possibly go wrong. Liam took a step toward me.

"What if we hurt each other?"

"We probably will," he admitted, and I blanched, ready to back away.

He grabbed my hand before I could retreat and clung tight, his words urgent and so sincere. "That's how love works, Cass. We're going to try our best. We're going to make mistakes. But we're going to work really hard to always forgive, and when I stop being the person who makes you the happiest in the world, you can go. I won't chase you down. Does that work?"

"Love?" My voice was nothing more than a croak. "You just said…" I couldn't bring myself to repeat it a second time, but Liam wasn't fazed.

"I guess I did." He reached up and tucked a strand of hair behind my ear and all I could do was stare back at him, drowning in his gaze. I'd never known such strength and tenderness could exist in one place—not for me. "I love you, Cassie Franklin," he whispered.

"I..." The words hung there, close enough to touch. But I held them back, too terrified to push them out of my mouth.

Instead of letting his disappointment show, Liam put his finger to my lips, silencing me. "Show me," he whispered.

I exhaled, brushing my mouth lightly over his. "That I can do."

CHAPTER TWENTY-SEVEN

LIAM

CASSIE'S mouth was magic. It didn't matter that she hadn't said the words back to me because everything those lips did next convinced me it was only a matter of time until she spoke them out loud. She loved me. Every kiss, every nip and tickle she left along my skin, was evidence.

When she dipped lower, pulling my shirt up to trail kisses down my abdomen, I grabbed her wrists, yanking her upright. "Pick a room."

Her eyes lit with delight, and it was all I could do not to take her right here in the kitchen bent over the breakfast bar. Normally, I wouldn't hesitate, but today it was going to be slow. "Pick a comfortable room," I corrected. "We're going to be at this a while."

"The spare bedroom," she said softly. "I want to show you something."

"Lead the way."

She grabbed my wrist and led me down the hall to a spare room I remembered as mostly empty and white walled. The only other time I'd seen it had been when I'd prowled through the house looking for an intruder that first night. But when she opened the door for me and stepped in, I realized a lot had changed since then.

Color.

There was color everywhere. On canvases propped along the baseboards and on every wall including the window frame. Bright, sweeping oranges and yellows for sunsets. Dark, lush greens and browns for forests. It all blended together in a representation of emotion in a way I'd never seen. Abstract but also a visceral definition of form that left me speechless.

"Cassie, this is amazing," I managed, staring at what she'd created before finally turning back to her with wide eyes.

She shrugged, much like I had when she'd complimented my woodworking. "It's fun. And I'm enjoying doing something for no other reason than pleasure."

I stared at her, completely blown away by the raw talent and depth and sincerity in the woman I'd come to know. And the desire that had been momentarily shoved aside sprang back to life, curling in my gut and hardening my cock instantly. I reached for, pulling her against my chest.

"That's good to hear," I breathed, pulling her hair aside so that I could plant a lingering kiss on her throat. "Because I've got something else we can do purely for the pleasure of it."

She leaned in, sighing as I kissed a trail from her chin to ear and back again. "I've missed you," she said. When her lips turned toward mine, I crashed my mouth against hers, suddenly a lot hungrier now.

Maybe this wouldn't be slow after all.

Cassie broke the kiss, reaching for my pants and yanking them open. She coaxed my erection free, stroking it so that my balls tightened and my knees went weak. "Fuck me," I breathed.

"That's my plan."

I smirked. Two could play at this game.

I reached for her, but she slid away, her hand still working up and down on my cock. She slid to her knees, her big blue eyes staring up at me, and I groaned in anticipation. Moving slowly, her tongue made small circles over the tip of my dick, and I shuddered.

"Holy shit," I managed, my head falling backward as she began tracing lines up and down the length of my cock with her tongue. The moment her mouth closed over me, my breath whooshed out, and I had to catch myself to stay upright. Nope. At this rate, it definitely wouldn't take long at all.

The sensation of Cassie's mouth around me was insane. She sucked and pulled, and I grabbed a handful of her hair, holding it out of her face and using the pressure of my squeezing hand to brace the tension that was building fast. Really fucking fast.

I couldn't take much more of this.

"My turn," I growled, pulling out of her mouth and falling to my knees before her. I didn't give her a chance to argue before I grabbed her and eased her back onto the carpet, rising up over her and yanking her shorts off. I spread her legs and pulled her panties aside, leaning in and delving my tongue between her folds fast enough to make her ass jump up off the floor.

She gasped, but I didn't let up. If she was going full speed ahead, so was I.

My tongue was insistent as I licked and sucked at her clit then probed her folds until her wetness dripped from both of us. When she whimpered, her hips bucking and rocking toward me, I knew she was just as close as I was. With one hand, I reached up and found her already taut nipple inside her shirt. I plucked at it, pulling lightly and running the pad of my thumb over the hardened tip. With my other hand, I slid two fingers inside her.

"Liam," she warned.

I kept licking and pumping my fingers into her until I felt the muscles in her thighs tense.

"Liam," she said again, louder now. More insistent.

My cock jumped and throbbed, aching to be inside her.

At the last second, I pulled my fingers out of her and sat up, yanking her panties off and sliding into her so fast, we both inhaled sharply. Cassie gasped and my breath caught, my chest tightening and my dick hardening even more.

I slid farther, burying myself inside her as far as I could go. Cassie was completely taut, her hips pushed against mine. I stared down at her, neither one of us moving an inch, and let myself get lost in the liquid warmth of her blue eyes.

So much heat. Inside and out, it was all I could feel from her. Passion and heat and need. "Liam, I…"

She trailed off, just like she had earlier, but I didn't care. I didn't need to hear it. Not now, like this. Not when I could literally fucking feel the truth in her. In answer, I let myself fall over her, my mouth crashing to hers and making it impossible for her to talk.

Moving slowly at first, I eased back a little and then rocked lightly against her. She whimpered, her nails digging into my back. "No more talking," I told her, my mouth barely releasing hers as I spoke. "Just coming."

Her answering moan was exactly right.

"Faster," she breathed and I complied, pushing against her harder now. Faster, in and out, I lost myself in her, until the rhythm of our bodies was all that existed. I reached around with one hand, cupping her ass and holding her against me as she grinded her hips, meeting every one of my thrusts with her own.

"Liam, I'm going to…"

I felt it the moment she tensed. A split second where her body wasn't her own anymore. Tension, pressure, and pure passion—and then she came apart. Exploding into an orgasm that I felt all the way through me. My cock throbbed as her walls contracted against it, and then I went with her, crashing over the edge of my own release and falling, falling with only Cassie there to catch me at the bottom.

CHAPTER TWENTY-EIGHT

CASSIE

I stood on the sidewalk, watching the progress of the crane currently lifting the sign into place over the entrance to Liam's store. The sun had set behind the building just enough not to blind me, and I watched as the crew communicated about centering the rectangular display and then leveling it out before securing it into place. It was the last step before Liam opened next week. After three weeks of preparation, we were actually ahead of schedule. I was so proud of him—a fact I mentioned often. Mostly to make up for the fact that it was still too terrifying to tell him the one thing I really wanted to say. And Liam never pushed me or made me feel bad for it. In fact, he seemed perfectly fine with my lack of response and used it as a challenge for a much more physical response instead. I'd lost count of how many times I'd *shown* him my feelings lately.

"Looking good." A pair of arms covered in sawdust slid around my waist from behind.

I turned and offered my mouth for a kiss. "They've done a great job," I agreed.

"I wasn't talking about the sign." He grinned and slid around to face me, his arms still holding me tight.

"Such a smooth talker," I teased. "Is that how you're going to treat all your customers?"

He scoffed. "Of course not. I have you to charm them."

My eyes widened. "I think you have me mixed up with someone else. I am not your employee, and I am most definitely not charming."

He nibbled my ear. "Job's yours if you want it."

His easy offer left me speechless. Not because I didn't want it. I was touched that he'd extended the invite, especially after how terrified he'd been when I'd offered to help him negotiate the lease a few weeks back. A lot had changed, not the least of which was my need for control. Apparently, Liam was noticing that too.

When I didn't answer, he leaned in and planted a kiss on the tip of my nose. "You are very charming when you want to be. Lucky for me, I'm the only one in the world you want to charm. Otherwise, we'd all be in trouble, and I'd probably have a lawsuit of my own to deal with."

"Very funny." I tried not to let his comment make me think of Evan, but it was a losing battle.

"Sorry," Liam said, squeezing my hand.

"It's fine."

"Have you heard from your dad?"

I shook my head.

Liam had been gently pushing me to reach out, but so far, I hadn't tried. My dad was the one who needed to apologize. Until he did that, I wasn't sure what there was to even say. I knew Liam had a sort of "life's too short" outlook when it came to that stuff, but I wasn't quite there yet.

"Are you ready for all this?" I asked, changing the subject

as we turned to face the store again. We watched as the crew put the finishing touches on the sign.

"I don't know. I guess. I mean, I did sign a two-year lease so I have to be, right?"

"One thing I know for sure: you don't have to do anything in this life that you don't want to."

He smiled at me. "Spoken like a true rebel."

"I'm trying."

And I was. With each new passing day, I got further from the old Cassie and more acquainted with the new one. When I wasn't with Liam, I spent my spare time finding things that brought me pleasure. I was planning a second tattoo and considering taking art lessons at some point. Mostly, I was just breathing easier. And wearing more tank tops thanks to the fact that I was now on day twenty-two without the rash. And the panic. Mostly.

"Speaking of rebels, Jess called," I said, and Liam's expression turned annoyed—a reaction I was starting to suspect was more out of habit for them both than actual dislike. "She thinks you should have a party for your opening."

"Of course she does."

"And apparently Jamie agrees."

"If there's one thing those two can agree on, it's a party."

"So is that a yes?"

He hesitated.

"If you don't want the attention, we can skip it," I began.

"No, let's do it."

"Are you sure?"

"Yeah." He glanced back at the sign. "Publicity for doing what I love is something I want to get used to."

I beamed up at him. "I'm really proud of you." He was never going to want the spotlight for what had happened to him in the military, and I couldn't blame him there. But for this, he deserved it.

He wiggled his brows. "How about instead of going out with Jess tonight, you and I step into the back room and you can show me how proud—"

I laughed, swatting at him. "You're so bad."

He darted in for another kiss. "You love it."

I felt my face flush with warmth. "I do. If I bring you breakfast tomorrow, does that make me a good girlfriend?"

"Yes. But if you *are* breakfast tomorrow, it makes you an even better one. Have a good time tonight," he said, sending me off with another kiss that made it very tempting to take him up on his offer to go back inside. But in the end, I managed to untangle myself and promised to see him in the morning. By the time I drove away, Liam's sign had lit up in my rearview, and I was still smiling.

CHAPTER TWENTY-NINE

LIAM

MY earache, a dull throb that had persisted since last night, suddenly turned sharp, and I grunted at the stabbing sensation coming from inside my ear canal. When it didn't pass, I signaled to Jamie to lower the table he was helping me haul into the shop space I'd rented. The moment it was out of my grip, I doubled back outside, and fumbled in the cab of the truck for the eardrops the doc had prescribed. After a couple of drops, the pain dialed back again, leaving me dizzy but able walk. Sort of. I leaned back against the building, breathing and wincing with the pain that had migrated from my ears to my head.

Jamie stepped out, squinting into the morning sun, and crossed his arms over his chest, studying me. "You look like shit, bro."

"Your encouragement is noted." I leaned my head against the brick and closed my eyes, concentrating on my heart rate. After the sign had gone up last night, I'd cut out and gone back to the shop to work on the last pieces. Jamie had arrived bright and early to help me begin bringing them over, but the earache that had only been an annoying background issue for weeks was suddenly much more pronounced today. It hurt like hell—enough that I wasn't playing it off anymore when Jamie asked how I felt.

"I'm serious," Jamie said now, real concern lacing his words. "What did the doc say?"

"To call him if the drops didn't help the pain," I admitted.

"Uh-huh." Jamie's brows rose. "Let me guess, you're getting to that."

I shrugged. "It's on my list of things to do."

His look was like an entire lecture wrapped in a glare. "Bro."

I held up a hand to stop him. "Don't start with me. You sound like Sophie."

"For good reason. You're being stupid."

"Again with the encouragement. I just have to get this stuff loaded for the opening and then I can take a break."

"And if your ears explode or some shit before all your customers can come buy your wood?" He ignored his own joke—a sure sign he was pissed. "I hate to point out the obvious, but no Liam, no customers."

When I didn't answer, he sighed. "You're going to make me say it, aren't you?"

"Say what?"

"How much I love you and can't live without you. If something happens to you—"

"Nothing is going to happen." I shoved off the building, pushing past him to unload the next item from the truck.

Jamie blocked me, his nostrils flaring. I'd gotten to him. "Your balance is still giving you problems, isn't it?"

I sighed and gave up on the nightstand I'd been trying to grab. "I have fluid in my ears."

"Fluid," he repeated. "Have you told anyone? Sophie? Cassie?"

I shook my head and Jamie cursed. "Doc isn't sure what it's from," I told him. "He gave me these drops, but they aren't doing much."

"And you didn't think that was important enough to follow up on?"

"I think I'm opening a new business and in between that I'm having the best sex of my life. I'm a little busy. I'll get to it."

Jamie shook his head. "Get to it soon, bro."

"Yes, Dad."

"Don't even joke with me, man," he warned. "We'll wrestle it out like we did in high school. The only way you're getting out of that headlock will be to answer the question 'who's your daddy?'"

"What makes you think you'll get me into a headlock?"

"Please." He scoffed. "I always whooped your ass…"

His mouth kept moving, but the sound was suddenly gone.

I blinked, tugging at my ears when they began to tingle. Then they began to hurt again. Not a little. A lot.

As I tugged, the sound returned, but it wasn't the same. Everything sounded garbled—like I was hearing it from underwater.

"Dude." I formed the word, but when it came out, I had no idea how it sounded.

I stumbled, a wave of dizziness washing over me. My chest tightened as I sucked in a startled breath. What the fuck was happening to me?

Jamie's hand closed around my elbow. I swayed and he grabbed me, holding me upright. I looked up and found him watching me, worry lines around his eyes and mouth. His mouth was moving again but I couldn't make out the words.

"I can't hear," I told him, wincing at the pain in my head. "And I can't stand."

Jamie replied with something unintelligible.

He helped lower me to the ground, and I sat, watching as he whipped out his phone, pressing buttons too fast for me to see. A second later, he began talking again, his eyes glued to mine.

Another wave of dizziness hit me.

I leaned my head back against the brick wall, breathing slowly in and out.

The pain in my ear intensified, and I cringed, pulling and tugging at my earlobe. But it only made the pain worse. "Fuck," I muttered, my stomach roiling with the pain that radiated out into the rest of my head and down into my body. This was almost worse than the explosion itself.

Jamie tapped me, and I opened my eyes, unsure how long I'd been sitting here now. The pain screamed through my skull, making it hard to concentrate. His mouth was moving, but I couldn't understand the words.

Another face joined his. I took in the uniform and the bag he set beside him. A medic. Good.

The guy asked me a question. I shook my head, looking to Jamie. Talking made everything hurt worse. I let him explain. After a minute of some crazy hand gestures on Jamie's part, the medic nodded and then began a quick vital check while two more medics appeared behind him with a stretcher.

I groaned, but by the time they'd finished checking me out and given the green light for me to move onto the thin mattress on wheels, I didn't fight it. Right now, I wanted to get to a doctor as fast as possible. The quicker I got to one, the quicker they could make this pain stop. Or, at least that's what I hoped.

CHAPTER THIRTY

CASSIE

I woke to the sound of my phone ringing. Grumbling about manners and good sense, I picked it up, fully expecting it to be Liam or even Jess bothering me this early in the morning. But the display read Dad and I sat up quickly, worried, nervous, and then worried again in the split second before I answered it.

"Hello? Dad? Is everything okay?"

"Hi, Cassie. Everything's fine."

I frowned. "Why are you calling me so early?"

"It's eight," he said.

"I know."

"On a weekday." The way he said it made his point clear: a month ago, this would not have been early for me. I remained silent, annoyed already. "Anyway," he said after a beat. "I need to tell you something. About the company. And Evan and—"

"I don't care."

"Excuse me?"

"Whatever thing you're going to tell me, if it involves Evan, I don't care."

"He's gone," my dad said simply, and I blinked.

"What do you mean?"

"There's a sexual harassment suit filed against him. Your assistant—"

"Oh, God. Bev." A sick feeling churned instantly in my gut. I threw the covers back, jumping out of bed and heading for the stairs. I was going to need a lot of coffee for this story.

While I waited for the coffee to brew, my father talked. This time, I let him, still cringing every time he said Evan's name. "She says it's been building for a few weeks now. Apparently, it started with offhanded comments around the office and after she agreed to one date, it escalated pretty quickly. It didn't get out of hand, though," my father assured me. "She put a stop to it and got out of there before it could get too far."

"Obviously, if he was sexually harassing her, it was already out of hand," I snapped.

"Right. Of course. I meant that—"

"That what? He didn't rape her so everything's okay?"

"You don't have to be crass." The first hint of annoyance colored his tone which only made me furious.

"I'm calling it what it is, Dad. Stating facts. That's not crass just because you prefer to live in denial."

He didn't answer, and I was getting exhausted over what felt like an argument we'd had thousands of times now. I poured my coffee and pinched the bridge of my nose against the headache already forming.

"Why are you telling me this?" I asked quietly.

"Because Evan's gone and he won't be back."

"Good. Finally. But what does that have to do with me?"

My dad's hesitation was the closest thing to an apology I knew I'd ever get. "I'd like you to come in. So we can talk about this in person."

So many quick retorts flashed through my mind, but I didn't say any of them. My dad was silent too and I recognized it for what it was: a negotiating tactic. Once a deal was laid out, the first one to speak lost the edge. In sales, the first one to speak was the one to pay. Sadly, I realized now, it was also a description that fit our relationship perfectly.

"I don't think—" I began, but a beeping in my ear startled me.

I checked the screen. "Dad, I have to call you back."

"Cass—"

"Bye."

I hung up with him and answered the incoming call. "Jess?"

"Cassie," she said on a sigh, her voice a terrifying mixture of fear and desperation.

"What's wrong?" I asked, my conversation with my dad already forgotten.

"Liam's in the hospital."

No preamble. No lead-up. Just the facts.

I went perfectly still.

My hands turned instantly cold despite one of them being wrapped around my warm mug. I remained frozen, not even sure I'd heard her right. But in the background, I could hear the jingling of her car keys followed by the slam of her front door, and I realized she was serious.

Setting my coffee aside, I jumped off the barstool and raced upstairs to my closet for clothes. Still holding the phone, I said, "What happened?"

"Jamie said his hearing's gone, he's in a lot of pain, and he can't stand without losing his balance. It's a buildup of fluid, I think. Someone tossed around the word meningitis. They're talking about surgery."

"Shit." I'd known his ear was bothering him, but I hadn't realized—

"Jamie said to hurry," Jess said and her voice was grim.

"I'm leaving in thirty seconds," I promised. "Meet you there in ten."

Jess hung up without answering.

I tore through my clothes, grabbing a pair of jeans and stepping into them as fast as I could. The sweatshirt nearby was covered in paint but it would have to do. I threw it on, not bothering with a bra, and then raced downstairs, stopping at the door to grab my purse and slide into some flats.

Then I yanked open my front door and ran for my car.

All I could think about was Liam. His ears—the ears we'd helped fix—were failing him. Just like my father had failed me. Just like I'd failed to tell Liam how I truly felt. Fury and fear both rose in me, making it hard to breathe around the sheer volume of it all, but not just at Franklin Industries. I was angry at myself. For not having the guts to say the words. For not understanding what Liam meant about how life was short and we never really knew how much time we'd have. And fear. Fear that I'd never get that chance again.

My hands shook as I fumbled with the button on my key fob that would unlock my door. I didn't see the two figures standing at the bumper until one of them cleared their throat and my head whipped toward the sound. I stopped with my driver's side door cracked, my hand tight around the handle.

"Who are you?" I demanded, taking in their nondescript dark pants and nearly matching blazers. I didn't have time for a couple of Jehovah's Witness' right now.

But the man deferred to the woman, so I glanced from him to her—and stopped as she removed her aviators and recognition dawned. My hands fell limp at my sides.

"Bev?" I asked incredulously.

She offered a tight smile that didn't feel like a smile at all. Then she reached into her blazer and pulled out a shiny badge, flashing it for me. "It's Agent Perez, actually. And we're going to need you to come with us. Now."

CHAPTER THIRTY-ONE

LIAM

WITH the first real breath I was aware of drawing, I groaned. It wasn't until halfway through that I realized my head was no longer pounding to the beat of my own heart. Reflex, I guess. It had hurt so bad before I awoke that I'd just expected it to hurt again. In the absence of the pain, I forced my eyes open and then quickly closed them again. The lights overhead were bright. Much brighter than my bedroom.

Fucking shit.

I opened my eyes again, looking around quickly as my eyes adjusted fully to the well-lit and sterile hospital room. A quick tug on my arm revealed an IV line hooked into the crook of my elbow. I followed the line to a bag of clear liquid that hung from the hook on my right.

This wasn't my bedroom. I wasn't home. Hell, I wasn't even sure I was alive. I groaned again, the sound of my own voice garbled in my ears. Somewhere nearby, a chair creaked and then grated against the floor as it was shoved away. The sound of it echoed harshly, sending waves of pain into my skull before it all quieted again. I winced.

Sophie's face appeared over mine. Followed by my parents.

"Liam," my mother said, tears already forming in her brown eyes as she bent closer. "You're awake. He's awake," she announced even though my dad and Sophie were both already smiling down at me and fully aware of that fact on their own. Her words were slurred and it took me a minute to realize she wasn't drunk or too tired to talk. It was my hearing that was wrong.

My dad's arm came around my mom's shoulders and squeezed. "I told you," he said, and I wondered how serious things had been if Mom hadn't been convinced I'd wake up.

Sophie answered the question before I could ask. I concentrated on her lips as they moved, wanting to be sure I heard her right. "Your implant broke inside your eardrum and the fluid that was in your ears leaked into your brain cavity. The doctors have mentioned meningitis but they need to run another test before they can confirm it."

"Meningitis?" That wasn't something I expected.

"You were in surgery for a few hours."

"Surgery?" I frowned.

She nodded. "They replaced your implant. After the anesthesia wore off and you still hadn't woken. We weren't sure..."

Sophie didn't finish the sentence, but I understood what they'd feared. I reached for her hand. She offered it and squeezed me lightly, smiling. "Glad I'm back," I said.

She nodded wordlessly, tears slipping down her cheeks in silent tracks.

"It doesn't hurt," I assured her.

She attempted a smile. "That's because you're being pumped full of the good stuff," she said, pointing to the IV line.

"Nice." I breathed deeply, enjoying the numbness. "Where's Cassie?" I asked, earning a strange look from Sophie that put me on edge.

"She never showed up."

"Did someone call her?" I asked.

"Jess did," Sophie said quietly.

"And?" I demanded. For a second, I was too surprised to be hurt by the fact that she hadn't shown. Something must have happened.

But Sophie exchanged a look with my mom and then shook her head sadly. "She never showed up. We've tried calling her a bunch of times but she hasn't answered her phone. Jess went to her house but Cassie wasn't there. Sorry, Liam."

I blew out a breath.

For a moment, no one else said anything.

"Do you want me to call her again?" Sophie asked.

"No." I fell back against the pillow, wondering what the hell could have possibly been more important to my girl than being here when I woke up. But at the pounding in my head, I let it go.

I spent the next twenty minutes being fussed over by my parents. Sophie left to find a doctor and returned with two.

"Overachiever," I muttered and she grinned.

After that, it was a flurry of medical jargon, test results, tests ordered, and a diagnosis that kept using the word "oxygen therapy" as a possible treatment option for the fluid still lingering on my brain. The new implant made it possible to hear but underneath their voices was a buzzing that was hard to ignore. I knew from the first time it would subside eventually.

"I'm down for whatever you think will help," I told the doctor.

My mother spoke up. "Any word on whether the treatment

will be covered by insurance?"

My mom and the doc shared a look. "It's a little complicated," the doctor said uncertainly. "The implant was donated by a private company so your insurance needs some time to work out whose financial responsibility it is now that the equipment has malfunctioned—"

"Are you saying his medical treatment isn't being covered by anyone?" my mother demanded. "He is a war hero."

The doctor shifted his weight, clearly uncomfortable with being the messenger here. "We've reached out to Franklin Industries with no luck. Until we hear back from someone who will claim financial responsibility, we can't move forward on a treatment."

My dad swore. My mother shot him a look: disapproving but not disagreeing.

I sighed. "Thanks, doc." The man nodded and took that as his cue to disappear.

Within seconds, all the medical staff had cleared out and we were alone again.

All I could think about was Cassie. Where the hell had she gone? And what was more important than this?

Eventually, my mother went from quietly ranting about insurance companies and returned to fussing over me. But whatever drugs they'd given me were kicking in again and my eyelids drooped, making it hard to keep up with her questions.

"Guys, he's literally falling asleep here." Sophie's voice cut into my mom's monologue about a dairy-free diet proven to help reduce mucus. I wasn't sure how that helped my ears.

"Oh. Right. Sorry. We'll let you rest." My mom bent and kissed my forehead, smoothing my hair back before my dad tugged her away.

"We'll come back in the morning," he said.

I nodded, already starting to drift.

Sophie waved and then they were all gone. I was asleep before they'd shut the door, still wondering where Cassie had gone.

CHAPTER THIRTY-TWO

CASSIE

I rubbed my palms on my jeans and then ran a hand over my hair, fidgeting with the ends of it while stale coffee churned in my stomach. This had already taken entirely too long, and I was drained from the emotional roller coaster. Between my desperation to get to Liam and the shock then fury over what I'd been dragged into thanks to my father and Evan, I wasn't sure whether I wanted to scream or cry anymore.

I shot a glance at Bev who was seated across from me in the small interview room, but she didn't look up from her paperwork. Looking at her now, she seemed like a completely different person from the girl I thought I knew. Probably because she was. Her dangly, gold earrings were gone, along with the hipster business suits she'd worn when I'd known her as my assistant. In the place of all that, she still wore the black blazer with pants to match and a plain white blouse. Her lipstick was gone now too and when she looked up from the files in front of her, the half-clueless expression of her receptionist persona had been replaced with impassivity. There was an edge to her now that screamed competence. And danger if you crossed her.

Agent Perez. A complete stranger who now held my fate in her hands.

Even with all of this hanging over me, all I wanted was to give my statement and get the hell out of here so I could find Liam and make sure he was okay. He'd clearly been keeping this from me, playing off his earaches as normal for the healing process. Probably not wanting to scare me. I'd seen those drops he'd been using, but he'd acted like it was all routine. I swore that from now on, I'd be more involved in his medical care. He was going to be okay. I was going to make sure of it. Just as soon as I found out whether I was facing prison time or not.

Finally, Bev looked up from the briefing she was reading and her gaze settled on me. "Well, it looks like your written statement includes everything my bosses wanted confirmed. It all lines up with the information your father gave us too. So that's good news."

"And the bad news?" I asked.

"Well, you're out of a job for starters. Your father will lose the company, that's a given," she said, and I nodded, my shoulders tight.

"Was he involved in the...?"

"Embezzling?" she asked. "Yes and no. Your dad has a habit of getting his hands on a lot of money and then losing it again pretty quickly. Honestly, your company's financials are some of the craziest I've ever seen and I've been doing this for a while now."

I wondered how long "a while" was considering she looked no older than me. But I decided not to ask. Better not to question her until she was done questioning me.

She continued, "But he's given us everything we needed on

Evan and that's what we wanted from the start, so he's in the clear on whatever shady money management practices he might have had." She pinned me with a look that meant business. "This time. Next time, we won't be so lenient on him."

I nodded. "I understand. Does that mean you aren't filing charges?"

"Not against your father. His testimony, and the dissolution of the company, will satisfy us. He won't be allowed to enter into a company of this type again, according to the deal he's making, but he won't go to prison. Evan, on the other hand, isn't so lucky. His embezzling is a habit he apparently brought with him from his previous job. Not to mention the assault and the lawsuit he buried there before he came to work for you."

"Speaking of assault, are you okay?" I asked quietly.

Bev softened an inch. "I'm fine," she assured me. "His harassment only sealed the case against him, so it has a silver lining there. Besides, I can handle myself, but thank you for asking."

"I can't believe you're a federal agent," I said. "I feel like such a jerk for making you do all that filing."

"It was part of the cover while we investigated," she explained. "Besides, all things considered, you were a decent boss."

"I was a bitch."

"I like to call it being a hard ass." She offered a crooked smile, and I realized she and I had a lot more in common than I'd once thought. Then she gestured to the recorder between us. "Shall we begin?"

I took a deep breath. "Ask me anything," I said.

Bev set up the recorder and then went to work, asking me questions about my employment with the company, my duties, and my knowledge of the financial inner workings. I answered everything as truthfully as I could and by the end, I felt an empty sort of relief. That time in my life was absolutely over, no matter what came next.

And I was more than okay with that.

When we were finished, Bev packed up her paperwork and we stood. I resisted the urge to scratch at my arm, but for once, it didn't feel red or inflamed. "So, what's the verdict?" I asked. "How much trouble do you think I'll be in?"

Bev patted my shoulder. "None."

"Really?" My relief left a sweet taste in my throat.

"Really. Cassie, you didn't do anything wrong. Your name isn't on any of the documents including financial reports and business deals. I just wanted to get some more background for our case with Evan. You have nothing to worry about."

"Thank you," I told her as I followed her back out to the waiting area I'd passed on the way in. "I mean it. I appreciate everything."

Bev's expression clouded as she spotted something over my shoulder. "Don't thank me yet."

"What?"

She nodded. "Looks like you're not off the hook completely. There's someone waiting for you."

I turned and spotted my father standing in the middle of the empty waiting area. He didn't say a word, and I knew he was waiting for me to make the first move. If walking out was that move, I knew he'd let me.

"I'll see you later," Bev said and walked away.

I took a deep breath, and when Bev was gone, I turned to my dad.

"Cassandra." He sounded a bit surprised that I'd actually approached him. That made two of us. "It's good to see you."

I didn't answer.

"How's Liam?"

"I don't know. I've been here. Wait." I frowned. "How do you know about Liam?"

"I got a call from the hospital about his... He's fine," he assured me when he read my panicked expression.

I exhaled. "Do you know what happened?"

"His implant burst, leaking fluid into his ear canal which created some complications for him, including some fluid on his brain, but he'll recover."

My shoulders sagged. "I have to go to him."

"Before you go, I..." He frowned. "There's something I need to tell you."

"Okay."

"I lied to you. About Evan and the deal for purchasing our shares."

"What do you mean?"

"The sale never went through. It was Evan's idea to tell you that. To push you out. I went along because, well, by the time Evan came to me with his idea, I knew about Bev. Knew who she was. What she was doing there. I agreed to work with them if it meant taking Evan down and keeping myself out of prison. But I couldn't have you there. Not when I couldn't guarantee you wouldn't be implicated. I just needed to go along with Evan's wishes.

"He wanted your job. Wanted to hurt you. And after what you said about me, about your mother, I did too, I guess. I'm sorry for that. But I wanted you to know that I never would have fired you. That company, the legacy, was yours. Nothing would have changed that. What I did, I did it to protect you."

All the air left the room and my knees buckled. Dad watched me carefully and when I took a step toward the chairs lining the wall, he grabbed my elbow, guiding me into the closest one. "Are you okay? What's wrong? Is it a panic attack?" he asked.

"No, I… You've never apologized to me before."

"Oh." He looked away. "Well. I'm overdue on a lot of things, I guess."

"Is this why you called me to come in to the office this morning?"

"Yes." He sighed. "I wanted to explain everything then, but I chickened out. Work has always been our thing together, and I thought if you came into the office, it would give me the boost I needed to apologize for everything in person."

"Dad, work has been our thing because we didn't have anything else."

"You're right. I see that now."

Silence fell between us, and I struggled to find the right words. My insides were torn in a million different directions over what he'd just told me. An apology wasn't going to fix everything between us but it was a start—and it was something I never, ever thought I'd get.

Besides, Liam had taught me that in life, there were no guarantees. And I wasn't going to take anything for granted.

"I'm sorry too," I said finally.

Dad looked up again, eyes wide. "For what?"

"For saying what I said. For bringing Mom into it."

He shook his head. "You weren't wrong. If your mother were alive, she'd kick my ass."

I didn't argue.

"What will you do now?" I asked.

For a long moment, he didn't answer. He simply sat staring at the far wall, lost. Finally, he turned back to me, his expression a mixture of sadness and acceptance. "I don't know yet. I guess we'll start over."

"No." I shook my head, my voice as gentle as I could make it. His firing me in order to protect me didn't erase all the times before it when he'd shut me down or tried to sell me out in order to make another dollar. I wasn't sure if he'd try it again, after everything that had happened, but I wasn't going to let myself find out.

"Not we," I told him. "You. You'll start over Dad. I can't do it with you. Not anymore."

He nodded slowly, as if he'd expected it, and I let out the breath I'd been holding. "Of course." His voice was ragged. "I wouldn't expect you to."

Despite every hard word and impossible expectation he'd ever given me, my heart ached. I sat up straighter and leaned over, wrapping my arms around him in a hug.

He stiffened, and I waited for him to pull away completely. I couldn't remember the last time Dad and I had hugged. But a second later, his arms came around me too and he squeezed. "You're better than I deserve," he said against my ear. "I love you."

A jolt of surprise shot through me at his words. All at once, the tears I'd been holding back finally spilled over and streamed down my cheeks. I hugged him harder, overwhelmed and a complete mess—and happy. Happier than I'd been in a long time. And also devastatingly sad that it had taken so long for him to say it. For me to say it. For me to feel it—for anyone.

"I love you too," I whispered.

The moment I said the words, something inside me softened. My heart opened, and every scary thing I'd felt for Liam came pouring out. I'd been such an idiot before—too scared to let him in and my feelings out. And now, it was all I wanted to say—to every single person I cared about. Because Liam was right, you never knew when they wouldn't be around to hear it anymore. And this, I realized, was exactly who the real Cassie Franklin was: someone who felt everything deeply. And someone who wasn't afraid to show it.

CHAPTER THIRTY-THREE

LIAM

THE sound of a wrapper being torn open urged me awake instantly. A sharp ringing in my ears followed and then subsided slowly. I blinked, trying to get my bearings, but the room swam before me. Dizzy didn't even begin to cover it. In the mostly dark room, a nurse stood beside my bed. She smiled when she saw me, her expression friendly as she worked on changing out my bag of fluids and adding some injection into my IV. The wrapper that had woken me sat discarded. The needle it had held was a lot less exciting than the candy bar I'd dreamt it was.

"What's that?" I asked, still groggy.

"Antibiotic. It'll help with any leftover infection," she explained. "How are you feeling?"

I looked around the room again as it all came back to me. Still no Cassie. I sat back. "Fine. Where's my family?"

She frowned as if it were obvious. "They said they'll be back in the morning. They said you were awake when they left. That they told you goodbye first."

"Right. I forgot." Damn drugs. "It's not morning?"

Now, her lips curved upward in an amused smile. "Not for another fourteen hours or so."

I frowned, hating that I didn't even know what day it was, much less what time.

"You have a couple of friends in the waiting room," she said. "Can I send them in for a bit or do you want to sleep?"

Despite her casual tone, I tensed in anticipation. Cassie? "Send them in," I told her.

She finished up with a vitals check and then jotted some notes onto a clipboard on the counter. I thought about asking her for more information about my recovery, but then she said something that completely threw me off.

"Your name keeps coming up on the news today. You're pretty popular from what I can tell." She nodded up at the television mounted across the room. The sound was too low for me to pick out actual words—apparently, that's what that buzzing noise was.

I ignored it. If I heard "Liam Porter, war hero" one more time, I'd rip the new implant out myself and happily remain deaf forever.

The nurse must have taken the hint and left.

A moment later, the door opened and Jamie and Jess walked in. I tried not to let my disappointment show. "He lives!" Jamie announced, walking over and throwing his arms around me in a bear hug.

When he pulled away, Jess frowned down at me. "You look like shit."

"I'm in the hospital. What's your excuse?" I shot back.

Her lips twitched and I had the sense we'd just bonded somehow. That girl was so damn weird.

"How are you feeling?" Jamie asked, pulling a chair over beside my bed. The legs scraped over the floor, and I winced at the pain it sent pulsing through my skull.

"Jamie," Jess hissed, gesturing from me to the chair.

He stopped, his expression falling. "Sorry," he said.

I sighed. "It's fine. I'll be okay. The implant ruptured. Fluid leaked into my—"

"We know," they said in unison and then glared at each other.

"How do you know?"

"Your mom filled us in," Jamie explained. When I continued to give him a blank look, he added, "Those drugs you're on are apparently no joke. We came to see you for about five seconds earlier today but you passed out and they made us leave."

"Don't worry, though," Jess said brightly. "I took your picture while you were drooling. For posterity."

I decided to pretend I hadn't heard her. At least until I could move enough to chase her down if she was serious. "Do either of you know where Cassie is or why she hasn't shown up yet?" I asked instead.

They exchanged a glance, but not like the sad, confused one my mom and Sophie had shared earlier. This was too devious. I didn't trust it for a second.

"If you know something," I began.

"Oh, look. What's that?" Jess interrupted, completely ignoring me and looking pointedly at the television across the room.

"I don't know and I don't care," I said, my temper heating. "Can someone please tell me where the hell my girlfriend is?"

Jamie didn't meet my eyes. "Uh. She had to run an errand."

"Yeah, you'll see her in a second." Jess wandered closer to the television, but something in her voice felt off.

"So you've talked to her?" I sat up straighter—or tried to. A headache bloomed immediately, and I forced myself to remain still.

Jess shot another glance at Jamie and my suspicions were confirmed. Whatever they were up to, they were in on it together. Interesting. I'd never seen them team up on anything before. "Yeah," Jess said, waving me off, "But let's talk after the news. I want to see this."

My lips parted, ready to tell her to turn it off, but when I finally looked up at it, the scene stopped me cold. "Can you turn it up?"

Jess reached for the remote and hit the volume.

"More," I said.

She cranked it up and then handed me the remote, shaking her head. I knew it was loud as hell, but I couldn't hear it otherwise. And I didn't give two shits what Jess thought about it either because currently on screen was a group of reporters gathered on what looked like the front lawn of this very hospital. Standing before them, with a hundred microphones pointed at her perfectly composed and solemn face was Cassie—and standing beside her was her father.

CHAPTER THIRTY-FOUR

CASSIE

I waited until the cameraman gave us the nod. When he did, I smoothed my sweaty palms against my jeans one last time and then followed my father onto the makeshift stage they'd constructed for us to give our statement. I'd leaked just enough of what we'd intended to do so that every major news outlet in both Charleston and Summerville had shown up to hear it. And even though it's what I wanted, I was also pretty close to throwing up on them all.

My father's hand squeezed mine one last time and then he stepped forward, smoothing his jacket and tie and still managing to look imposing despite the fact that he'd just lost everything. Off to the side, hospital officials stood solemnly, waiting for us to finish so my father could sign the necessary paperwork required to make his promises official.

For now, I watched as he cleared his throat and the hum of voices died down, all of them waiting for him to speak. "Thank you all for coming," he began. "My name is Donald Franklin and up until today you knew me as CEO of Franklin Industries, a private research firm that developed and supplied medical technology to those who needed it. Tomorrow, you will read about a scandal. One that, I'm embarrassed to admit, went on right underneath my nose at my own company. An embezzlement scheme that robbed me of my money, my company, and my upstanding reputation. As a result of my partnership with federal agents, the guilty party has been brought to justice."

I tried not to roll my eyes. Even now, my father was still painting himself the good guy and the victim. I shouldn't have been surprised.

"But that's not what I called you all here for today. My daughter's friend, Liam Porter, is in this very hospital right now, recovering from nearly losing his hearing. And maybe even his life."

Murmurs. Some soft, some loud. A reporter or two shouted a question but my dad ignored them. "In the course of the investigation, it was brought to my attention that part of the embezzlement scheme involved investing in faulty equipment. That equipment was then developed and donated to Liam. A cochlear implant. Franklin Industries has always been about saving lives, and I regret that I must stand here before you today to take responsibility for my part in harming a life instead. Liam was the unfortunate collateral damage, and I should have paid more attention to what was happening."

I blinked, a little surprised my father had used the words "responsibility" or "regret."

"As I said, Liam is in this very hospital and has just come out of surgery to replace the defective implant that malfunctioned while in his ear canal and nearly killed him. And I stand before you today ready to make amends for my part in his unfortunate medical mishap. I will personally be covering

Liam's medical expenses for his full treatment and recovery from here on out. I know this doesn't make up for what happened to him as a result of Franklin Industries' careless oversight, but justice will be served elsewhere and you can rest assured the guilty party will never be free to do this again."

More murmurs. This time, drowned out by shouted questions.

But my father simply ended it with a quick "thank you" and then stepped back beside me. This time, I reached for his hand, squeezing it in silent appreciation. Finally, he'd done the right thing.

Now it was my turn.

Slowly, with much less confidence than my father had shown, I stepped to the podium. Looking out over the sea of faces, I watched as they all squinted and then finally began to recognize me. I couldn't blame them. In my sweatshirt and jeans, I wasn't exactly the Cassie Franklin they'd come to know. My dad had offered to let me change first, but I'd wanted them to see me like this. It was part of the message. Showing them all how I'd changed. Obviously, it was going to take more than jeans though.

I took a steadying breath and leaned toward the microphone. "Thank you all for coming," I began.

I blinked as a few cameras flashed.

The silence stretched.

"You can do this, Cassandra," my dad whispered from behind me and that gave me all the courage I needed.

"My name is Cassie Franklin. I am the daughter of Donald Franklin, and up until recently I was an employee at Franklin Industries." The introduction was for them, but the rest was for Liam. I looked directly into the closest camera, hoping like hell it was the one he was watching, and continued.

"I've spent the entire day in an interview room at a federal agency with the girl I thought I knew as my assistant. Turns out, she was someone else entirely, and thanks to her and the statements we've given, the man responsible for what happened with Liam's faulty implant is behind bars. I'd like to publicly apologize to Liam and offer my sincerest sympathies to him and his family. He didn't deserve to be caught up in this, and I'm truly sorry that it turned out this way."

Another breath.

I kept my eyes on the camera and said, "Liam, if you're watching this, I love you. I know it's taken me way too long to say that. Or to smile. Or to let go, but I know it now. I love you so much for being the one to draw all of those things out of me. For pushing me to discover who I was. Not who everyone else said I should be. And for loving me without needing me to be anything for you. I can't imagine my life without you. Please don't be pissed that I'm up here putting you in the spotlight again. You told me you didn't mind the attention as long as it was for the things you cared about. I hope that includes me."

The moment I shut my mouth and stepped away from the podium, the crowd exploded. I heard every question imaginable hurled my way.

"Is Liam suing Franklin Industries?"

"Are you suing Franklin Industries?"

"Are you angry at your father for firing you?"

"Are you still paying Liam to pretend to be your boyfriend so people will like you?"

"Are you making this announcement so we will like you?"

I rolled my eyes and let the hospital officials lead us back inside where security was waiting to hold off the press. We rounded the corner into the patient wing, just down the hall from Liam's room, and I stopped, blowing out a deep breath.

My father spoke quietly to the administrative rep about payment arrangements and release forms that needed signing.

I leaned against the wall, closing my eyes while I concentrated on breathing normally again. Someone bumped my shoulder and I opened my eyes to find Jess grinning at me.

"You did awesome," she said.

"You think so?" I asked, barely able to remember what I'd thought about during those ten minutes, much less anything I'd just said.

"Definitely," she agreed and I exhaled again.

"Did he see it?"

"Yep."

I studied her for some clue about his reaction, but she was unreadable. "I hope he's not mad."

Jess snorted. "You just publicly denounced your own company and threw your dad under the bus," Jess said. "If Liam can't appreciate that, I'll—"

"Do not say kill him," I interrupted.

Jess grinned. "Absolutely not. That would be too easy. My style is much more evil than that."

"I can only imagine…" I trailed off as I spotted Liam's door. It was open and from the limited view, I could see him moving around in bed. A second later, Jamie emerged and shot me a thumbs up.

Jess nudged me again. "We'll wait here."

"Are you sure?" I asked, shooting a glance at my dad. He paused his conversation to nod at me encouragingly.

Jess nudged me forward. "Go. We'll keep an eye out. Make sure none of the press sneak past security."

"Thanks."

I turned and headed for Liam's room, my heart pounding. While I walked, I tried counting to ten to calm my nerves, but it was no use. No amount of counting was going to do it. Only laying eyes on him, seeing that he was okay, was going to be enough. Even if he was pissed at me for that press conference, he was alive. That was all that mattered.

When I realized that, I ran the rest of the way and shoved the door aside.

Liam turned to look at me, the TV remote hanging limply in his hand. I looked from him to the television where the news channel was still panning to all the reporters gathered while replaying my statement in the corner of the screen. My stomach tightened.

I approached him slowly. "You saw it?" I asked.

He nodded. "Oh yeah."

My heart leaped. "You can hear me?"

He nodded again. "Loud and clear."

"Thank God," I said.

When he held out his hand, inviting me closer, I nearly leaped on to the thin mattress with him. Careful of his IV line, I threw my arms around him, making sure not to touch his ear or face as I hugged him tight. Instead, I pressed my cheek to his chest, enjoying the sound of his beating heart. Whatever came next, I had this.

CHAPTER THIRTY-FIVE

LIAM

"I was so worried," she said, her words muffled, but I heard them well enough. Her arms tightened around me, and even if I hadn't heard her speech just now, I would have forgiven her for not being here earlier. Just feeling her pressed against me, knowing she cared, would have been enough. But then she'd gone and said the words I'd wanted to hear—and she'd said them in front of the entire damned world.

"I was pretty pissed when you weren't here," I admitted.

She drew away, her expression full of earnest apology. "I know. I am so sorry for that. The agents were waiting for me outside my house this morning."

"Did you get arrested?"

"I was escorted downtown," she said, using her fingers to air quote the last words.

My brows shot up, wiggling as I asked, "With handcuffs?"

She laughed. "Seriously? I am trying to explain and apologize here and you want to talk about handcuffs?"

"With you, I'll always want to talk about handcuffs." She

shook her head and I added more seriously, "But first, tell me what happened."

I listened as she told me everything that had happened to her from the moment Bev had shown up at her house to bring her in for questioning. I still couldn't believe I'd missed that one. My instincts should have been better. But Bev was good, I'd give her that.

"I'm really sorry, Liam," Cassie said when she was finished with her story.

"It's fine."

"It's not. I should have been here. Not just this time but the other times too. I've left you hanging over and over again and you don't deserve that. You deserve someone who shows up. I swear, it won't happen again."

"I deserve *you*." I leaned over and kissed her, silencing any more apologies. Now that she was here, and it was all over, I just wanted to touch her. To feel her against me. And to remember how it felt to hear her tell the entire world that she loved me.

"How are you feeling?" she asked.

I frowned and decided to go with honesty. "Like my head's been filled with acid. Not the good kind."

Her lips twitched. "Hopefully the oxygen treatments will help with that."

"Your father's paying for the treatments?" I asked, remembering what he'd said during his speech earlier.

She nodded and her near-smile vanished. "It's the least he can do." She paused and then said, "He apologized for cutting me out. Apparently, he was in on the investigation and he didn't want me to get caught up in it so he shut me out to protect me."

"Wow."

"Yeah."

"Are you guys good now?"

She shrugged. "Good enough. He'll start over. Find some new thing to invest in."

"And you? Will you work with him?"

"Not a chance. In fact, I think I'd rather work for myself than risk getting in with the wrong people again." She winced. "God, I can't believe what happened to you because of Evan's greed. I am so sorry, Liam."

"I told you, stop apologizing," I said. "You've said enough. I saw your speech remember?"

She winced. "On a scale of one to ten, how pissed are you?"

I chuckled. "I'd say a zero."

"You're not mad?" She sat up, her eyes wide. Relief was clear, and I realized she must have been pretty worried.

"What would I be mad about?"

"The publicity. Putting you in the spotlight," she admitted. "I know how much you hate that."

"But I love you," I said, reaching for her hair. Or her face. Something. I just needed to touch her. "So that makes it worth it. Besides, you completely outed yourself. Jeans and a sweatshirt? Professing love for someone? You can't go back to ice princess now. Your reputation is completely ruined. You have nowhere else to go but stick with me."

Her hand came up to cover mine where I held her cheek against my palm. She smiled softly. "I love you."

I went still. "What did you say?" Even though she'd said it for the cameras, it was different hearing her say it here, just for me.

"I love you," she repeated. "So much. And I'm so sorry it took me forever to say it back."

I felt my insides warming, chasing away the worst of the pain and drowning out whatever disappointment I'd felt earlier. "Not forever," I told her, bringing her close enough that I could kiss her without splitting my head open from the headache that followed any move I made. "That's still ahead of us."

"I hope so," she said softly and then our words were silenced by our mouths moving together. Softly at first but then it wasn't long before she broke off, chest heaving with labored breaths. Her cheeks were flushed and her lashes lowered as she shook her head.

"You need to rest," she said.

"Come on. Haven't you heard of physical therapy?"

She laughed—and the sound was like music to my ears.

EPILOGUE

LIAM

I stepped back to admire the precision of the lines I'd routed along the edge of the headboard, and something wet touched my cheek. I turned, my eyes widening when I spotted Cassie— and the paintbrush in her hand. Its tip was coated in blue paint, and I realized belatedly now my cheek was too.

"You didn't," I said darkly, and she giggled.

"I did."

"We're expecting guests in two hours, woman."

"I know, but I'm done with that last piece you wanted me to accent for you, and all I can think about is how we never got that sexy, body painting night I wanted."

"You're pure evil, you know that," I said, my cock already twitching at the image of her naked and painted and splayed out for me.

My store was too lit up for this conversation, thanks to the party preparations we'd already made. In fact, Jamie and Jess had made a last minute run for more champagne and would be back any minute. But I didn't give a shit. Not with Cassie proposing this.

"Okay. That's it. Staff meeting in the supply closet. Now."

"I'm not sure I like the look in your eyes, *boss*," she said, taking a step back.

But it was too late now. I grabbed her wrist, yanking her closer. Ignoring her protests, I tossed her over my shoulder and took off for the stock room.

"What are you doing?" she demanded.

I kept my hand firmly on her ass as I walked in and shut the door behind us. "Exactly what you wanted," I told her, returning her to her feet.

Before she could react, I reached up and turned on the light, grabbing the paint brush out of her hands.

Her eyes went wide. "Okay, wait. Let's think about this. Maybe you're right. People are coming—"

"No, not people," I said, reaching out and painting a thin line down the center of her cleavage. With my other hand, I pinned her in place before she could wriggle away, enjoying the sound of her laughter as she struggled against me—and the fact that the sound of it was crystal clear in my newly healed ears. "The only one coming right now is you," I breathed, my mouth close enough to her throat that I could feel when goose bumps rose along her skin at my words.

"Am I?" she asked softly, turning her mouth to meet mine. Her hands ran up my chest and over my shoulders, locking around my neck as she pushed off the door where I held her and rocked her hips into mine. "Because I think you're forgetting it takes two here."

I grinned. "Not the way we're going to do it."

"What are you…?"

I reached behind me and grabbed the little bag I'd stashed here earlier. When I held it up, Cassie stared at it—and blinked.

"What is that?"

I opened the bag and pulled out a cookie. "Macadamia nut. Your favorite," I said, holding it out for her. "With how much you claim to love them, I was curious."

"Curious about what?"

"Whether your face when you eat these looks anything like your face when I eat you." I didn't miss the heat that crept into her cheeks as I said the words.

She shook her head, laughing as she took the cookie from me. "I guess we're about to find out." But instead of taking a bite, she reached for the button on my pants, her free hand already going to work on sliding them down.

"What are you doing?" I asked.

In my ear, she breathed, "Show me your O face and I'll show you mine."

It was a tie.

ABOUT THE AUTHOR

Heather Hildenbrand was born and raised in a small town in northern Virginia where she was homeschooled through high school. (She's only slightly socially awkward as a result.) She writes romance of all kinds with plenty of abs and angst. Her most frequent hobbies are riding motorcycles and avoiding killer slugs.

Find out more at www.heatherhildenbrand.com.

ALSO BY HEATHER HILDENBRAND

Remembrance: She's the cure that could save him … if only she could remember how. A New Adult Paranormal Romance with "Witches, Werewolves, and WTF?!"

Whisper: A standalone New Adult Fantasy Romance full of loss and true love and justice served. There's also a hot Cherokee warrior involved.

A Risk Worth Taking: A New Adult Contemporary Romance with southern charm and a hippie farmer capable of causing swoon and heartbreak in the same breath.

Dirty Blood: A Young Adult Paranormal Romance about a girl who falls in love with a werewolf, only to find out she's a Hunter, born and bred to kill the very thing she means to save.

Imitation: A Young Adult Sci-Fi Romance with life or death choices and a heroine mired in a conspiracy so deep, even a motorcycle-riding bodyguard can't pull her out.

Bitter Rivalry: Two long lost sisters are reunited and forced to compete for the alpha role in their pack. The winner has been promised to the vampire prince. One sister wants to kiss him; the other wants to kill him. Can siblings survive rivalry and forbidden love?

Made in the USA
Columbia, SC
03 April 2018